MAYA IN MULTICOLOR

SWATI TEERDHALA

HYPERION

Los Angeles   New York

First Edition, March 2025
10 9 8 7 6 5 4 3 2 1
FAC-004510-24361
Printed in the United States of America

This book is set in Laurentian Pro/Monotype
Designed by Zareen Johnson
Stock images: Holi powder pots 2425867051/Shutterstock

Library of Congress Cataloging-in-Publication Control Number: 2024010378
ISBN 978-1-368-09612-6

Visit www.HyperionTeens.com

For all the women in the world who bridge the old world and the new, looking for themselves in the process.

PROLOGUE
FOUR MONTHS EARLIER

There was something about the first week of freshman year that smelled like promises and hope, or at the very least, fresh coffee.

Okay, slightly burnt coffee, but Maya would take it. It was college coffee.

She gratefully took the steaming cup from the yawning boy behind the counter at the Neadham library, the main and also most stunning library on campus. When Maya had imagined her first year at Neadham University, she had visualized herself walking the university's green lawn–lined paths and studying in this glass-domed library atrium.

What she hadn't envisioned was how difficult it would be to juggle her newly acquired coffee with the stack of notebooks tucked in her arms. Especially because the coffee was particularly hot. Maya tried to move her fingers around the cup, but every inch was like touching burning concrete.

She spotted a table to the side and made a beeline for it, but a group of students exited one of the study rooms at that exact moment. Maya barely avoided running into them, and all her carefully arranged notebooks went flying.

They landed in a heap on the gleaming mahogany floor.

Welp. Hopefully no one had seen that, though it wasn't like anyone *knew* her yet. She was probably in the clear. Maya let out a deep sigh, put her coffee down to claim her spot, and went back to get her belongings.

She was reaching to pick up her notebook when she realized, a bit too late, that someone else was doing the same thing. At the same time.

"Is this yours?"

She looked up into bright hazel eyes that gazed at her curiously from under a head of dark curls. And then he smiled. Dimples. He had heart-melting dimples.

"Uh, yes, thank you," she said, feeling herself start to blush. She was done for, wasn't she?

"They don't double-line their cups here," he said. "I found that out yesterday. How are your fingers?"

"Mildly burned," she said. "I might lose my fingerprints, but I guess it's a fair trade-off for coffee."

He laughed, holding out a hand to help her up, which she took. She accepted the rest of her notebooks from this boy.

"I'm Thomas," he said.

"Maya."

She turned to go, when Thomas stepped in front of her. "Would you be interested in ice cream? I heard Goldie's does a sundae you can't miss." He grinned.

Maya looked back at the table she had snagged to study and then at Thomas. Meeting a cute boy the first week? One who seemed to be interested in her? She wouldn't deny that she had dreamed of a college romance, but she hadn't expected an opportunity to present itself so quickly. Or at all, really.

This was a stroke of good luck, one that she probably shouldn't turn away. Plus, Maya put stock in meet-cutes and she was pretty sure she had just been in one—in the Neadham library of all places. That had to be a sign from the universe, didn't it?

College was off to a great start.

"Sure, I'd love that," she said, a slow grin curling up her face.

What did she have to lose?

CHAPTER 1
PRESENT DAY

There were three things Maya loved—freshly cut peonies, chocolate chip cookies right out of the oven, and new possibilities. So far, today had delivered only one of those.

Another whiff of Cheetos and funky boy smell passed by Maya as she walked to the kitchen of her small dorm suite, carefully balancing two trays of cookie dough in each hand. She had been testing out a new batch of double chocolate chip cookies and this was her best yet, she thought. Jana, her roommate and new best friend, seemed to agree, given that she was licking the bowl of batter Maya had left behind.

Jana had decided to join her tonight after Maya had discovered that the baking date she had planned with Thomas had turned into another all-dorm-hall gaming tournament.

In the living room. Of *her* two-bedroom dorm suite.

Thomas had started out as the perfect first-semester romance, especially after her high school history. They had a definite meet-cute, and they had spent one entire blissful week eating ice cream together before she had decided he was it.

Reality had set in pretty quickly. She was a homebody who loved baking and every type of cozy activity you could imagine, but she did want to leave the living room to go on a date occasionally. Thomas, apparently, didn't feel the same way.

Especially since he could just ask her, his exclusive-but-no-labels-please "girlfriend," for use of her lottery-drawn dorm suite. Or not ask her, like tonight. It wasn't the first time he had turned one of their dates into a gaming night, but she was growing alarmed by the number of times it was happening now, like it had just become a routine.

Maya wasn't sure what to be more annoyed by: the fact that he still wouldn't call her his girlfriend, the expectation that he and his friends could use her suite, or that he had "forgotten" he had promised to help her bake tonight for her TA discussion. She was starting to get tired of always having to remind him of things outside of gaming and coding, especially when she wasn't even technically his girlfriend.

Jana popped the oven door open, and Maya gave her a thankful nod before sliding the trays in.

"Batch three in the making," Jana said, tossing her short, bobbed hair back.

"How is batch two?" Maya asked, waving at the countertop filled with cookies.

Jana bit into a cookie. "Best yet, babe." She took another bite and groaned, very loudly. Maya was the type of person who would cook for ten people even if only five people were coming over, just to make sure that everyone had seconds—and Jana would eat anything. Maya gave another round of thanks to the universe for that roommate forum glitch that had accidentally given her Jana's name.

It had been a stroke of random good fortune, really. Jana had been initially paired with Michelle Sanders, but due to the similar initials and a technical snafu in the Neadham intra-web, Jana had ended up with Maya Sastry instead. They weren't a natural fit on paper, given that Jana's love of punk rock and dislike of order were somewhat opposed to Maya's folk-pop obsession and no-nonsense business major. But it worked, like balanced scales. Or that teaspoon of salt you needed in baking.

A cheer went up from the common room couches and there was a series of thunderous cheers and high fives.

"What happened?" Jana asked, mouth half-full.

Maya rolled her eyes and put on her best British documentarian voice. "That particular cry is that of the *Homo sapiens* male playing a virtual battle game of swords. I believe it signals the defeat of a level, indicating a rise in their position in the virtual arena. The pack has been fed. Or something."

Jana frowned in their direction.

"You think if we put on our cutest heels and walked in front of the TV they'd notice?"

"Unlikely," Maya said.

Jana cleared her throat and lowered her elbows to the counter. She tilted her head at Maya and fluttered her long, mascaraed lashes at her. "Babe, you know I adore you and support you, but when *exactly* are we going to get our living room back? I know I promised not to get involved, but, *Maya*."

Maya sighed. "Yes, Thomas said he said he'd help me get these cookies ready for our class discussion tomorrow. But he forgot. He said he accidentally planned over it"—Jana's eyebrow rose—"and I believe him. I can't force him to miss that now, can I?"

Jana made a face that Maya interpreted as *You can't.*

No, she couldn't. Plus, she didn't want to force him. She would lose all her credibility as a cool girlfriend or, well, potential girlfriend, if she did that. And she knew she was so close to getting him to say it.

If she were being honest, and she didn't always want to be, part of her had kept hoping that Thomas might finally give her the official girlfriend title all last semester. She just needed to be patient.

"Anyway, you're a lifesaver for helping me out," Maya continued. "My TA seemed so excited by the idea of my double chocolate cookies after he tried them that one time."

"Of course. But I don't mean tonight. I mean forever."

Maya winced and tried to avoid answering by stuffing a cookie in her mouth.

"I know—" She had tried to talk to Thomas about it, but he always looked so sad whenever she tried to take back their living room. But Maya had to admit, she wasn't very good at disappointing people, even if those people had disappointed her first.

"Babe, your inertia is real bad," Jana said.

Maya blinked at her in confusion. "Huh?"

"I was listening to this podcast about it. It happens a lot to people early on in college. They find someone who is good enough and then they just stay together for four years. No forward movement. Total inertia."

Maya looked over at Thomas. He was smack-dab in the middle of the couch, squeezed in between two of his friends from down the dorm hall. Meeting Thomas, and then dating Thomas, had kind of just . . . happened, especially after the heartbreak that had been her senior year of high school. It had been nice to be wanted. Thomas texted her back, and he looked nothing like the boy who had given her air promises and half lies her senior year of high school. He had seemed like a total catch. And then somehow she had blinked her eyes and a semester had gone by, most of it spent watching Thomas play video games with his friends.

Maya had entered college with a plan—major in business, join the Hindu Student Association to keep in touch with her roots, go to three athletic games a season to tell her kids about, and find real love. So far, she had only managed to do the first, mostly because Thomas just wasn't interested in the others, and they tended to do what he liked. That was just because he was more opinionated.

But they didn't do anything. Ever. And sometimes when he spoke, her thoughts drifted off, and she started to daydream about Harry Styles in that one music video. Wind in his hair, adventure sparkling in his eyes. Totally focused on the object of his affection.

She couldn't remember the last time Thomas had taken any interest in what she liked to do. Or even asked her what she liked to do. Plus, there was the whole matter of still not calling her his girlfriend, though she did all the work of being one: hosting his gaming tournaments, helping him study for his literature class he hated, even baking his favorite peanut butter cookies (which she hated). She figured he would eventually come around.

Was that inertia?

Jana pointedly looked at the living room, where Thomas had slouched so far down into the couch that he had almost morphed into it. "What is this, like, the fifth time he's bailed on you for gaming? Or forced you to stay home? I still remember you saying you couldn't come to the stoplight party at Sigma Chi because you had to, and I quote, 'support your man during his first video game tourney.' How'd that turn out for you?"

"Hey," Maya said. She swatted at Jana. "Not fair."

Jana was right. But she didn't have to be so smug about it. Despite their differing exteriors, they both had the same sense of humor and love for their family, and after they had met the first week of orientation, they had been inseparable. Meeting Jana was one thing Maya didn't regret about first semester.

"But the truth," Jana said, swatting her back.

"Whoa, are you guys having a catfight?" a voice said. One of Thomas's friends, Ronnie, was standing on the other side of the kitchen island, his hand in the huge tub of cheesy puffs that the guys had been sharing.

Maya rolled her eyes. Jana popped the rest of the cookie in her mouth and winked at him. "Yup, wanna join?"

Ronnie's eyes almost bugged out.

Maya shook her head and pulled Jana away. "You're going to give him an early heart attack," she whispered. To Ronnie, she said, "We're baking cookies. Keep out of the kitchen and I might give you all some later."

Ronnie looked appreciatively at the cookies and then at Maya before he left. "Best not-girlfriend ever."

Jana made a face. "Wait, did he just say what I think he said?"

Maya's entire body froze in icy awareness, and at the same time her cheeks heated into an angry flush. Had he really— Yes, Ronnie had said that, which meant that Thomas—

She should have seen red. She should have seen some sort of warm toasty orange, but instead, Maya had a flash-forward of her life.

She was still here, still watching Thomas play video games with his friends, still stuck in the kitchen after being stood up for the hundredth time, but now she had gray hair and wrinkles as she handed out cookies and made excuses for her not-boyfriend. One who clearly never had any intention to give her the title. So much so that he had even told his friends!

"Ow, Maya." Jana shook her hand off, and Maya realized she had just death-gripped Jana's hand.

"I need to get out. Now," Maya said, her voice frantic. She was not going to become another victim of boy inertia. She had things to do! She had a plan once!

To be fair, she had let Thomas take the lead and she had thought it was for the best. It was only during winter break that she had realized how much she had actually missed. Spending time with Thomas had become doing everything Thomas wanted to do, and now . . . she was here.

This was not who Maya wanted to be. In all her dreams of her future, Maya had never seen herself here, waiting for a boy to realize she was good enough to be his girlfriend, letting him walk all over her life. And worse, losing out on her college experience in order to make him happy.

Maya had come to Neadham University for a reason; she had chosen this white-stone-and-green-ivy campus, this community, on purpose.

No more inertia. It was time for her to evolve to New Maya. Maya 2.0, if you will.

Jana smiled. "I thought you'd never ask." She took another bite of cookie. "You need a plan."

"I know," Maya mumbled, ducking her head. "I started working on one during winter break. But it wasn't supposed to be anything . . ."

Jana's eyebrows rose to her hairline. "Show me."

Maya hesitated, and then grabbed her laptop and pulled up the document titled "Maya's Master Plan." She frowned and quickly crossed out the Step One she had in the document.

"My new Step One?" Maya said. She paused, and then whispered as she typed. "End things with Thomas. I'm done waiting." Jana threw her a silent, mini high five. "Which means this is now Step Two. Do the things I've been wanting to do, like be more active in HSA. Or check out the fencing club. Or join the a cappella group. Or apply to study abroad."

"That is a lot of things," Jana said.

"Well, I had a lot of ideas as I was sitting at home, hearing everyone else's college stories at our neighborhood holiday party." Maya bit her lip. Winter break had not been the best for her confidence. "I just knew I couldn't come back this semester and do the same thing, you know? You found your little niche at Neadham with your engineering frat and the film festival, but I haven't yet."

Jana patted Maya on the shoulder gently. "And you will, too."

Maya nodded, a little slowly. "Yeah, but only if I make an effort. Which is why I applied to be on the event committee this semester for HSA." She took a big breath. "I was going to take whatever event I could get that would fit around the gaming tournaments I had promised to host with Thomas—"

Jana glared at her.

Maya hurried on. "But not anymore. Which means I could . . . I could help with Holi. Could you imagine if I got to help plan Holi this year, as a freshman?"

She had been . . . imagining it. A lot. The Hindu festival of Holi meant a lot to her—the love, the bright colors and sense of fun, the way it symbolized spring and rebirth. It felt even more poignant to her now as she envisioned her own rebirth as New Maya. She had attended the famous Holi Mela at Neadham, *the* collegiate Holi experience in Virginia as a junior with her family, and that experience, the way it made her feel like she could have a home away from home, had been the moment she had decided to come to Neadham. Seeing the way the community came together, the joy and fun of it all, it had spun together this dream for her, of her four years of college and what they could be.

Jana's eyes went wide. "What? You sneaky little— Okay, I'm super proud of you. And yes, now you can do any of that. You could do India Day or Diwali, too."

"Don't get too excited," Maya said, rubbing her arm. "Their event chair is notoriously picky."

Jana leaned in. "Well, maybe not anymore . . . since Preetam resigned. I heard it from Lily in Comp Sci, who heard it from Robert in—" Maya gave her an impatient look. "Anyway, the spot for event chair is now open, but since it's the middle of the year, they're going to wait until the end of the semester election. But that means they're going to need a lot of volunteers since the spring semester is so packed with events."

"Wait," Maya said slowly. "He resigned? The spot is open?"

"That is what I just said." Jana waved a hand in front of Maya's face. "Are you short-circuiting? I thought you'd be happy."

Maya's brain began to whir. There had been another step she had added to her plan, one that she hadn't thought was possible before—until now. She turned her laptop to face Jana with a big flourish. She scrolled down to the very edge of the document where she had typed, almost as an afterthought, the words *Become HSA's event chair* and, after several ellipses, *to inspire and grow our community.*

"Then this must be my sign from the universe," Maya said, worrying her lip. "I had imagined it would be more of a junior-year thing, but . . . what if I could try for it this year?"

"Yes," Jana said before Maya could even fully finish her question. "Why not! It's college."

Maya nodded. "True. Why not? I like that." She typed the phrase on the top of the "Maya's Master Plan" document, right under the title.

"And this is your dream, isn't it?" Jana said. "You told me during orientation that you wanted to be the next event chair for HSA."

Maya flushed. "Only after you told me you want to win the Neadham Film Festival." She nodded slowly. "But yes, if I could become the HSA event chair, I'd have an amazing résumé for any event-planning internships later. And I mean, I love event planning. . . ." She really did, and had, since the first mermaid birthday party she had helped plan for her sixth-grade best friend. There was something about bringing moments and celebrations to life, something that felt so real and fulfilling.

"Wow, you've really been thinking about this," Jana said, looking impressed. "That holiday party must have sucked."

She didn't know how to tell Jana that it really, really had. Still, Maya had only started jotting down ideas. She hadn't finished her master plan, and she hadn't been sure she was going to. Until now.

Maya glanced at the clock. "Don't you have—"

"Oh crap," Jana said, bolting upward. "I've got a study group for Natural Language Processing at eight." She pecked Maya's cheek before speeding toward the door. "I'll see you tomorrow, same time, same place."

Maya barely had time to wave before Jana had disappeared. She held back a sigh, especially now that she was left alone here with the boys and the knowledge that Thomas had told them all that this was a non-relationship. The feeling of betrayal stuck in her throat.

She thought back to Ari, and senior year of high school, before quickly shutting that door. Nothing good would come of that. But the feeling followed her the rest of the night, even after the gaming tournament had started to wind down.

At last, there was a moment when Thomas was by himself.

Thomas looked up from his controllers, a lazy smile on his face. "Hey, Maya, those cookies were dope."

"How was the game?" she asked, taking the seat next to him. She sank in and reminded herself to fluff up the seat cushions later.

Thomas leaned back against her couch, spreading his arms out wide. "Great. I demolished them, but that was expected." He looked at her, and she knew that was her cue to tell him he was brilliant.

Something held her tongue, though, some part of her that was finally fed up. Thomas was brilliant, but for once, she didn't want to be the one making him feel better.

"I'm not surprised," she said finally, in a conciliatory way.

Thomas sat back, looking pleased. "The game descended into total guerilla-warfare tactics. Brian led a revolt by recruiting players to back him up as he tried to go sniper on the other team, but I had the rocket launcher, which meant that it was a bad play. Really bad strat work. I couldn't let that stand, you know. Mutiny has to be put down, so I took care of him later in the game."

"Isn't Brian on your team? Couldn't you have just convinced him?" Maya asked.

Thomas shrugged, looking supremely unconcerned. He definitely had a bit of a vicious side in his gaming, which was so at odds with his laid-back persona that his friends had taken to calling him Toxic Thomas when they played certain games. That was another thing that Maya didn't get. It was just a game, wasn't it? Thomas hadn't reacted well when she had mentioned that once.

"Do you want to hear what I did tonight?" Maya said.

"Um . . . yeah," he said, looking a little distracted. "One second." He typed something in his phone and then turned to her.

Wow, his full attention. She hadn't been expecting that.

Maya cleared her throat. "So, Jana said that the event chair for HSA just resigned, which means it's going to be open for election at the end of the semester. If I get on the event committee this semester, then I could run for the position—"

"Event chair?" Thomas said, his eyes half on the screen. "Are you sure you could handle that?"

Maya found herself deflating, just a little. "You know, I planned a lot of events in high school for our community—"

"High school is so basic." Thomas reached over and patted her arm. "I built a website for our fantasy football league back then." He rolled his eyes. "But now? I've been asked to build the backend for a couple apps, a dating app, a gaming community. It's another level."

"I mean as your girlfriend—"

"Babe, you know I'm not ready for that word," Thomas chided. "Anyway, I have another tournament next weekend. I know you wanted to go to that basketball game, but basketball is so played out. I'm thinking of inviting the boys over here, and you could make those cookies again? The ones with—"

Maya couldn't believe it. Somehow in one sentence he had hit on everything she had been worried about. This whole time Maya had told herself that he just needed a little push, a little convincing. She had hosted, she had baked, she had tried to get that A-plus gold star from him.

"You told them all, didn't you?" she said.

Thomas blinked at her. "Huh?"

"Your friends?" Maya's cheeks flushed. "Ronnie called me your not-girlfriend."

"What?" Thomas said. He shrugged. "Ronnie asked what the deal was, and I told him we don't like labels. You know how I feel about them."

"What about me? What about what I want?" Maya said.

"Look, I know you were told by society that you need to have a label and define things—"

"Hold on," Maya said. "I told you I wanted a real relationship. Official. You told me you weren't ready yet; I said fine." She shook her head. "But you were never going to get serious about me, were you? It's one thing that you won't say we're together, it's another thing to go flaunting it around."

Suddenly, it all clicked together for her. That knowing look in Ronnie's eyes, all of theirs. Had it been pity this whole time? Had they known?

Jana was right, no meet-cute was worth this.

The words bubbled up out of her like an overflowing teakettle, her annoyance and disappointment and fear all mixed together inside her chest.

"We need to talk."

CHAPTER 2

T he next day, Maya found Jana at the local coffee shop, the one that was right on the corner of the town's Main Street and University Drive. Maya dropped her backpack into the seat opposite Jana and shoved a coffee cup in her face with Jana's order—double shot of espresso and a splash of hazelnut syrup.

Jana took it gratefully but then turned a suspicious eye to her. "You look surprisingly happy for a pre-coffee morning."

"Well," Maya said, sliding onto the couch next to Jana, shooing her over to make space. She turned to her, a half smile on her face. "I did it. I am officially no longer inertia-ed. If that's a word. I'm fully moving again."

Jana blinked at her for a few seconds. "For real?"

When Maya nodded, Jana squealed so loud that the three tables nearby turned to glare at them. Maya waved at them sheepishly.

"I knew you could do it!" Jana said. "How do you feel?"

"Like that time you had to tell off that slacker in your Engineering group project. Exhausted, a little queasy, but like it was the right thing to do." Maya bit her lip. "I think."

"It was absolutely the right thing to do," Jana said.

"I guess?" Maya said. She had felt so sure of it when sitting on the couch, but a night alone with her racing thoughts had her second-guessing herself.

What if she couldn't find anyone else? What if she had been too harsh in her assessment? Maybe he really hadn't meant to tell his friends. Also, what if he was right and she wasn't capable of event—

"Yes," Jana said, grabbing her arms and squeezing. She stared her down so Maya couldn't look away. "Trust yourself."

"But I don't," Maya said, shaking her head. "I don't trust myself at all. I wore cutoff overalls on the first day of high school. I decided to get bangs in the summer when I have thick, flat hair. I let myself be duped into falling for the biggest player in our entire high school, and he went right ahead and played me. And even with Thomas, I thought if I could show him how good of a girlfriend I could be, he would change his mind." She paused, biting the outer edge of her lip. "You think I did the right thing?"

"Maya," Jana said. "It's not about what I think. Though, yes, I do think that."

Maya bit back a sigh. Jana just didn't get it. Maya had never been the one to get picked first for the kickball team or asked to homecoming. She wasn't full of confidence like Jana or Thomas or Ari, but apparently she was drawn to those sorts of people like a moth to the flame, hoping to catch some of their light. That had been why she had stuck with Thomas so long, wasn't it?

He was brilliant, and somehow she was hoping he would finally see her. She had always been the girl who would keep waiting, keep hoping, whether it was as the last kid to stop believing in Santa Claus or as the only one who kept believing that their high school might actually get a new gymnasium.

If Thomas had been a bad decision, it had been hers. She had made the mistake. What if she just kept making more? Maya swallowed that thought for now.

"Anyway, he took it . . . very poorly, which I found surprising," she said. "He said that I was making him feel like the bad guy for not labeling something before he was ready, and batch three is now defunct because he stole them and ran away in a huff after I told him I wasn't kidding."

The sounds of the coffee shop drifted over them in the ensuing silence. Jana blinked at her rapidly, her mouth forming words without sounds. Then she burst into laughter. "Oh my god, are you serious?" Jana's laughs bubbled over and then petered out. She brushed a tear from her eye. "I needed that. I am so blessed to receive that image. Anytime I'm bored in Electrical Engineering 101, I'll think of Thomas running away like Cookie Monster."

Maya's lips quirked a little at that. Leave it to Jana to find the funny in the morose. It's why they worked together, and, well, she had to admit it had been a little funny in hindsight. Though now she'd never know if batch three had been better than batch two.

"He must have been pissed," Jana continued, chortling in bursts.

"If nothing else, that reaction is all you need to remind yourself that you made the right call. And also the fact that, ugh, he tried to blame you."

Maya grinned and took a sip of Jana's coffee, before making a face. Blergh, that was not good.

"How was the film festival?" Maya said, pushing Jana's shoulder lightly. "Tell me all about it."

Jana's eyes lit up and she gave Maya a play-by-play of the film screening she had gone to the night before, as well as the question-and-answer session afterward. "And the director, Vandana Kumar, was talking about the fight choreography and how the VFX supported it, and it was just so cool to see a desi woman on stage talking about such things."

It was rare to see a South Asian woman pursuing a nontraditional career, especially in the arts, and Maya and Jana had bonded over their mutual "different" career aspirations early on, from Maya's event-planning dreams to Jana's desire to open up a VFX studio.

Maya made a face. "I'm so sorry I wasn't there. I should've come. I should've broken up with Thomas later. How can I make it up to you?"

"Dude," Jana said, lifting her eyebrow. "It's okay. You had some massive Stockholm syndrome."

"Well, that doesn't feel fair—"

"Just come to the next thing with me," Jana said, leaning back on the couch. "All the next things— Wait, actually, I do have a way for you to make it up to me." There was a twinkle in Jana's eye that Maya wasn't sure if she should be scared of. With Jana, that was usually a yes. "You know the plan you put together for yourself? Now that you're single, maybe you could be the subject of my next documentary. . . ."

"Now I'm scared," Maya said, backing away from her a little. "You know I'm crap in front of the camera. I freeze up."

Jana tossed her hair back and pouted. "You said you wanted to make it up to me."

Ugh, she was right.

"And anyway, you want to put yourself out there, find your niche, right? HSA makes sense. But what about everything else? What about dating? I don't want you to get inertia-fied after Thomas."

"I don't, either," Maya admitted. Sure, she was feeling a little sad about Thomas, but that was normal after spending all your time with one person. But another part of her felt ready to fly, to try new things, meet new people. Probably not a very long flight, but still.

"All right, then. Step One," Jana said.

"I already have a Step One. And Two."

"Fine. Step Three." Jana rolled her eyes. "Remember that girl I met the first week at that foam party?"

"Ugh, the one where you came back covered in weird green goo I had to shampoo out of your hair for you?" Maya said.

"Yup," Jana said, with a fond smile. "Exactly. Well, she's a junior and I've run into her a few times. Apparently, she launched this college-wide dating app and everyone's on it. She was telling me that the app has an eighty-five percent success rate."

Maya frowned. "Like eighty-five percent of people get matched?"

Jana waved her half cookie at her. "Yup, yup. It's called Meet'em@ Neadham, and it's totally student-run. So, no creeps." Jana paused. "Well, I probably can't promise that, but at least you know you're not being catfished. That girl Suki was saying developing the app is like her job application for next year, so she's all about making sure it's a safe community."

"I don't know," Maya said. "It doesn't sound very . . . romantic."

It didn't sound romantic at all. Not like a cute dimpled boy picking her notebook up from the ground, or—

"Like knocking heads in the Neadham library?" Jana said, raising an eyebrow.

Maya held her hands up. "Okay, fair point. Meet-cute does not equal compatibility or relationship. But a dating app sounds so . . . clinical."

Maya had always imagined her true love would find her organically, like in the olden times. The traditional, old-fashioned, time-tested way, one that Maya wouldn't be able to mess up.

"How about this?" Jana said. "You can screen people ahead of time. Chat with them first, get to know them. You know, actual dating. I think it would be good for you."

"And that's all you want me to do?" Maya said, biting her lip. She fiddled with the top of her coffee cup, feeling a pinch of anxiety. "Join an app?"

"Join an app," Jana said, nodding eagerly. "Maybe talk to a few people. And then maybe be interviewed about it for my documentary."

Okay, that didn't sound too bad. Usually, she was a bit more of a traditionalist about these things but . . . look where that had led her. Heartache, missed opportunities, and stolen cookies. Maya was almost positive she wouldn't get any bites on this Meet'em@ Neadham thing, but if it made Jana feel better, she would do it. Even if she hated the thought of being interviewed. Jana had her back throughout the entire semester and in a sense, she owed it to her.

Jana made a sad face at her coffee cup. "It's empty."

"That does tend to happen," Maya said. "Another one? On me?"

"If you missing my film events means free coffee, I'm in," Jana said. "Only joking. But I will take another cup."

Maya stuck her tongue out at Jana and swiped their two cups, tossing them out as she headed to the front of the coffee shop. Her phone buzzed and she reached for it. There was a small part of her that hoped it was Thomas, texting saying that he had made a mistake and he wanted to be fully official, maybe even finally learn the name of one of the bands she liked—but it was just a notification that her problem set for Statistics 102 was due tomorrow.

Ugh. She hated that that was her first reaction. She had dumped Thomas and yet here she was, waiting for a text from him.

Maybe Jana was right that dating and playing the field a bit more might be good for her. But how did she make sure another Thomas, or Ari, didn't happen again? A girl could only be disappointed so many times. Maya was staring so hard at her phone, lost in thought, that she didn't notice the broad shoulders in front of her. Not until they swung around, right into her.

She stumbled back, and two strong arms caught her, preventing her from falling on her butt in front of the entire coffee shop.

"Whoa there, you okay?" a voice said, so deep and husky it sounded like bottled smoke.

The voice was attached to a very attractive young man in a tailored button-down that only seemed to highlight the arms that had just caught her. His hair was thick, luxurious, the kind that you wanted to run your hands through, and while she was sure there was some sort of imperfection in his face, Maya couldn't find it at that moment. This was not your typical college boy; he was a triple chocolate ganache cake, a luxury car, the kind you'd stare at but never dream you could actually drive.

"I'm good, thanks for that," Maya said, trying to cover her embarrassment with a laugh. It took her a second to realize she was still in his arms, and she pulled away, straightening herself. "That could have been bad."

The broad-shouldered boy flashed her a smile, opening his mouth as if he were about to say something, which made Maya realize she wanted him to say something, especially to her. But then a tall girl in white jeans appeared at his elbow.

"Nishant! I was looking for you." The girl's perfect blowout bounced as she wrapped her arm around Nishant's, ignoring Maya entirely after a quick glance.

The boy, Nishant, barely looked at her before walking away—or being dragged away, by the tall girl.

Huh. He had nearly knocked her to the ground and then barely looked at her or apologized. Though she guessed he *had* caught her. She really couldn't afford a broken phone screen, so she'd give him that.

Maya was about to walk away when she realized he had dropped something. She bent down and picked up a flyer that had WINTERFEST FT. DJ NISH emblazoned on the front in bright block letters.

She stepped toward him.

"Hey! You—"

She didn't mean to overhear, but the girl's voice carried as she tossed her hair. "Who was that?" she said, her tone playful. "Did you find another study partner already?"

He turned away from Maya, but she could still hear his voice. "You have nothing to worry about," he said, a little too emphatically.

Maya didn't hear the girl's response because she had already turned on her heel. Maybe she was a little on edge, or maybe she had taken thirty seconds and run away with it in her head, but she hadn't expected his response. He had entirely dismissed her, after smiling and catching her in that magical, meet-cute way.

Maybe Thomas hadn't been the problem; maybe *she* had been. Maybe if Maya had been someone a little more gorgeous, or put-together, or *something* . . . she wouldn't be the one being dismissed. She bet that girl never had to convince a boy to call her his girlfriend.

Maya hadn't been the belle of her high school, or ever been very good at getting boys to notice her. The few attempts at romance in her life had failed spectacularly, in different ways. Despite being the one to end things with Thomas, she still felt a little raw. She hadn't wanted to do it; she would've preferred if he had wanted to be in a real relationship with her, if he had called her his girlfriend in front of his friends, if he had cared.

But he hadn't.

The common denominator was her. Her heart, her decisions.

She thought Nishant had smiled at her. . . .

Maya had gotten it so wrong. Clearly, her heart couldn't be trusted. Clearly, she couldn't be trusted with her own dating life. Maybe every decision she had ever made had been a mistake. Maybe this whole plan would burst into—

Okay, there. She took a deep, calming breath, wadded up the flyer, and tossed it into the nearest trash can. No spiraling today. And then she finally realized why that boy had looked so familiar as the image on the flyer stared back at her.

Nishant Rai. DJ Nish.

Two years above her and notorious, not just as the best DJ but also as one of the hottest guys on grounds. Even in her socially absent semester she had managed to hear about DJ Nish at the one or two HSA meetings she had been to, always by a lovestruck girl hoping to catch his attention.

Maya had enough experience with boys like that, built as a vehicle for heartbreak for girls like her. Green eyes and dark hair flashed across her mind, but she pushed it away quickly. This was not the time to think about Ari.

It was a good thing that Nishant had revealed himself. A good, firm reminder to her heart that he was a no-fly zone.

Anyway, not like she'd ever really talk to him again.

Maya firmly put Nishant Rai out of her mind as she walked up to the barista and ordered Jana's drink and an extra cupcake for them to share. She carried both back to Jana, who was eyeing her.

"What was that?" Jana asked. She had that expression on her face that Maya hated. The curious one.

"Nothing."

"Who was that guy?" Jana said, clearly not taking any hints from Maya. "He was—"

"Nishant Rai. DJ Nish."

It took a second for Jana to register her words. "Wait, *that's* him? DJ Nish? He's like the—"

"Unofficial social chair for all brown people at Neadham? Playboy

DJ of the junior class? Yup," Maya said. He was also kind of a jack-ass, which she did not mention. Her ego was already fragile enough at the moment after Thomas, and Nishant's dismissal of her only added fuel to that fire.

"Were you guys having a moment—"

"No."

"Are you going to let me finish a sentence?" Jana said. "Anyway, I'm not sure the 'two-date wonder' is exactly what you're looking for, though—" A thoughtful, slightly devious look crossed her face. "Maybe he is? A nice whirlwind romance could be exactly what you need."

"No, thank you," Maya said. "I've got to focus on event chair and looking for a real relationship, not someone who's going to waste my time for another semester." And seeing that it was pretty clear he was very *not* interested in her, she thought that was a fair point. "Like, sure, he's hot, I have eyes. But he's just going to—" She stopped, her heart constricting at old memories. "I'm not inter-ested in being another one of his two-date wonders."

Jana made a face. "You know, he went out with Imogen? Broke her heart. She was positive they were going on a third date. They had hit it off, and he had even helped her with some student coun-cil problem she had, but nope."

"Imogen?" Maya gasped. "She's the coolest and so—"

"Gorgeous? Carefree? Amazing?" Jana said. "I know! Is he really going to do better than her?"

Maya shook her head because it was actually unthinkable. Imogen was tall, willowy, with a carefree vibe that captured hearts wherever she went. She and Maya had bonded over their mutual love of period films and historical romances, but that's where their similarities ended. Imogen was not the type of girl to miss out on her first semester.

If Imogen wasn't good enough for Nishant, who was? Probably no one. Another boy out there to be a heartbreaker, as if it were a full-time occupation.

"That's ridiculous," Maya said. "I can't believe there are guys like that out there. I wonder if the two-date thing is a hard-and-fast rule."

"Apparently," Jana said. "It's like clockwork. And there seems to be an endless supply of girls who enjoy the challenge."

Ugh. That would never be her. Maya had spent enough time trying to get the wrong boys to like her. Nishant seemed like the type of boy who would never be happy.

"No, thank you," Maya said. "I'll stay away from that mess."

"Fair," Jana said. "Though I do still think a whirlwind romance would do you good. Try something new and all."

"I mean isn't that what I'm doing? I said I'll start to date," Maya said defensively, stirring her coffee. She conveniently brushed over the fact that she had just made that decision. Getting dismissed by the hottest guy on campus right after the guy you were seeing refused to commit was a lot for a girl to take.

Jana raised an eyebrow. "You did now. And how exactly are you going to do that?"

Maya traced the rim of her cup with her finger. "Um, by . . . putting myself out there? Where do people meet dates these days? What about mixers?"

Jana's eyebrows shot up even higher. "Mixers? What decade are we in? I'd say frat parties are the modern-day equivalent, but not quite effective." She leaned in. "You know, if you really want to date and you want to find someone who isn't a total waste of time, doesn't a dating app make sense?"

Damn, she had a point. Maya bit her lip. She wasn't against dating apps as a principle, but something about it felt so new, so untested.

Her own parents had met at a university mixer years ago, so she had thought that might be something that would happen to her, but look where that had gotten her. Her meet-cute had not been a happily ever after. Maybe sussing potential dates out ahead of time was a good idea.

Maybe her head needed to drive the car, not her heart.

"You might have a point," Maya said. "I'm looking for someone I could see myself with long-term, so . . ." She took a deep breath, wondering if she was really going to do this. This felt like jumping off a cliff—a very tall one with rocks jutting out under the crest of the waves. But wasn't this the point of trying to become Maya 2.0? "Okay, I'll try the scary app."

Jana blinked at her, taking a second to ingest her words. Her eyes went wide. "Wait, really? I love this new Maya. Plus, this is going to be great for my documentary." She whipped out her phone and pointed at Maya's phone, telling her what to do.

Maya followed her instructions, letting Jana pick her photo (her with windswept hair the summer before college in Florida with her family) but wrote her own bio (short, sweet, simple), though she did let Jana give input as she did her first swipe through.

Okay, this was . . . addictive.

High school had seemed like such a small pond, but Neadham

was not, a fact that Maya had wished she had known at the beginning of last semester. She even recognized a few of the boys from her classes. There had been this whole world at her fingertips, and she hadn't even known.

Maya tried not to beat herself up again, instead focusing on the smorgasbord in front of her.

"Oooh, that guy's a total hottie," Jana said, looking over her shoulder. "He's got that hair curl you know I love."

"Mhm," Maya said. Her own gaze went a little hazy. This was an entirely new learning experience. "And he's into traveling. He went to Costa Rica over winter break. So, check mark for wanting to leave the living room."

"Very high bar you've set there," Jana said, deadpan. "Send him a message."

"No, I couldn't—"

"I dare you. Just say hi. Literally."

Maya frowned at the phone. Was it really that easy? She typed in *Hi* and sent it, immediately feeling silly. He wasn't going to reply. Now what?

"This is the worst part," Jana said, leaning back in her chair. "Waiting. But that's why we have that cupcake."

She handed her a fork, and Maya was just about to tear into it alongside Jana, when a very specific trill went off. The ringtone she had set for Meet'em@Neadham. Maya checked her notifications.

To her utter surprise, Hair Curl had already responded.

She bit back a grin. What an instant ego boost.

A girl could get used to this.

CHAPTER 3

The HSA meeting was in the chem auditorium, the largest classroom in all of Neadham. It was in one of the older buildings, which meant wooden walls and rickety seats that creaked whenever you sat on them. The premed kids always complained about all the new buildings going to the business school, but Maya guessed that was the perk of having hedge fund managers as alumni.

Maya and Jana elbowed their way through a group of tall bhangra dance team boys who were practicing their latest routine and another group complaining loudly about the most recent Organic Chemistry exam. Maya dodged the a cappella group practicing in the corner and eyed two spots at the front of the auditorium. The meeting wasn't as crowded as normal—this one was for people interested in the committees for the spring semester, which meant only two handfuls of people. Jana had decided to tag along as an "anthropological study."

They slid into the seats with a few minutes to spare, which was good, because Maya's phone was trilling off the hook.

"Can you please call your mom back, or whatever else is causing that horrible racket?" Jana said.

"It's not my mom," Maya said. She lowered her voice. "It's Meet'em. My notifications are going crazy. Probably because I went . . . a little overboard."

That seemed to intrigue Jana, who leaned in, eyes gleaming. "Overboard how, exactly?"

"Um . . ." Maya said, biting her lip. "I may have stayed up every night for the past week messaging boys on Meet'em. I told you I was studying for the exam for Econ 102 . . . but the exam is actually next week and I'm totally fine on it."

Jana shook her head, laughing. "Wow, girl, you are obsessed. Even I didn't do that in the beginning."

Maya groaned, throwing her head of curls into her hands. She peeked out of her fingers at Jana. "The validation is so immediate! And I feel cool for once! I can compose flirty, snappy messages instead of freezing like a deer in headlights when talking to a cute boy, and I can ask them tough questions ahead of time, maybe even do a little cyber-stalking. I think the app was made for me," she finished, in a rush.

"Okay, let's slow our roll a little," Jana said. "You're in the honeymoon phase; I bet you haven't even gotten a weird text or photo yet."

Maya waved Jana's comment away. "Yeah, I have, and they're

super weird, but I expected that. You have to sift through some junk to find treasure. The entire university is on the app, so it makes sense that not everyone's going to be a fit, but everyone on the forums says it's far better than any of the other apps, and no one uses anything else at Neadham. Plus, this is like a much more safe and easy way to suss people out. I might even have a few coffee dates for next week!"

"Oh boy," Jana said, looking a little worried. "I think I've created a monster."

"No, this is all thanks to you," Maya said. She swiped to the Meet'em app and scrolled through her messages. "There is no way I could have met all these people in real life. This app is a godsend. It's the perfect thing for my new plan. For new Maya. Maya 2.0? I'm workshopping the name."

Jana's lips were pursed, and she looked a little skeptical. "You're welcome, I guess? You know what, you *are* welcome. I am mildly worried you're developing an addiction, but I guess that's better than what happened before, so . . . I'll take it?"

Maya grinned at her. "I'm not addicted. I can stop at any time." Another trill rang out, and she looked down at her phone.

"Uh-huh," Jana said, observing her like an animal in a zoo. "Might want to silence that. Think the meeting is starting."

Maya turned off the sound and tucked her phone away just as the meeting began. She wasn't sure if it was just her, but she felt excitement buzzing up her arms. Her plan was going along swimmingly, and if she could get a spot on the event committee, it would catapult her plan into the success stratosphere. A boost she could really use right now.

It had been a week since she had broken up with Thomas, and she felt good about the decision . . . but not all the time. She hadn't told Jana, but she had been *this close* to texting him a few nights ago after one of the Meet'em boys she had liked had ghosted her. Thankfully, she had caught herself quickly. Her ego had been wounded, that was all. Now, texting Thomas? That would be a mistake any way she looked at it.

"And as I'm sure you've all heard, because the one thing desi people can never do is keep secrets, Preetam will be resigning his post as event chair for the rest of year. He's decided to study abroad in Barcelona, which I'm sure is going to be horrible." Zane, the HSA president, laughed at his own joke, garnering a few chuckles on the side. He paced as he talked, close to where they both sat. Round wire-frame glasses sat on the top of his head, and he wore a half frown on his face like he had been born with it.

"See? I told you," Jana whispered into her ear.

"Which means this meeting is going to go a little differently than normal," Zane continued. "We have a solid turnout this year." Maya swiveled around with him, looking out at the rest of the crowd. She counted about ten to fifteen people, and she could assume only half of them would be interested in events, which gave her some decent odds for being picked for a committee.

She had gone over all her application answers while crossing her fingers *and* toes. They had been solid answers, if she did say so herself, and she had been the event chair of two clubs in high school. Hopefully, that would be good enough, but this was college and she had felt like she was behind from the first day she had walked onto the quad.

But that was the Old Maya. Maya 1.0.

Zane called out five names, a few of which she recognized,

including Pooja Kapoor and Nishant Rai. Maya resisted the urge to look for Nishant—out of curiosity, nothing more, of course. She hadn't forgotten their run-in the week before or the way he had ignored her. That was all.

And then Maya heard her own name.

"These five applications stood out," Zane said. "And since we're down an event chair, we're going to try something different and have each of you head up one of the events for this semester."

She bit back a gasp just as Jana squeezed her arm. Maya resisted the urge to clean out her ears. Had she heard that right? It was unexpected, to say the least. A surprising vote of confidence that buoyed her.

"Maya?" Maya started at Zane's voice, nearly jumping out of her seat. "Sorry to put you on the spot, but you had the best application," Zane said. "So you get first pick of your committee."

"What?" Maya said, nearly dropping the pencil in her hand.

She had the best application? That couldn't be true. She was about to ask why, but Jana poked her, nodding at the podium in the front.

"You get first pick," Zane repeated. "Valentine's Day dance, spring formal, India Day—"

"What about Holi?"

Maya said it before she could even fully think it through. Though once the words were out, they felt right. A murmur went through the small crowd.

"Holi?" Zane said, surprise laced through his voice like Maya had just said she had a third head. "You sure?" He lowered his voice a little, locking eyes with her. "I know the Holi Mela was one of the first and biggest Neadham events, but I feel like I should let you know, since you're a first-year, that the Athletics Office has been gunning for Holi so they can make room for more sports recruitment events. It wasn't very attended the past year, and they think it isn't worth the trouble, especially with the amount of cleanup required. We were thinking of canceling it."

"No," Maya said, a little more forcefully than she meant. "You can't. We can't. It's one of the best events on the Neadham spring calendar. The whole Lewiston community comes."

She racked her brain, trying to find a way to convince him. She had gotten this far, and she knew she could plan a Holi like no other. Sure, she could do the other events, but there was nothing like Holi.

Maya could still remember the first time she had played Holi, when she was five.

Her normally composed dad had chased after her mom with a small bowl of colored powder, smiles and laughs filling the air as loved ones turned into faux enemies for an hour. The goal was to get gulal, the colored powder, on everyone you could. The water balloons and water guns just added to the atmosphere of fun and joy.

She had always loved that about Holi. It was a time of rebirth and renewal. But even though she had loved playing Holi with gulal, her favorite tradition was the Holika Dahan, same as her grandmother's. In India, they would light a huge bonfire the night before Holi, to symbolize the defeat of evil and the triumph of good. Here in America, with her grandmother, they would make a small wood fire and toss anything that hadn't served them that year as a way of starting fresh.

Maya remembered one particular cathartic Holi when she had tossed all her SAT study papers into the fire.

She still did the ritual every year, even after her grandmother had passed away. She missed her grandmother with a fierce ache in her heart, but holding on to these traditions made her feel like there was still a part of her grandmother there. That she wasn't fully gone but lived on in their memory.

So, yeah, Holi meant a lot to her. And more so, the Neadham Holi Mela did as well. It had been the first time she realized that event planning could be a job—she had seen an article in the state newspaper on Neadham's Holi and the student organizer, Neelam Rao, who now owned the biggest Indian event planning company in NYC.

When her grandmother had brought her to the Neadham Holi six years ago, it was when she had decided to apply to Neadham. Not a lot of things came full circle in life, but Maya felt this could be one of those moments.

She just had to make it happen.

Maya took a deep breath and held Zane's gaze. "We should give it another shot. We could . . . revitalize Holi by turning it into a Holi Mela and bring that traditional vibe back into it." When Zane didn't laugh, she kept going. The words flowed out of her like they'd always been hers. "Not just colors on a random soccer field, but a real, old-fashioned mela. From top to bottom. We can show the administration that they were wrong. I've done this before at our high school. And I can handle marketing, too."

A beat of silence fell, and Maya held her breath. Finally, Zane nodded. "It's worth a shot. I hate the idea of giving that slot up to the Athletics Office anyway." Zane looked a little intrigued. "I'm curious to see what you do."

Maya sat back, a wide smile plastered on her face like she had just gotten the last ice-cream scoop of her favorite flavor. Part of her couldn't believe it.

Holi. She was going to bring back Holi to Neadham. A rebirth just as she was going through her own.

Fitting, wasn't it?

Jana squeezed her arm. "Look at that, you've got some fire in you," she said, looking appreciatively at Maya. "I like this side of you."

"Me too," Maya whispered.

Now she just had to pull it off. But for once, she didn't let her worry crush her like normal. Instead, she let herself bask in the moment.

"Okay, done," Zane said, continuing down the line. "Anjali gets Valentine's Day. Spring formal is gone. Guess that leaves you with India Day as well, Nishant. It's a big event, so it can definitely be a two-person job—"

"Don't I get a pick?" Nishant said drily, his voice punctuating the air. Maya turned and found him this time, sitting in the corner, his arms crossed.

Zane sighed, looking like he was doing his best not to roll his eyes. "Sure, Nishant. Go ahead. What's your pick? Though we all know—"

"Holi," he said, staring ahead.

Maya heard a garbled noise, and then realized it had come from her own mouth.

"Two people for Holi?" Zane rubbed his head. "I couldn't get anyone to plan it last year, and now two people?"

"We don't need—" Maya said.

"If we're going to make the one-hour event that was Holi into an actual event, one that's worthy of changing the administration's mind, you'll need the best on it. You know what I can do." He nodded at Zane, who looked a little resigned already. "And she's a freshman, and while I think she has a solid vision, I'm an upperclassman and I have more direct experience with the Neadham administration and student community."

No. No, no, no. Maya's triumph started to get a dingy gray tone. She was more than capable; she could do this. By herself.

"All right, you make a compelling case, Mr. Rai," Zane said. He gestured at Nishant, who nodded. "But it's up to Maya to decide if she wants a partner. Whatever she says goes."

"Can I think about it?" she said.

Zane nodded.

Maya tried to ignore the spark that shot through her body. She hadn't forgotten the way he had ignored her, or his reputation.

Normally, she might welcome help, but now Maya knew one thing. Nishant Rai would be an obstacle.

And she wouldn't be able to avoid him now.

CHAPTER 4

The meeting wrapped up shortly after, but Maya rushed to the exit, and when she was finally out into the fresh air, she took a deep breath. The sky was a hazy pink and blue, hinting at the sunset that would follow, and chatting students walked to and fro, on their way to dinner at the nearby dining hall.

She had done it. She was planning Holi, of all things.

Even if it was going to be a total from-the-ground-up creation of a new event, and it could be a massive challenge, and she might fail utterly, and then Holi would be canceled forever at Neadham and it would be all her fault and—

Maya held a hand to her chest, willing her heart to beat a little slower. Anxiety was Old Maya, not New Maya. Or that's what she was going to tell herself starting now.

She could do this.

It would all be worth it in the end when she had pulled off the most perfect, most nostalgic and traditional Holi Mela that would make everyone think of their childhood in the best way possible. Which would put her in the running, or even lead, for event chair. And to do it for her grandmother's favorite holiday, well, that was the icing on top. A fitting tribute to the one person who had always believed in Maya.

Zane came out of the chem building with Pooja, the two of them chatting about something she couldn't hear.

"Hey," Zane said, both of them catching up to Maya. "Sorry you got put on the spot like that. You don't have to decide if you want to work with him until the next meeting. Say the word, and I can put him on another committee. But to be fair, Nishant has a bit of an eye for events, and his family owns an event planning company, so he might actually be helpful."

Oh, she hadn't actually realized that. Her curiosity was piqued, but her interest quickly soured—a DJ in an event planning family? Good for him. His parents must have thought it a coup, unlike her two engineer parents, who looked at her baking and event planning as odd hobbies rather than a possible life path.

"I appreciate that," Maya said. True, she wasn't looking forward to working with Nishant, but she would act like a professional and put her personal qualms aside. Or at least pretend to, for now. Her actual plan was to give it a fair(ish) shot and then regretfully tell Zane that it did not work out. "Let's see how the meeting goes next week, and I'll let you know."

Nishant passed by in the corner of her eye, his arm tossed around a new girl she didn't recognize. And not the one from the coffee shop. It had only been a few days, but Maya supposed she must have hit her two-date capacity already.

Zane snorted. "He's moved on from Emilia, has he? No surprise there." He noticed the question on Maya's face. "Ah, we went to the same high school, so I've known Nishant for a while."

He waved goodbye, mentioning he was meeting someone on University Avenue, where all the actual restaurants and bars were.

"Dinner?" Jana said, coming up from behind and looping her arm through Maya's. "Celebrate your major win today?"

"Yes, please, I'm starving," Maya said. Plus, the dining hall was doing mac and cheese that night. Thomas never wanted to go. Who didn't like mac and cheese?

"And you promised to help me with my Bollywood 101 homework," Jana said.

"I still can't believe you haven't seen *DDLJ*."

Jana shrugged and pulled her toward the dining hall. "You can yell at me about it over fries and mac and cheese."

A trill rang from Maya's phone, and she glanced at her notifications. Surfer boy had responded, and she couldn't help the smile that crept onto her face.

She hated to admit it, but she was starting to perk up every time she heard a trill, even if it wasn't a successful message. There were a thousand tries with Meet'em@Neadham, like a video game where you could restart the level. Jana was right; it was addictive. Was this what Thomas had loved about gaming?

For the first time, Maya felt like she had some control when it came to her love life, and *that* was what was truly addicting.

And she didn't think she'd ever let it go.

———— ✍ ————

The sun was shining overhead when Maya finally made it out of her Econ 102 exam, her brain filled with macroeconomics numbers and facts and . . . she really needed something sugary sweet, stat.

She headed for the local coffee shop, the one with the cinnamon rolls she loved, and texted Jana to meet her there. Jana would need the rush as well, especially because she had just finished a Comp Sci 102 exam with Professor Turnbull, who was known to make students cry during exams.

Maya wound her way out of the econ building. The lawn was filled with students who had probably also finished their exams, and she could hear the raucous noises of flag football from the corner. There was some sort of music practice on the left lawn, maybe the concert orchestra, and Maya noted that they were playing Bach. Guess her piano lessons had turned out to be useful after all.

She should tell Isaac, the music major she had been texting with—wasn't he in the chamber group? Maya ducked her head to message him and check her Meet'em app DMs as she walked. Particularly that guy with wavy hair who said he was into historical novels. Even better, she could finally set up that date with SoCal, the cute surfer guy from LA who she had been texting late last night with. He had hinted that he wanted to grab her coffee, and even Maya could tell the ball was in her court, and she actually wanted to pick it up.

For the first time, she was excited about dating. Not just about getting the chance to meet SoCal, but also the chance to see what was out there and find the person who was exactly right for her. She would not be falling into the Thomas trap again. Nope, nuh-uh.

Maya hummed to herself as she clicked open the app and began to swipe. And that's when she noticed it.

"Oh no," she said, her eyes widening. "Oh no, oh no, oh no."

Her previous filled-to-the-brim message inbox for Meet'em@ Neadham was gone.

As was her entire account.

"Okay, explain again, without the hyperventilating?" Jana said. She sat back in her chair and crossed her arms.

Maya rubbed her temples and took another calming sip of chamomile tea. She had rushed them over to the coffee shop and cornered their favorite couch, the one with the soft, peeling leather and proximity to the large windows that looked over University Avenue. The three empty drink cups and muffin wrapper were indicative of her mental state.

"Like I told you," Maya said, "I tried to log into Meet'em when I got out of the exam, and poof, everything was gone. I was going to ask out SoCal, because he kind of hinted I should, and now he'll think something horrible has happened to me. Or worse, that I'm ghosting him!"

"Let me see your phone," Jana said, frowning.

Maya handed her phone to Jana. Jana tapped into Meet'em and saw the horrible evidence—a blank, empty screen where flirty, perfectly crafted messages and potential life partners had once been. Now there was a little pop-up that alerted her that she had been reported in bright red block letters.

"I tried to log in, and every single time it said I've been blocked for violating community rules, whatever the hell that means."

"There's only one explanation," Jana said, shaking her head. "Given that you are you and you would never do something to violate the community guidelines . . . Thomas." She narrowed her eyes. "That weasel."

Maya sighed. "Jana, we don't know that it was Thomas. This would be a pretty big thing to do. It would take effort, and why would he waste time doing all of this? We're broken up."

"That's exactly why he would. Because he's mad you broke up with him," she said, glaring at the phone. "I know he did it. I'll prove it." She had her scary face on, and if it *was* Thomas, Maya felt a little sorry for what Jana might do to him.

Maya let out a deep sigh. This was the last thing she needed right now. Not that she ever needed a potentially vengeful ex, but still.

For the first time in months, she had been starting to feel good. Great, even. If nothing else, like she was getting her life back on track.

And now?

"What am I going to do?" Maya groaned into her hands. She glanced down at her phone with a frown. Was this some sign from the universe? Some horrible, crap-wrapped sign?

Maybe she was destined to be single. Maybe it was a sign that her mother was right and dating apps were the worst modern invention. Maybe Thomas was right and she couldn't handle all of this, all this newness and putting herself out there. Maybe . . . it was bad luck.

Maya grabbed a small chocolate muffin from their pile of acquired drinks and baked goods and stuffed it in her face. "If it was Thomas, that sucks. A lot. Honestly, the first time I dump someone—not even dump, because I tried my best to be gentle about it—"

"You're making it sound like it was your fault," Jana said. "You know it's not your fault, right? If he did this? His friends literally call him Toxic Thomas when they play games."

"Yeah, yeah," Maya said, taking another monster bite. The chocolate was working, but not quick enough. Was there a way to inject chocolate into her veins?

"Don't worry, if it was him, he'll face my wrath," Jana said. She took a sip of her drink, and then made a face. She had accidentally grabbed Maya's chamomile tea. "Anyway, I can set you up with—"

"No."

"Maya, you didn't even let me finish—"

"No," Maya said firmly. "I'll appeal the ban, or whatever you do, and get back on the app." She swallowed roughly. What the hell was she supposed to do now? Maya couldn't just . . . meet people normally. That was something Confident, Sexy Maya could do, which was basically Imaginary Maya.

There was a reason she had gotten addicted to Meet'em in the past week. In a few clicks she had been able to learn everything she needed to know about a person to make sure they'd be a fit, instead of learning a semester into the relationship and getting Cheeto stains on her favorite blue pillows.

"You know, I only forced you to join Meet'em because you needed a change. I was honestly surprised you took to it so quickly. I thought you were all about doing things the old-fashioned way. That's why you still haven't gotten a new phone, isn't it?" Jana said, glancing down at Maya's ancient phone, which still sported a large crack she had gotten two months ago after an unfortunate incident with the corner late-night sandwich shop cash register.

Maya pursed her lips. "It works just fine the way it is! Who needs all those new, weirdly human emoji things?"

"Point," Jana said. "But still, why not let yourself meet someone the old way? What about that cute guy in your Econ 102 class?"

"Nope," Maya said. "He went to Coachella last year with his mother."

Jana snorted. "That's the truth, right there."

Maya sighed. "Look, Jana. I don't need an IRL connection." Especially because none of those had worked out for her in the past. "I need my access to Meet'em back. Stat."

"Hoookay, you sound like an addict," Jana said. "But I feel you. I'll talk to Suki again; maybe I can convince her to get dinner with us and you can plead your case."

Maya squeezed Jana into a hug. "Yes, thank you, I was feeling so helpless."

"And I mean it," Jana said. "If this was Thomas, and I will find out, no one will be able to save him." A thoughtful, downright devious look crossed Jana's face. "Ooh, that could be a great documentary subject. An investigation. Not to make your life a whole thing, but . . ."

"It's fine, might as well use material that's right in front of you," Maya said. She looked down at the phone in her lap and gripped her phone tighter. "If it was Thomas, I won't let him bring me down."

"That's the spirit!" Jana said. She tapped her coffee cup against Maya's mug in a faux cheers, a huge smile on her face.

Maya laughed and sank back into the couch.

———❦———

Maya walked into the HSA event committee meeting with a cloud over her head.

She had tried for the past week to get her dating ban repealed, but nothing had worked. Jana hadn't even been able to convince the founder, Suki, to get dinner with them so Maya could plead her case. Apparently, they had a zero-strikes policy, and she took their community reporting very seriously. Even though she suspected Thomas, Jana had no proof. Which left Maya high and dry.

"Hey, Maya!"

Maya turned around to see Zane. They had been emailing back and forth about Holi, Zane providing some of the administrative context from the past two years and generally giving her an overview. Honestly, it had been the only saving light in the past week of the Meet'em ban. It had given her something to focus on other than her disastrous love life.

"Hope my emails were helpful," he said. "You know my philosophy is to get as many thoughts together as possible!"

Maya did know that, since they had been the main cause of her stress this past week aside from the Meet'em debacle. Zane, with his glasses and keen expression, was literally the human embodiment of a Socratic seminar. His emails had revealed that pretty early on, and his frantic in-person energy ported over digitally as well.

"I'll check in with you guys later!" Zane said before running off, just as Nishant entered the room. Maya sucked in a breath, wondering why it felt like all the air had disappeared. He was in a black

T-shirt and jeans, and somehow he made even that basic outfit look good.

"Hey, Maya," Nishant said, sidling up to her. "I'm Nishant."

Damn him for having a low, smooth voice that would make Idris Elba jealous. And wavy, thick hair you could definitely dream about running your hands through.

If only the rest of him fit.

"I know. We met. Last week," Maya said.

He gave her a languid smile. "I do remember that but wasn't sure if you would."

What was she supposed to say to that? Either way, she felt like she had walked into some sort of trap.

"Anyway," she said, taking a seat. "Let's start. Zane mentioned you had a ton of ideas. So, hit me."

She took out her notebook. The best way to handle this was to be professional. Planning the Holi Mela was something she was excited to do, and she wasn't going to let anyone ruin it. Maybe, possibly, he might have a good idea, which she would write down, and then that would be it.

"Getting right down to it?" Nishant raised an eyebrow as he leaned against the desk nearby. He couldn't even sit down properly, how annoying. "Okay. Get ready for it. Here's my vision. We turn the Holi Mela into the hashtag HoliFest. Lights and cameras everywhere. Think EDM festival meets old-fashioned Holi dance party with bhang."

Bhang? Maya had had a taste of a bhang drink—milk mixed with ground edibles—once in India and she had almost eaten all the mangoes on her grandmother's mango tree after, peel and everything. She knew people all around India drank it during Holi to celebrate, but she hadn't really enjoyed her experience with it.

But what really got her goat was the other things he had said.

Nishant continued. "We can add a five-K Color Run, maybe make the bonfire boozy. Plus, that's around the time of spring break—so we might as well make it a lit party. And I can DJ, of course."

"Wait, are you serious?" Maya said. She knew she was being just a little rude, but she couldn't help herself. "You want to make Holi *lit*?"

Nishant blinked at her slowly, his stupid long eyelashes fluttering. "Why not?"

"Because it's Holi."

"And?"

And Holi was her holiday. He could go make Diwali all "lit" or whatever. Of course he would think of taking one of the best holidays and turning it into some souped-up, annoyingly loud EDM festival. Holi wasn't just a day of colored powder and water guns; it symbolized so much more to so many people.

To her.

Holi had been her thing with her grandmother, and bringing that slice of home here . . . that was what she wanted to do. That's how she was going to become the next event chair, by bringing the traditional events from their community to life here at Neadham. The HSA had been a fixture of the Neadham community for two decades, and she wasn't going to be the one to ruin all of that by changing things drastically.

She'd had enough change for a while.

Nishant kept looking at her, waiting, with that unnerving stare of his. Screw being professional.

"You know what?" she said. "This isn't going to work. It's

an . . . interesting idea, but not what I'm thinking and definitely not how I'm hoping to plan this event. I'll tell Zane it just wasn't a fit."

"What's the big deal?" he said, looking annoyed. "So I'm suggesting we modernize Holi. That's what the future is all about. Don't be all dadi on me."

Maya began to see red. Had he just told her not to go all *grandma* on him? She had called her grandmother *Amamma*, but she knew what *dadi* meant.

First of all, that hit a little too close to home. And second, there was nothing wrong with being traditional. There was a reason these things lasted. There was a reason she had fallen in love with Neadham Holi, as had so many other people. How could you top that?

"What's the big deal?" Maya sucked in her breath and then let it out. "You're stomping all over Holi! It's known as the festival of colors, not the festival of bad music and earplugs. Holi is the festival of renewal. A time to celebrate life and love, just as spring starts to bloom. It's traditional and nostalgic. And you—"

She pointed an accusing finger at him.

Nishant stared at her and then her finger. Maya set her hand down, realizing she might look a little unhinged.

There was no way she was going to consider working with Nishant if he wanted to turn their Holi festival into the second coming of E-Zoo. DJ Nish was not taking over. Not if Grandma Maya had anything to say about it.

"I'm sorry, but no," Maya said, taking a deep, calming breath. "I know Zane was suggesting we could be partners, but partners should at least agree on a plan, and clearly we're on opposite ends of this. This just wouldn't be a good fit."

Something shifted in Nishant's face from before, an expression she couldn't pinpoint. He seemed almost nervous.

"Hey, look, give me a chance here. I really want to help plan this event, and I'm positive I can help bring it into the future. We could make the Holi Mela the top club event at Neadham for the entire year if we do this," he said.

"What if it doesn't need to be pushed into the future? What if it's totally happy right here?" Maya asked, hands on hips.

Nishant pursed his full lips, looking a little confused. Okay, so that wasn't a great comeback, but she was a little flustered. She had come here expecting to put pen to paper on planning her first HSA event, and Holi, no less.

And he had to come in and ruin it all. It wasn't that she was against having a partner. She was just against *this* partner, his #HoliFest.

Plus, he had called her a grandma.

"How's it going, Maya?" Zane asked, popping up behind Nishant. They both jumped.

Maya plastered on a smile immediately. "Great!" she said. "We're talking through Nishant's ideas." She didn't want Zane to regret giving her the chance to plan Holi, even if he had said her application was the best one.

"Fantastic!" Zane said. He nodded at the two of them and walked away.

"Crap," Maya muttered. Even Zane was Team Nishant.

"Give me a chance," Nishant said, putting on a pouty face. It was sort of adorable, which only made Maya more annoyed. "You're right, we don't have to push it into the future. Or not that much. But I know I can help make this event successful. I know more people will want to attend if we offer them something new, like a music festival. You should consider that."

Maya gave him an uncertain look. It probably wasn't fair to hold his complete dismissal of her at the café against him. Or him calling her a grandma, though she felt a bit more justified about that.

She did really hate his idea, though . . . but she wasn't able to completely dismiss his point. Attendance was the most important thing.

"I know a lot of people, which will be really useful if you want to actually make the Holi festival the best club event at Neadham," he continued.

"You said you wanted to do that, not me," Maya said grumpily. "I just want to put on a wonderful Holi Mela, the way it used to be. People want a slice of home here at Neadham, and we can bring that to them. I think that's how we get those attendance numbers up again. Not with all this newfangled stuff, but by delivering a better version of the classic experience they used to love. That's what Neadham wants."

Nishant stepped closer, and Maya had to resist the urge to step back as well. He was a little too close for comfort now, close enough that she could smell his earthy cologne. It didn't immediately make her want to gag, which she saw as a betrayal from her body.

"Maybe, but what if they also want more? Are you telling me you don't want to plan the best event this university has seen this year?" he said softly. "You don't want to show them how wrong they were for underestimating Holi? And the HSA?"

Damn it. He had figured her out perfectly. Of course she wanted to plan the best event. Of course she wanted to show off Holi and make the administrators eat crow. Who wouldn't?

"I'll figure something out on my own," Maya said, now a bit unsure. Was it a mistake to turn down Nishant's help?

Maybe she could salvage this situation. He wasn't wrong about knowing everyone. Even in her one semester at Neadham, she knew that Nishant was a man around campus. Doors opened for him. She did really love the idea of making Holi the best club event of the year, and maybe she could use a partner.

She had her principles, but she was also practical. Maya wanted to win.

But what was he really after here? Why did he want to plan Holi so badly? Even Zane didn't get it. Holi was underfunded and hanging on by a thread. Maya knew her motivations, but what about Nishant's?

Her phone pinged and Maya sneaked a peek at her screen. Her frown turned into a scowl when she saw the notification.

ACCOUNT DELETION APPEAL—DENIED.

Great. Just absolutely fan-freaking-tastic. This day was getting worse and worse.

Nishant leaned over her shoulder and Maya hid her phone. Last thing she needed right now was for Nishant to find out that she had gotten kicked off Meet'em—that would mean embarrassment of epic proportions. He knew every cute guy on campus, and it would probably only take two days before he told all of them and ruined her entire dating pool.

"Everything okay? You look a little—" he said.

"I'm fine," she said, with a deep sigh.

"Fine?" Nishant said. "Are you only fine because you just got banned from the one dating app on grounds?"

"What?" Maya said, stumbling back. "That was private! Did you just read my message?"

Nishant shrugged. "I may have also heard that someone was massively banned yesterday at dinner with my comp sci friends. No name was given, but with your reaction and that familiar trilling noise . . ."

Damn it. He was good. Also, he had comp sci friends? That was range.

"And now everyone is going to know," she said, unable to hold back the despair in her voice. "And I'll never get a date again and I'll be a pariah forever."

Oops, she hadn't meant to say that last part out loud. Nishant looked at her thoughtfully, his head cocked and his eyes assessing.

"And why would they need to know?" Nishant started to grin. "What if I have an offer for you?"

She tilted her head at him. "And that would be?"

Nishant shifted on his feet, and she was reminded again of how tall and big he was. Made her feel like I was standing next to a sunflower.

"What if I was your dating app?"

"Huh?" Maya couldn't help but blink at him in confusion.

"Like a matchmaker," Nishant said. "You know, *Fiddler on the Roof*?"

Maya was surprised he knew any musical theater. Score one to Nishant for surprising her—and for having good taste.

"You want to find dates for me?" Maya said, a little disbelieving.

"Screen the general boy population for me?"

"Sure. I'll be your unofficial matchmaker," he said. "And in return, I'm your co-chair for planning the Holi Mela."

Ah, there was the catch.

Was it worth it? Maya bit her lip, glancing down at her now very empty notification screen. Her request had been flat-out denied, and she knew that she wasn't ever going to be the girl who could just walk up to people in random places and strike up a conversation. That was one traditional route that had never quite worked out for her. She needed help, that she knew for sure, especially after Meet'em. She couldn't date from her heart anymore.

Maya snuck a look at Nishant. But she hadn't accounted for him staring back. Nishant looked down at her with that annoying little smirk of his, his eyes focused and intent on hers as if he was seeing her for the first time.

And maybe it wouldn't be bad to have an upperclassman as a partner in planning Holi, especially when it came to marketing.

"Fifty-one percent to forty-nine percent," Maya said, coming to a decision. "The fifty-one being me, obviously."

Nishant gave her an appraising look. "Drives a hard bargain. I'll add it to my list for matchmaking. Fine, forty-nine percent."

"And the dates only count if they're in real life and last more than, like, half an hour or something—"

"All right." Nishant paused. "I think I can make that work."

"Then I suppose we have a deal," Maya said, sticking out her hand. "We can go over the terms in finer detail later."

He took her hand, his enveloping hers, and shook it.

Nishant glanced at her. "I'm curious. How exactly did you get kicked off Meet'em?"

"I'm not sure, but my best friend thinks . . . well, she thinks it was an ex. Kind of ex."

Nishant paused and raised his eyebrow at her. "Damn, girl. Not such a dadi after all."

Maya flushed. Okay, that had come out sounding cooler or more interesting than what actually happened, but she didn't have time to explain. Nor did she really feel like justifying herself to Nishant Rai.

"You cannot tell anyone," she hissed. She could feel her cheeks heating, and it only got worse when Nishant stepped closer to her. "And stop calling me a dadi."

"Fine, I won't tell anyone about your heartbreaking ways," Nishant said.

Once it was all said and done, Maya realized what she had agreed to—two months in close contact with Nishant Rai. And she had put her entire love life's future in his hands.

She only hoped she hadn't just made a terrible, terrible mistake.

CHAPTER 5

Nishant Rai: Hey, this is Nishant.

Nishant Rai: We should meet up soon to start planning.

Nishant Rai: Hello?

Maya Sastry: If you promise not to call me a dadi again.

Nishant Rai: No promises.

M aya spent most of that night pacing the kitchen as a batch of lemon pound cake muffins baked, going over her conversation, and deal, with Nishant ad nauseam. What had she been thinking? And what must he be thinking now? Why had she agreed to work with someone who thought she was a grandma?

Her thoughts swirled around her head like a storm of gnats. When her timer went off, she slapped her oven mitts on, pulled out the muffins to cool, and then proceeded to scream into the muffins.

Jana happened to walk in at that moment. Her eyes went wide. "Everything okay over there?"

Maya groaned in response. Plus, her muffin experiment hadn't worked. Half of them were deflated, despite the extra baking soda she had put in.

"I'm going to take that as a no," Jana said. She put her keys on the wall hook and dropped her bag onto the ground. "Those muffins smell amazing."

Maya managed a small thank-you before she slouched onto one of the barstools that surrounded the kitchen island. Their little dorm apartment was stuffed to the gills with things, from cleaning supplies to the old baking pans Maya had brought from her family home to all their textbooks. Maya had been grateful that Neadham even had full kitchens, even though they were tiny. Without baking, she would have definitely lost her mind sometime in the second week of first semester.

But apparently that had happened this week instead.

"I think I just made the biggest mistake of my life," Maya said.

"Bigger than Thomas?" Jana countered.

Had he really been that bad and she had missed it? Maya thought back to their first meeting, the ice creams after. They had started out so good, but maybe that was always the case.

Maya gave her a look; Jana shrugged in response. "I really didn't like him," Jana said, before peering at the muffins.

"They're cooling," Maya said. "Hands off."

"So if I tried to eat one, I would probably burn my mouth?" she said, still eyeing the muffins.

"Yes, Jana." Maya nudged the muffins out of her way. "Please don't do that again. You couldn't taste anything for a week last time."

Jana let out an aggrieved sigh and turned her full attention to Maya. She flipped her short, curly hair out of her eyes. "Fine. Then distract me with your drama. What's up? What's this new mistake? I thought everything was going well with the Holi Mela planning."

"It was," Maya admitted. "Until yesterday."

She gave her a quick recap.

"Let me get this straight," Jana said, as Maya finished her story. Her mouth was open in a comical way, like a cartoon. "*Nishant Rai* wants to help plan the Holi Mela? Why? He doesn't really seem the type to care about a Hindu festival."

Maya threw her hands up. "No idea! But he seemed really passionate about it and wouldn't let it go, so . . . I made that deal. And now I'm majorly regretting it. Plus, he called me a dadi."

"That's brilli— That sucks. He sucks. So much." Jana stifled a laugh, but not quick enough that it didn't earn a glare from Maya. "Um, what I was trying to say is that you are definitely not a grandma, though you do love baking and knitting quite a lot, and you are a bit of a traditionalist—" Another glare from Maya. "Anyway, what I was trying to say was that the *deal* was brilliant. I'm surprised he offered it." She rested her chin on her palm. "Something smells fishy here."

"Maybe he really wants to make this #HoliFest happen."

Jana pointed a finger into her open mouth and mimed gagging.

"Thank you," Maya said. "I agree."

"Don't get me wrong, I love music festivals," Jana said. "But I'm trying to show some solidarity with you." She eyed the muffins again.

"You don't actually think it's a horrible idea?" Maya said. "Holi isn't about all of that nonsense."

"Holi is the arrival of spring. What's more spring vibes than a party? And people in India have a blast for Holi. They're leagues ahead of our celebrations here," Jana countered. She reached for a muffin, and Maya swatted her hand away. "Anyway, you're a real stickler about these things sometimes. Maybe trying something different won't be so bad."

"It's not just that," Maya said slowly. "My grandmother used to love Holi, and she would always do it a certain way. Part of me wants to bring that to Neadham, to all the other students who may have been a little homesick like me. I want to make them fall in love with the Neadham Holi I did." Her shoulders drooped. "I know that sounds a little sad, I guess—"

"No, I get it," Jana said. She pulled her into a quick, surprising hug, one so fast that Maya thought maybe she had imagined it. Jana was not really a hugger. "That's really thoughtful of you. And I do think a lot of people would appreciate that."

Maya relaxed a little at her support, enough that she actually considered what Jana had said. Holi was about the arrival of spring, the triumph of good over evil, about the renewal of the earth. But it was already a party.

What was more fun than throwing colored powder at each other? Messing with a good thing could be a problem anyway. It's not like she was against innovation, but maybe only in small ways? Trying a new color powder brand. Maybe a scavenger hunt. Something safer. Something that wouldn't get her branded as the worst event planner ever. Or disappoint the memory of her grandmother.

This event would have her name on it. It had to be good. It had to be good enough for event chair, too.

"Stop pre-worrying," Jana said. She tilted her head at Maya and raised an eyebrow. "It's going to be great. No matter what you end up doing. Now, can I have one of those damn muffins?"

Jana was seconds away from snatching one, so Maya helped her to it. "I'm terrified about pulling this off."

"Don't be." A very pleased moan came from Jana, who was already three-quarters of the way done with the muffin. "These are amazing. They look a little busted, but . . ." She took another bite. "So freaking good."

Maya tilted her head at the muffins. "They were a little busted."

Huh, maybe that was a sign. Something that didn't look so great on the outside turned out to be delicious. Maybe she had a chance here after all.

And if it could help her become HSA event chair and to find an actual relationship, a real romance, she'd have to take the chance. No matter how scary.

Maya took out her phone and found Nishant's number, and before she could think about it too much, she sent him a quick text to plan for their first meeting.

There. She had done it.

Maya tried not to worry about the rest.

Maya found Nishant lounging on the quad, a notebook resting on his lap as he tapped a pencil to whatever beats were playing through his massive headphones. DJ headphones. The pretentious kind, too, which didn't surprise Maya.

And of course, he was one of those people who actually did their work outside. Maya was an indoors gremlin when it came to studying. She needed darkness and solitude to do her best work. One more way they were complete opposites.

Oh, and she wasn't a huge asshole.

She sighed internally. It didn't matter, did it? They were working together on this event, so she would need to put aside all of that. Or at least try to. Zane had sent her a text earlier that day asking for a status update and all Maya had been able to do was send him back a series of thumbs-up emojis and a quick timeline for the event date approval, which was coming up.

"Are you standing there, staring at me, for a reason? I mean, I know I look good today and all . . ." Nishant said. He had taken off his headphones and was now looking straight at her. Maya flushed, but she had no idea why. She hadn't done anything wrong. Maya had to resist the very, very strong urge to cross her arms across her chest in defiance.

He was so irritating, especially because he was totally right. Nishant did look good today. Dark jeans and a white Henley, his hair swooped back under a baseball cap. Not her typical look, but he had style—the cap was flat-brimmed and all in neutral tones, and the Henley fit snug, showing off those broad shoulders of his. Add that to the slight dimple in his cheek, even as he smirked, and Nishant was a problem.

"I know you love to spend time in front of the mirror staring at yourself, but the rest of us have better things to do," Maya blurted out. She almost slapped her hand over her mouth, she was so surprised.

Sure, she had been thinking that, but first-semester Maya would have never said that. What had possessed her?

She was considering apologizing, which would be absolutely mortifying, when Nishant blinked rapidly and then broke out into laughter.

"You think I look this good from dressing in the dark?" he said, trailing into a small chuckle. "Of course I spend my time in front of the mirror. You're welcome."

She rolled her eyes, relaxing. He was so annoying. Even if he was right.

"I didn't thank you," she said, taking a seat next to him on the blanket he had laid out. She took care not to sit on the grass, especially because these pants could not afford any grass stains.

He leaned over to her. "I could see it in your eyes. You were undressing me."

Maya sputtered. "I was not. How could—"

"Relax," he said, winking at her. "You're not the first."

Well. She was now annoyed, hot, and bothered. A combination she hadn't expected this morning and definitely hadn't dressed for. Why exactly had the universe decided to give this man an ego along with his good looks? It wasn't fair. Everything probably fell into his lap without him even having to try, just because he oozed that confidence that everyone lapped up. And then there were people like her, those who had to build that confidence, little by little.

When she looked up, Nishant was still staring at her in that unnerving way, like he knew everything she was thinking.

Maya distracted herself by getting her things out of her backpack, taking the moment to re-collect herself. They were partners, forced to work together. She would get through this, if and only if she remembered who exactly she was partnered with. She let out a breath.

She turned around to find Nishant still looking at her, almost expectantly.

"I started to put together an event proposal," Maya said, breezing past Nishant's last comment. She pulled out the folder Zane had given her and held it out to Nishant.

He looked . . . almost disappointed? That she hadn't engaged in his pointless banter and pseudo flirting? He hid it quickly and took the folder from her. He hung his headphones around his neck, which was actually a good look for him, and flipped through the papers.

"First, we'll need to get approval from the Activities Office for the event date," he said. "Thanks for that email with the timeline."

Maya nodded. "Since it's already the third week of January, we only have two months till the event. Holi is in mid-March this year, which buys us some time."

That was the thing about Holi—it was based on the lunar calendar, so it fell on different dates every year. Maya remembered the one year it was in February and there was a light dusting of snow on the playing field. Her fuzzy hat had been completely demolished by gulal that year.

"A little," he said. "But there's a lot to do. Once we get the date approved, we'll need to finalize a venue and vendors. Performances, too. Then there's marketing. I see you have that all in your project plan here, but you're only planning for one afternoon. Aren't we trying to make Holi big at Neadham again? Redeem it? I have a few vendors and new event spaces in mind, so I'll—"

"Whoa, whoa." Maya glanced up, surprised. "What's wrong with the soccer field they started the event on?"

He shrugged. "I'm sure you remember what Zane said. Last year was not the best showing. I think we need to consider a wider range of options, if we really want to make this the best event possible."

She also wanted to make this the best event possible, but that meant making sure they had a solid footing. People expected Holi to be on the soccer field, expected certain vendors. *That's* how they were going to make this the best event possible, by returning it to its glory.

"What's wrong with the existing options?" she said, frowning.

"What's right with them?" he retorted.

Maya opened her mouth, but nothing came out. What a ridiculous question! She didn't need to prove something right that had already worked. It was tested. It could be trusted. The outcome spoke for itself.

"Look, Holi was one of Neadham's main events for a long time. I agree we need to spruce it up, but—" she said.

"We don't need to spruce it up. We need to completely change it up," Nishant said. "Reimagine it. We shouldn't be doing things the same way for the sake of it. That's not how you get to the best. We have to innovate. People will show up to an EDM Holi music festival, but they're not going to come to the same old event."

That didn't even make any sense. People loved Holi at Neadham. She had loved Holi at Neadham. Sure, they could update the vendors and she did want to add a Mela—a fair and performances—but it had to make sense.

Ugh. He was so frustrating. Was that why he never went on a third date? Because he didn't want to "do things the same way for the sake of it"? The thought alone made her even more annoyed. Leave it to a man to assume he knew better than everyone else, just because he happened to be hot and charming.

"There's a reason why it's tradition. Why it's been done that way," she said. "Because it's a *good* idea."

He shrugged. "Says who?"

"Tons of people!" Maya said, barely resisting the urge to throw her hands up. Was he trying to get a rise out of her, or did that just come naturally to him? "People who want to be successful."

"So you're saying you can only be successful if you do things the way others tell you to? What about what we think?"

"No," she said. "I didn't say that. I'm saying innovation for the sake of it isn't necessarily right, either."

He gave her a look that said she basically had. Maya felt her cheeks heat. She should've known not to trust two-date wonder DJ Nish. She didn't even like EDM music, which was his whole thing. How was she supposed to get along with him? How were they supposed to plan this?

Nishant held up his hands in a conciliatory gesture. "Look, we're on the same team here."

She glowered at him.

"Really, we are. And we're not so different. I mean, look at you. You got kicked off the app and now you're letting yourself be matchmade."

"Oh, is that another dadi move?" she said, unable to hide the sarcasm in her voice. "Too traditional for you?"

Nishant didn't even have the decency to look chastised. A coiling grin lit up his face. "Yeah, it is, but it's also a good solution. An innovation."

"Huh?" Maya said, unable to hide her confusion.

"You had a problem and found a new way to solve it. Innovation," he said. "Look at that, Maya."

Huh. Was that a compliment? Maya couldn't tell, and given that she wasn't really holding a lot of goodwill for him at the moment, she decided not to assume.

"Maybe," she said. "But an EDM festival doesn't solve our problem, either. Okay, fine, so Zane said attendance was a problem. The Activities Office doesn't want to invest in the cleanup. How does that scream *We need to add a messy, random EDM festival?*"

"How does it say *We need to keep everything the same?*" he challenged.

Maya pinched the bridge of her nose. "I'm not— Ugh."

"Maya," he said, his voice low and warm enough that it made her look up. "I'm not trying to be a pain—"

"You just are?" she muttered.

"I heard that."

She gave him a pointed look. "Nishant. I chose to plan Holi on purpose. I don't want to mess this up. People love Holi at Neadham, and I want to bring that back, bring back that Mela and fun aspect."

He nodded. "And I respect that. But if you want our event to reach the next level, we'll need to do more."

Our. Our event. Somehow the words cut through her cloud of annoyance.

Maya blew out a frustrated sigh. She couldn't say he was entirely wrong. Or right. And she was mildly regretting her decision to partner up with him, dating or no dating. But she couldn't deny that he did seem to care.

"Think about it," he said. "We bring back the Holi Mela, but we add a fun, updated music festival."

It was the first time he had mentioned their ideas together, instead of competing with each other. Not this or that, but something in between.

Still, she didn't want to run their timeline till the edge by trying to change things up.

"We only have two months left for us to plan," she said.

"Then we're going to be spending a lot of time together, aren't we?" Nishant said, not looking up from the papers.

"Maybe not," she said. "We don't have to. We could do the work and just . . . text a lot." It sounded stupid even to her own ears, a bad attempt at an excuse.

"What? Why would we do that? Are you scared of me?" he said. The way he raised his eyebrow indicated that it was a joke, but he had also clearly noted the tenor of her voice.

"No," she said immediately. "Scared? Of you?" She scoffed. "What's so scary about you?"

Nishant didn't say anything to that, tucking a grin away instead. "Maybe you're scared by how much you like me already."

What was she supposed to say to that? Such clear and unabashed flirting? It was like the man couldn't help himself. But she knew better than to fall for it.

She wasn't his type, and plus, she was a dadi.

"I've heard about your dating rep around the school, so nice try," she said.

Nishant chuckled, but it was a little harsher than his laugh before.

She glanced up. "My dating rep, eh?" There was something about the way he said that, something that Maya couldn't place.

"I'd have to be a recluse not to hear it. You know how the HSA talks."

Maybe it had been a little mean to bring that up, but he seemed proud of it. Cultivated it. The two-date rule wasn't a coincidence. What about that whole mirror bit from before? Why flirt with her?

"So, what exactly have you heard?" Nishant said. His eyebrow had shot up again.

"Nothing," she said automatically. Wow, she sounded so naive. Like a total freshman. She could feel her cheeks burn, and she wondered why she had even opened her mouth. Nishant Rai seemed to bring out the worst in her. "Forget I said anything."

"Don't worry," he said, after a beat. "I'm sure I've heard it all before. I highly doubt you're going to surprise me here."

Maya peered at him over her papers. "Really? You've heard that you're considered a two-date wonder? That you leave a trail of broken hearts behind?"

Nishant shrugged. "Or I'm not stringing anyone along." He shifted. "I'm up-front about how I feel and don't lie. I've never gotten complaints."

"Because you also somehow convince them it was their idea," she said. "Months later, they start to wonder and talk."

"Nothing you're saying sounds that bad," he said. "I show people a good time and end on good terms."

Maya snorted. "How can you end something that never began?"

Nishant didn't deny it, but he didn't agree, either, instead looking at her with those inscrutable chocolate-brown eyes of his. It wasn't a fair thing to say, really, because it wasn't like she had ever been in a real relationship herself. But at least she wanted to be; she had tried. Nishant didn't even seem to try.

"Do you have a type, by the way? Figured I should get to know what you like if I'm going to find boys for you," he asked suddenly, leaning toward her. He had spread out his arms so that if she leaned back, she would brush against him. Maya made sure not to lean back.

"Huh? Me?" Maya looked around. "No, I don't really have a type."

It was true, she supposed. She didn't have a physical type. And she wasn't sure if she had a non-physical type, either. None of her exes had been that similar, other than for the fact that none of the relationships had really worked out.

But more precisely, maybe she had never taken the time to find out. Her heart kind of leapt first. Unavailable, that seemed to be her type.

"Everyone has a type," he said.

"Not me," Maya said, feeling the words more strongly now. It might just be because she felt feisty around Nishant.

"Maybe that's your problem," he said. "You don't know what you're looking for."

"That's not fair," she said. But then she considered it. Could he be right? Both of her last relationships had been guys who had come on strong to her first.

"What do you like?" he said. "What do you want?"

Maya was silent for a second, not because she didn't know, but because no guy had really ever asked her that before. She swallowed roughly, deciding to just go with it. "I like a good book that makes me want to cry, I like action movies about racing, I love to bake and try new food, I want to be event chair of the HSA, I want to have a good semester because the last one sucked, and I want us to plan this Holi festival and make it the best that Neadham has ever seen. Like you said."

It all tumbled out of her, and afterward, Maya wondered if there was a way to shove it back inside. Her cheeks burned, her chest squeezed—but Nishant didn't laugh.

He just nodded, as if the words she had spewed were all completely normal. No judgment, no mention of how baking must mean she ate too much sugar or if that was the reason why she was on the curvy side, no snide remark about her being bad at business, no *You like to cry?* Nothing at all but a simple nod.

"Well, that's a start," he said.

Maya was about to ask him about himself, though she was unsure how to do that in the same smooth way he had, but Nishant spoke up first.

"We have that deal, don't we?" He moved forward so that his broad chest covered her view of the left side of the quad. "I find you dates, you graciously let me help plan Holi. Just doing a little reconnaissance."

It sounded so pathetic when he said it like that.

"You help me wade through the dating pool," Maya corrected. "Like a . . . dating guide."

"A dating guide," he said. "I should put that on some business cards."

"Well, after this, maybe you can," Maya said. "Though you actually have to uphold your side of the deal for that."

Nishant turned to her, a grin on his face. "Oh, really? Well, good thing I'm a great dating guide. I've already got your first date set up for you. And it's tonight."

"What?" Maya said, her eyes growing wide.

"Tonight," he said casually. "That's fine, right? You did mention you weren't doing anything tonight."

Normally, she would have texted a guy for a few weeks before meeting up with them. Tonight was so soon. Panic crept back in.

"What's his name? And major? How do you know him?" she said.

"Anthony, biology major, second year. I know him through my roommate, who plays pickup basketball with him on the weekends." Nishant raised an eyebrow at her. "I can vouch for him, and if he does anything weird, I'm on speed dial."

That was surprisingly thoughtful, though she would probably rely on Jana in case of any emergencies. Then her brain started to worry about any potential emergencies. Meeting someone for the first time was already hard, but a total stranger? What had she been thinking?

But this was the traditional way. The old-fashioned way to meet people. Tried and tested. If it worked for millions of people before, it would work for her, too.

"I mean, if you're not ready, I can cancel it—" he said.

"No," Maya said, squaring her shoulders. She wasn't normally competitive, but something in Nishant's expression made her want to show him she wasn't scared. "You got me my first date." She turned a bright smile on. "I can't wait."

CHAPTER 6

Nishant Rai: Good luck on your date. I've got another one in the wings.

Maya Sastry: Already? Do you think this one won't work out?

Nishant Rai: It's only your first date.

Nishant Rai: Wait, were you thinking it would only take one date?

Maya couldn't remember the last blind date she had been on. Well, she could, and it didn't hold any sort of fond place in her mind. It actually lived in that deep part of her mind where she shoved all of her other incredibly embarrassing and mildly traumatic experiences.

Her friend had set her up with someone from their volunteering workshop, which she had taken as a sign of virtue. That is, until she had met him in person and he kept texting his ex in front of her. It had only gotten worse from there.

But she was here now, and Maya would make the most of it.

She took in a deep breath and pushed the door open to the café, immediately scanning the room for the bright blue shirt that Nishant had mentioned in his text. In the corner, a boy with a great smile and a blue button-down waved at her.

Maya waved back and put on her best first-date smile—smiley but not too smiley, with just enough mystery and, hopefully, a hint of seduction.

The closer Maya got, the more apparent it was that Nishant had done good work. Anthony was cute, in a clean-cut way, and seemed to have gotten dressed up for their date, if the pressed khakis and shiny brown loafers were any indication.

"Anthony?" she said.

"You must be Maya," he said, getting up to greet her. "You're even prettier than your photo."

Maya flushed at that. Anthony knew how to open up a date, that was for sure.

"Glad to hear I live up to my photo," Maya said, playing along.

Anthony reached his hand out like he was going to shake hands, but then pulled it back quickly. It was a slightly awkward but strangely endearing moment.

They locked eyes and both laughed. "First dates are weird, aren't they?" he said.

"Tell me about it."

She grinned at him. She could get behind this. He made space for her across the table, and she slid into the chair with ease.

Maya felt herself start to relax as Anthony chatted about the café and finding a table. Conversation was easy and she found herself staring into his eyes, drifting away as the possibilities of a future with this boy started to pepper her mind.

Nope. No, no. That was the Maya of old.

Maya 2.0 was here to play the field, to use her head. Even if by the second hour of their conversation she felt like maybe, possibly, this could work out. Maybe she was not the good-time type, especially because she could already see them walking hand in hand down the quad. Or getting ice cream together at Flurry's Café.

She ordered herself to snap out of it. This was exactly the sort of behavior that had gotten her into this whole mess in the first place.

New Maya wouldn't fall head over heels for the first boy to smile at her on a date. An okay blind date did not a romance make. She just had to keep telling herself that.

"So what do you like to do for fun?" Anthony said. "I'm a runner myself. Any interest in that? Or cross country?"

"Oh yeah," Maya found herself saying. It was like her mouth had a mind of its own. "I've never done cross country, but I do run."

Once. A year. While dying on the inside.

Maya didn't say any of that, she only smiled when he told her about a beautiful lake run a mile away from the grounds, near the swimming hole that all underclassmen went to, and nodded briefly when he mentioned loving hiking despite the fact that the one time she had approached a mountain she had broken her toe. Nature did not like her.

But it was like Old Maya, people-pleaser Maya, desperately romantic Maya, was the only one around. Like the new version she had just found of herself had frozen up, unable to speak.

They parted ways two hours later—Maya had a study group she had to get to, and Anthony said he had practice with his band.

She had made sure not to talk about her five conspiracy theories about *The Great British Bake Off* and had tried her best to come across as cool, chill Maya.

So, that hadn't been so bad. She had no idea if he liked her but—

"Hey," Anthony turned around suddenly. "I had a good time. Can I get your number? I'll plan that hiking trip."

New Maya instantly recoiled and wanted to take it back, maybe suggest going to that new bakery. But instead she found herself saying, "Sure."

She typed her number into his phone, all the while beating herself up for letting her heart take the reins.

Anthony waved goodbye, and she watched him walk down the road before she turned around and headed for her late-night study group. Was it the best date she had ever been on? No. Had she totally sold herself out in hope of a second date despite not knowing if he was a good match? Yes. But did she still feel like a kickass human right now for putting herself out there? Hell yes.

Her phone pinged with a text.

Nishant Rai: How'd it go?
Nishant Rai: Did I knock it out of the park or what.

Maya rolled her eyes but typed a message back.

Maya Sastry: Not bad. I think it went okay.

She bit her lip, the honesty bubbling out of her like an overflowing teakettle.

Maya Sastry: But he likes to hike. And I somehow
found myself agreeing to potentially go on a hiking date.
This is what you're working with.

Had that been too much? Too real? Then again, what did she have to lose being up-front with Nishant? Somehow without the pressure of impressing him, because she knew she never would, Maya felt a weight off. Like she could be herself.

Nishant Rai: I'm assuming you don't like hiking then?
Maya Sastry: I'd rather poke needles into my skin. The
only nature I like is the beach. Or maybe the woods at
sunrise. But mountains? We were not meant to scale
them!!
Nishant Rai: Might actually agree with you on that one.
Will strike hiking off the list. Maybe try telling Anthony
you don't actually like hiking next time.
Maya Sastry: What if he doesn't like me then? 😧
Nishant Rai: Then isn't that good to find out early?
Maya Sastry: But what if hiking is the only obstacle to
our lifelong romance? What if I can make it work?
Nishant Rai: You shouldn't have to.

Ugh, of course he would say that. Such a two-date-wonder thing to say.

But she could hear Jana's voice in her head, too, and even her own. Why was she twisting herself into shapes for a guy she didn't even know if she liked? If he was compatible or good for her? Old Maya needed to take a back seat with her dating, clearly. Maybe that's what Jana had been trying to tell her.

Nishant Rai: What do you think about hockey?
Maya Sastry: Ooh, I can get behind that.
Nishant Rai: So, I've found your "type."
Maya Sastry: What? No!
Nishant Rai: 😘 😘

But Maya couldn't help the laugh that bubbled out of her, even as Nishant sent increasingly more risqué emojis.

For the first time, Maya could see a new path laying itself out for her, even if becoming a whole new version of herself was exhausting work. Rome wasn't built in a day. But she had wanted this semester to be different, and to her surprise, Nishant might be the key to making that happen. Maybe this wouldn't be so bad.

Just maybe.

CHAPTER 7

Nishant Rai: Does Zane keep texting you random ideas?

Maya Sastry: All the time.

Nishant Rai: Is it bad that I muted the event committee group chat?

Maya Sastry: Yes. Because now he only talks to me.

Maya woke up late due to a faulty alarm, which meant that once she got to the Activities Office, she realized she had forgotten to brush her hair. She tried to comb it down, using the reflection of one of the hazy glass windows, to only minor success.

Today was their appointment for the approval of the event date, and given the administration's lukewarm feeling toward Holi, Maya had decided to pull out all the stops.

She turned the corner in Lewis Hall and saw a tall figure loung-ing against the wall near one of the glass cabinets with memora-bilia. Nishant didn't look as if *he* had forgotten to brush his hair. He was dressed more casually than Maya was used to seeing, in a long-sleeve crewneck and a puffer jacket, but he still looked good. Which she found supremely annoying this morning.

"You came?" she said, approaching him.

"Yes," Nishant said, narrowing his eyes at her. "Though you sound surprised. Were you hoping I wouldn't show up?"

Maya bit her lip and decided on the truth. "You didn't respond to my last text, you know, after we complained about Zane."

"Ah, sorry," he said. "I was out on a date." Maya tried not to make a face or imagine Nishant out on a date. "And have you forgotten our deal? Why didn't you tell me about this meeting before last night?"

Maya shot him a *Be quiet* look. Nishant looked around, spread-ing his arms wide to make the point that there was no one around.

She understood that, but you never knew when someone might just show up and overhear you. Maya was already in enough social hot water right now after getting banned from Meet'em. At din-ner with Jana the night before, she had met someone and he had mentioned the tale of some poor girl who had gotten banned from Meet'em, not realizing that said poor girl was sitting right in front of him.

The way things were working out for her, one of the administra-tors would overhear and use it as a reason to keep them from get-ting the date for Holi or something equally as horrible.

"I didn't forget," she said. "We only got the official event appointment yesterday." She frowned. "Zane mentioned it's a little unusual." The outer door shut, the bang resounding through the room. "We'll finish discussing later. Game face on, DJ Nish."

"It's never off," he said, winking at her.

Maya resisted the very strong urge to roll her eyes, especially because Nishant hadn't in fact done anything directly to her that warranted such a response. But she couldn't help the fact that he reminded her a bit of Ari—confidence that edged on arrogance, suave and smooth in that unhurried way. It didn't help endear him to her. If anything, it just slapped a big red warning sign on Nishant's forehead.

She straightened her back and adjusted the basket in her arms so that one of the muffins peeked out. Next to her, Nishant inhaled deeply and made a noise in the back of his throat.

"You brought muffins?" he said. "Blueberry? Damn, Maya, that's a move."

She sniffed. She wasn't sure why he expected any less; still, she noted the appreciation in his eyes with a hint of delight. The muffins were a timeless blend of Old and New Maya, both of whom wanted to get event chair.

"And what did you bring?" Maya said. "For the cause?"

"My smile."

Maya made a face. Fine, it was a devastatingly . . . decent smile, but really?

A head appeared from behind the doorway, glancing at both of them from behind thick eyeglasses. It was attached to a very stern-looking middle-aged woman who looked as if she hadn't taken a lunch break in ten years.

"Maya?" she said.

"And Nishant," he said, stepping forward. "We're *both* from the HSA."

Maya shot him an annoyed glance, but Nishant wasn't looking at her. The full force of his megawatt smile was focused on the administrator—Mrs. Catcher, if Maya remembered correctly.

"Fine, both of you come in," she said.

How typical. She had been here first and he had come swooping in, taking all of the attention.

Nishant was looking at her now, mouthing something she couldn't understand. She shook her head at him because what exactly was he trying to say? *Angels taste good?* He really needed to work on his fake communicating skills.

"Mrs. Catcher," Maya said, after they had shut the door, "thanks for making the time for us. We're so excited to get started on planning Holi this year, and the date is the first step."

Mrs. Catcher looked genuinely perplexed for a second. "Holi? Oh, the one where you throw colors at one another."

Maya bristled at that; Holi was so much more, but a gentle touch on her arm from Nishant stopped her from reacting.

"Yes, exactly," Nishant said.

"You're holding it this year? After the failure that was—" Mrs. Catcher cleared her throat. "After the low attendance of last year? HSA was supposed to have gotten notice that due to the attendance, their priority in date and venue selection had been lowered." She shuffled her papers. "You applied for March tenth? It's been given away."

What? Given away? Maya's stomach clenched, her heart beating faster. She hadn't realized it had gotten that bad, and by the way Nishant tensed up, he hadn't known that either. This was a disaster.

"Lowered, but not gone," Nishant said. Maya knocked her knee into him. What was he doing? They didn't need to rile Mrs. Catcher up. "Right?"

He leaned forward and smiled at Mrs. Catcher, who looked up from her papers at that exact moment. And then blushed. Actually blushed.

"Well," she said. "March tenth is a popular date. Both the morning and afternoon slots are taken. The Athletics Office wants to host an early recruitment mixer, and the French Club wants to hold a Mardi Gras Carnival."

"Well, the Athletics Office might have better luck hosting one after spring break," Maya said. Mrs. Catcher shrugged, looking nonplussed. "And isn't March tenth a little late for Mardi Gras?"

"That's when they submitted for, and they have a better attendance record with their event, plus they're donating part of their proceeds to the new renovation on the languages hall," Mrs. Catcher said, giving them an apologetic smile. Maya winced. That was going to be hard to compete with, and it was clear that Mrs. Catcher knew it, too.

But she looked a bit sorry for them, which might mean there was still an opening for them to slide through. Suddenly, Maya was very thankful she had thought ahead.

Maya slid the basket of muffins onto Mrs. Catcher's desk. "Oh, by the way, I had some extra muffins and I thought maybe you and the rest of the Activities Office might like the extras? Blueberry, and no nuts."

Nishant raised his eyebrow at her, mouthing the word *smooth* at her, which Maya actually understood this time. She didn't know what that said, but she could tell that Nishant was being sincere. She flushed a little at the praise before the indignation came. Of course she had moves.

Mrs. Catcher lit up. "Blueberry muffins? With a brown-sugar top? Did you use the recipe from Margaret Preston?"

"The *Bake Off* winner?" Maya said, perking up. "Modified, but yes! How did you know?"

"May I?" Mrs. Catcher gestured at the muffin basket and Maya nodded. Mrs. Catcher took one and turned it around in her hand. "It's such a unique recipe and I've been testing it myself."

"Exactly!" Maya said, leaning forward. "I added a bit more butter and a dollop of yogurt to this one because I wanted a more moist crumb."

"It worked," Mrs. Catcher said, with a full mouth. "Sorry, but this is delicious."

"I'm glad to hear that," Nishant said. "Maya is an excellent baker. Actually, we were thinking of bringing local food vendors and bakers, like Maya, to our brand-new Holi Mela."

What? How could he— Maya saw the glint in Nishant's eye and caught on.

"Oh yes," Maya said. "We're reimagining Holi this year . . . into the Holi Mela. We know last year was not the success we wanted, and we'd love to have our event, one of the biggest religious and traditional festivals for the HSA in the spring, really be a tentpole for the community. We also have a plan to donate part of the proceeds as well—it'll be ticketed for the first time."

Nishant nodded from the corner of her eye, which Maya

appreciated, because she was totally making this up on the fly.

"And we're going to have it over a weekend, with a wide variety of events that anyone and everyone can attend," he said. "Our Holi Mela will bring people together to celebrate the arrival of spring—with traditional aspects like the Holika Dahan bonfire, but also food, colors, and a huge music party—"

"And a celebration that everyone can enjoy," Maya amended, kicking Nishant. They still had to convince the Activities Office, and she hadn't actually agreed to the rest. Food, music, fine.

"What do you think?" Nishant said, throwing his best smile on.

Mrs. Catcher smiled back, but then it faltered as she glanced at her computer screen. "I do love what you're pitching me, and given the typical success of HSA's Diwali, I have hope you can pull it off. But that date is still not open."

Ugh, a gut punch. A huge letdown. Actually, this was all her fault and *she* had let down everyone—

"But I can offer you another date? March sixteenth?"

Maya looked over at Nishant before she could help herself. It would be the weekend before spring break, which would mean a lot more marketing to get people to come, but maybe, just maybe, they could pull it off?

It wasn't like they had a better option.

Nishant gave her a short nod, like he had reached the same conclusion.

"Could we also reserve the two dates around March sixteenth?" Nishant said. "I know it's unconventional, but we're planning a new type of event. Hopefully the best event of the spring schedule. Right, Maya?"

When he put it like that, she couldn't even frown at him, despite the fact that they had not confirmed a multiday event. But she found it hard to be too mad at him, given how desperately he was trying to make this work.

Mrs. Catcher tapped on her keyboard for a few moments and then turned to them. "Reserved. I got you the whole weekend."

The relief nearly overwhelmed Maya, and she had to hold herself up in her chair to keep from collapsing. There had been a part of her that really wasn't sure that they could fix this, and while this wasn't ideal, it was still a path forward.

"But getting an event space for that date with your lowered priority will still be tough," Mrs. Catcher warned, giving them a stern look. "You'll have to act quick. And the soccer field is already taken on the sixteenth."

All the air that had built up in Maya blew out. One step forward, two steps back.

The cards looked as if they were stacked a mile high against them. First the date, now the venue? Maya had been hoping to re-create the same Holi magic on the soccer field. Now it looked like Nishant was going to get what he had wanted.

"Noted," Maya said, trying to keep a smile on her face, even as that steady drumbeat of panic lifted in her chest.

"We appreciate the advice," Nishant said. "We'll do our best."

"I hope you enjoy the muffins," Maya said.

"Oh, I will," Mrs. Catcher said, pulling the basket toward her. Maya wasn't sure any muffins would actually leave Mrs. Catcher's office, but she didn't hold it against her, since hoarding the muffins was a very Maya thing to do.

Once they were outside the Activities Office and on the lawn,

Maya felt as if she could finally take a breath. Nishant paused beside her, and they both watched a group of students attempt to make a pyramid on the lawn.

"That did not go the way I had hoped," Maya said. "But at least we locked down a date."

"Looks like my smile did the trick," Nishant said. He looked at her with half-lidded eyes, his hands in his pockets.

"And my muffins," Maya countered. She squared her shoulders and gave him a challenging look. "You think that was a coincidence? Nope, I found Mrs. Catcher on social media and saw that she also liked baking and I took advantage of it."

Nishant tilted his head slightly, as if he were seeing her anew. "Okay, you're right. My smile and your muffins. It was a good play. Really. And I know it's not what you—or I—wanted, but it's something. Don't let it get you down."

Oh, that was a little unexpected. Ari would have never conceded a point like that or tried to reassure her. Or given her a compliment. Neither would Thomas.

"But Mrs. Catcher is right, we need to move on event spaces before every venue is booked. And I have something I want to show you."

She found herself nodding. "Okay."

Nishant looked a little surprised, like he had been waiting for a fight. But Maya found that she didn't feel like fighting. With the challenges stacking up, she felt glad that she had a partner at that moment.

"By the way," she said, trying to sound casual. "Zane mentioned you guys went to high school together."

"He's cool. We get dinner sometimes, whenever he can fit me in around his basketball obsession and HSA, but no, we're not that close. And no, I probably can't get an in with him."

"Huh? Why would you say that?" she said.

"Why are you asking unless you want me to set you up with him?" he said.

"No, no!" Maya said quickly. "I'm not interested in him like that." She quirked her mouth. "Though I am waiting on my next date."

"Yeah, yeah, it's coming." Nishant's expression smoothed out. "And, uh, good." He coughed lightly. "Because that would be weird, since Zane's kind of our boss."

"Yes, it would," Maya said. Her and Zane? What an odd thought. No, she was mainly thinking about event chair.

"Okay, well, solid teamwork, Maya," he said. "Told you we'd be good together." He gave her a quick wink before walking away.

Maya shook her head, a retort on the edge of her lips, but she also couldn't help but watch him go. Working with him hadn't been horrible. Maya was big enough to admit that Nishant had been an essential part in locking down their dates, and they had worked well together.

Nishant had been everything she had expected—charming, a little sales-y, flirty—and yet he had followed through. He had known about the meeting without her telling him, he had shown up, and weirdest of all, he had acted like a real partner. Committed, focused.

Was it possible?

Had she misread Nishant?

CHAPTER 8

Maya Sastry: Really? Come on, DJ Nish.
Nishant Rai: You said you liked hockey!
Maya Sastry: He said he hates reading! Even hockey can't make up for that.

When Maya had agreed to go to the first basketball game of the semester with Jana, she had imagined something a little different than the chaos in front of her. To be fair, Maya had only agreed because it seemed like an experience you should have your freshman year—and because of Nishant mentioning Zane was a huge Neadham basketball fan.

She and Nishant had finally agreed on a tentative event proposal after their spitball planning in Mrs. Catcher's office. *Tentative* being the key word. They'd find a way to meld their two ideas together, if only because Maya didn't want to waste any more time on opposite sides.

She had been trying to get some time with their HSA president, but he always seemed to be running to some class or other, and as they approached February it was high on her list. Plus, as Jana kept reminding her, she hadn't been to a basketball game yet because of Thomas, so she supposed this was a good way for New Maya to get a bit more experience. And as an event-chair hopeful, she needed to know what was going on in the Neadham social calendar.

Which is why Maya found herself outside in the chilly January air, watching two groups of upperclassmen boys throw foam fingers at one another from their tailgate tents. The basketball stadium was a half mile away from campus, which meant that she and Jana had walked over, since the buses would be stuffed with underclassmen. Shouts and thumping music filled the air, as did the strong smell of grilled meat.

The parking lot of the stadium was filled to the brim with people in bright green and gold, which oddly reminded Maya of a group of leprechauns. She was wearing the clashing colors herself and had even allowed Jana to paint a gold *N* on her face to show some school spirit and match the other painted tailgaters.

They were waiting by the edge of the arena for the rest of their group, and as always, Maya had insisted they be early.

"I don't think I've ever seen the stadium parking lot look so full before," Jana said.

Maya nodded. "Neadham goes all out for basketball games."

"And how would you know that?"

"I went to a game senior year of high school," Maya said. "Ha, that surprised you, didn't it?"

Jana tugged her beanie a bit lower to cover her ears. "You got me there."

"I visited Neadham a couple times before deciding to come here," Maya said. "My dad wanted to do his master's here when he came from India, but couldn't, so he was so excited when I said I was considering it. That's when I went to Holi here, too."

Jana nodded. "I remember you telling me that, but I didn't know about your dad. I bet he's so happy for you."

He was. It was part of the reason Maya was unwilling to lose another semester to a boy, because she had wanted to come to Neadham so badly. Already she had sent her dad a couple of photos of her decked out in gold and green. "He is," she agreed. "He made me agree to live-text him."

"By the way, why exactly are we here so early when we're not even tailgating?" Jana looked longingly over at a girl chowing down on a large hot dog and screaming the lyrics to the Neadham fight song.

"To get good spots," Maya said.

"You'd be right, if we weren't talking about college students. And anyway, you do know that the stadium seats are on the tickets?"

"Nope," Maya said, whipping the tickets out. "They have the section, but not the row or seat number, so it's fair game." She frowned. "I've been burned before assuming that college kids would play fair."

Jana raised an eyebrow.

"The *Into the Woods* performance last semester?" Maya said. "It's my favorite, you know that."

"You do love singing 'Agony' in the shower," Jana agreed.

"And I ended up having to sit behind this really tall guy who kept jumping in his seat. Never again," Maya said. "I may have gotten a little worried and spent half an hour researching the stadium."

Jana shook her head, sighing. "Well, we're here now. And we can't go in without all of the group, since we have their tickets." Maya knew her slightly anxious tendencies were not necessarily endearing, but Jana always took them in stride.

Maya glanced down at her watch, which told her that they were actually very early. "Should have thought about that."

Jana shrugged. "It's fine. Maybe this will cheer you up after that terrible date with that boy with the swoop-y hair."

"You mean Tyler." Maya made a face. "It started out so good, too. Until he spent thirty minutes telling me in detail about how he had broken his toe. I told Nishant I need more options."

"That you do," Jana said. "Though I'm proud of you for not pretending to be an orthopedic surgeon this time."

"Ugh, shut up. I'm working on it."

Someone came out of the stadium entrance and started to set up the lines, showing that they were now open. A few people bolted out of their cars straight into the line, surprising both of them. Maya sent Jana an *I was right* look, which only resulted in Jana rolling her eyes.

Jana looked down at her phone as it pinged, scanning the screen. "Good news, Imogen has the same brain as you, so they should be here in a few. Let's see if we can get in and get some snacks before the concession stand gets ridiculous. I can dip out and give them the tickets."

She and Maya got through the short line quickly and went straight to the concession stand. There was something about game concessions that always felt nostalgic for Maya, reminiscent of her dad taking her to football games and of the old county fairs in Virginia, where she grew up. Plus, she actually liked that fake yellow nacho cheese, especially with a huge soft pretzel. Maya noted the jalapeño poppers on the menu and grabbed Jana's arm.

"Did I miss out on jalapeño poppers for a whole semester?" she said, her eyes wide.

Jana laughed, tugging her arm back and shaking it out. "You've got a surprisingly strong grip. I never saw jalapeño poppers at the football arena concessions, so it's your lucky day."

Five minutes later, Maya bit into her first jalapeño popper and moaned. It was good. And bad. So bad it was good. So good it was bad.

"We can leave their tickets with will-call, so I went ahead and did that," Jana said. "Let's go get those perfect seats, you goon." Maya squealed and hugged Jana, accidentally getting some nacho cheese in her hair.

After they got the cheese out, they found the perfect seats—higher than the marching band, so they could see over the tubas, and low enough that they could still see the players' facial expressions, which Jana insisted was the best part.

A little while later their friends arrived, waving at them, each of them decked out in their own green-and-gold outfits. The announcer called the time, and a few minutes later, the game started. The Neadham basketball team wasn't exactly good, but they had been having the best season of the last decade apparently, so the seats were packed. A conversation was going on behind them about whether Neadham had a chance to make it into the regional conference, which turned into a very loud argument.

The lights started to strobe, and the Neadham basketball team ran onto the floor just in time. The chanting started from the top of the bleachers, filtering down. Everyone got to their feet and started singing the university song in a cacophony of noisemakers, bullhorns, and bad singing.

"NEADHAM, THE BEST OF 'EM, FIGHT, FIGHT, FIGHT—"

Maya found herself smiling. She couldn't believe she had missed this all first semester, so she threw herself into the chanting. She even managed to nudge Jana into participating in the wave when it came their way after a particularly spectacular three-point shot by Neadham.

Halftime hit and Maya made a beeline for the concession stand, mostly because she had finally caught sight of the wire-rimmed glasses she had been looking for—Zane. She told Jana she was going to the bathroom and dodged a few people to make it over to where he stood in line.

"Zane?"

He looked up and blinked for a few seconds before his face broke into a smile. "Maya? I didn't know you liked basketball."

"Who doesn't? Neadham is actually doing well this year," she said, sidling into a spot next to him and ignoring the glare from the girl behind her.

"Fair point," he said. "Did you see that three-pointer? Kemper was—"

"Amazing," Maya said. "He really nailed that shot."

Zane nodded excitedly, like he had been waiting for someone to say the same thing. Maya was not the biggest sports fan or the most knowledgeable, but even she had gotten into the excitement of the game.

"By the way, how's it going with you and Nishant? The partnership?" he asked as they trudged forward in line.

"Good!" Maya said.

"It's working out, then?" Zane said, leaning in.

Maya paused, unsure exactly how to answer that. It was going passably, if you didn't count the fight at their first meeting and the numerous cryptic texts about meeting him at a "potential location" tomorrow. And they had managed to get the date locked down when it had been in jeopardy.

Maya didn't think it would be a good idea to tell Zane that, especially because she was going to figure out a way to make it work. Somehow.

"Uh, it's going . . . well," she finally managed.

"Good, good," Zane said. "Just checking in."

"By the way," Maya said, "the date we submitted is cool?"

Zane nodded. "Great job on the date, by the way. I know it wasn't ideal, but you made it work. I was a little worried about your partnership initially, if I'm being honest," he said. He shook his head. "Nishant can be a lot to take on. He sent me a text mentioning a multiday event, though, which was exciting. Could be really cool actually."

Wait, what? They hadn't officially decided on the event and whether it should be multiday or not. And Nishant was already out here making promises? Suddenly, his event venue texts took on a sinister hue. He better not be planning ahead without her.

Maya tried not to grimace. "Nishant told you about the *potential* multiday event? Our main goal is to revive the Holi Mela, secondary is the multiday event."

"Oh yeah. I think it's a great goal," Zane said, mistaking her annoyance for worry. "Not to talk ill of past HSA presidents, but we let Holi fall off the radar in favor of Diwali and India Day. I'm actually really glad you took on this challenge, Maya. Definitely a surprise, but a good one."

"Oh," Maya said. "Thank you." This was the perfect opportunity to ask her question, even if she was still a little taken aback. "Zane, I have to ask, what would make Holi successful as an event?"

He blinked at her. "Meaning?"

"What would make the administration regret their decision to try to shut us down? And maybe, what would make a strong case for the next event chair?" Maya said, in a bit of a rush. Those were the two questions milling about in her mind for a week now. A week of her building up the courage and putting together a plan to ask.

Zane continued to give her that furrowed-brow, confused look, and then it cleared. His eyes widened and he let out a small chuckle. "Event chair, huh? You are not what I expected, Maya." He tilted his head. "I noticed you guys decided to make the event ticketed, which is smart. So, if you're asking what metric of success we'll need for Holi with the administration, which I think is exactly the right question, I'd say ticket sales of more than five hundred."

"And probably a small donation of some sort, maybe to the International Languages Institute? They're building a new wing," Maya said.

Zane gave her an assessing look. "Definite possibility. I'd also look into the Cultural Center, which not many clubs know about yet. It's a new project."

That sounded promising. Maya made a mental note to look into it.

"And, Maya," he said, "for your second question, I've got to be honest with you. Rising sophmores rarely get leadership positions and . . . there are other people making a play for event chair as well.

But if you can get over a thousand ticket sales, you could make Neadham's Holi Mela go down as the biggest comeback event for the college in recent history." Zane gave her a long look. "That is more than a worthy qualification for the next HSA event chair, even as a freshman."

They reached the front of the concession line, and Zane stepped forward to order his nachos with extra jalapeños and a side of ranch dressing. Maya had known aiming for event chair would be hard, but she hadn't quite anticipated how hard.

One thousand ticket sales. That was bigger than last year's Diwali festival, and that had been two events over the course of one Saturday. Maybe Nishant was right, maybe they would need to go bigger with a multiday event.

Because if there was one thing Maya knew for sure right then, it was that she was going to make Holi the comeback kid of the century.

Maya 2.0 wouldn't settle for anything less.

CHAPTER 9

Maya Sastry: This one was good!! He was nice, normal, and he had similar interests to me. No hiking, secret hatred of books, or other red flags.
Nishant Rai: Erm, I just found out he has a girlfriend at home.
Maya Sastry: *Sigh*

Maya got to the meeting place Nishant had sent her two minutes late, mostly because she kept worrying if she had turned the oven off in their apartment. She had. But the anxiety never disappeared, did it?

Plus, the little evil part of her wanted him to wait a bit, despite how much being late made her physically ill. She was still annoyed that he had talked to Zane about their plans without confirming with her first. Granted, he had been crucial in locking down their dates and he had surprised her by complimenting her at the end. Still. A girl had to have a few grudges. And once Nishant had returned to his fake flirty ways over text, it was easy to hold them.

The building that now loomed in front of Maya looked like a warehouse where government agents disappeared people. Not really her ideal meeting place, but Nishant had suggested it. Demanded it, really.

Speaking of him, where was he? She was late, but she wasn't that late. She tugged at the door, but it seemed shut well, and when she ducked around the building, there weren't any other doors or entrances. Maya walked up to that main slab of a door again and knocked, despite feeling very silly.

A few seconds later, a head popped out. "You made it," Nishant said, locking eyes with her.

"I did," she said. "Though this kinda looks like a place where someone gets murdered in a horror movie."

"That would be an old, creaky house," he said. "This is more CIA-black-site vibes."

"I was actually also thinking that," Maya said, narrowing her eyes at him.

Nishant laughed and waved her inside the building.

He was wearing a crumpled dark green Henley that showcased those shoulders of his, and a pair of light-wash, slightly ripped jeans. And not in a deliberate way, but more in an I've-worn-these-for-years-and have-put-these-through-hell way. Maya was surprised. She wasn't sure she had ever seen Nishant look anything but immaculate. Not that he didn't look good in this outfit, too.

Maya immediately shut the door on that. Or tried to. His jeans hugged him a little too well, something she couldn't help but notice as he walked in front of her.

"So, what exactly are you trying to show me here?" Maya said. "I don't buy that you thought this would be the best meeting spot, given that Umbra Coffee is right down the street."

"This," he said, stopping suddenly. Maya nearly ran into him.

Nishant threw his arms open, and Maya peered over his biceps. A vast warehouse space greeted them, completely bare, except for a small DJ booth off to the side. It had a second-floor balustrade that went around, overlooking the main area below and double doors at the back corner that looked as if they would open onto a catering kitchen.

"What is this place?" Maya said.

"A secret, until now. I needed a place to develop my new DJ set because my roommate is taking the MCAT this semester, and a buddy of mine told me this place is open." Nishant walked into the center of the room and spun around, his arms still wide. "Can you believe this is just sitting here on campus?"

Maya shook her head. "How does no one know about this?"

Somehow the creepy building outside had transformed into this kind of cool warehouse space. It reminded her of this club she had gone to (accidentally) in New York City. Jana would love this space, and Maya was surprised it wasn't already booked up until next year.

"What's the catch, then?" she asked. "There's got to be a catch. How has someone not found this space already?"

Nishant shrugged. "Not sure, but I'm not looking a gift horse in the mouth. My buddy says it was used by the art and architecture school before they got that new wing. It's a little rough, but it's got potential, doesn't it? Could be perfect for the music festival component."

Maya couldn't help the groan that came from her mouth. "Not this again."

"Wait, hear me out," he said, jogging over to her. "Let me show you my vision for this place."

Maya let out a deep, world-weary sigh while trying to put on her best teamwork hat. What did she really have to lose by hearing him out? She still wasn't positive this music festival was the right path forward, but he seemed so excited about it.

Nishant turned her toward the window, which looked out over a green area. "There's even a field nearby that the football team occasionally uses for training in the fall. I checked, it's totally free for our date. Think about it. We get the whole field for the event and it's right next door."

Hmm . . . okay. That was promising. He seemed sincere, and it wasn't in Maya's nature to be cynical in the face of such optimism. It was like poking a hole in a soufflé on purpose.

She was too much of a softie, she realized.

"I have to admit, it does sound intriguing," Maya started. "I remember Zane complaining about playing Holi last year with a bunch of Frisbees flying through the air. And while I'm not so sure about the music festival"—Nishant made a noise low in his throat—"I can say that this place would be an awesome venue. If we were to do it. Which we're not, at least not for sure."

"I'm going to have to find some way to convince you about the music festival, aren't I?" Nishant said. "Would it help if I gave you full control over the set list and performers? If we also had local performers? And some traditional ones? Made sure the set list all had South Asian artists and a good amount of fusion?"

"I thought you wanted Holi to be ultramodern," she said, dragging the last word out in a clearly contemptuous way. "No dadi vibes."

"Okay, I love my dadi, but I stand by that. And I'm trying to meet you halfway here," he said. "Maybe I reconsidered. Maybe you're not a dadi and I was being a little harsh."

Maya raised an eyebrow. The man could compromise. Would wonders never cease? She wasn't going to mention that she had brought up the idea of local performers at their first meeting.

"It would help," Maya said slowly. "How do we make sure the event feels cohesive? I'm not fully convinced."

"Then I'll find another way," Nishant said. Something in his voice made her look up at him. He was staring at her, his gaze intent. There didn't seem to be any anger or rancor, just an unabashed curiosity.

Maya wanted to hide. She broke their look first, pointing at the back doors. "That's the kitchen, I'm assuming?" Nishant nodded. "Wow, this place is really tricked out, isn't it?"

She shook her head. Nishant really did know this school well. Maya had thought that just meant the people, but now she was realizing he knew the nooks and crannies of campus also. This was not an area she had ever been in before, and if left to her own devices, she probably never would have made it out here. Maya hadn't gone much past University Drive in her first semester here, and even a month into her second one, she hadn't gone much farther. She resolved to change that.

"Do you spend a lot of time here?" Maya said, unable to hold back her curiosity.

"I only found the place two weeks ago," he said.

"No, I mean *here*," Maya said, waving her hand around. "Near the architecture school. Most undergrads never come here. Unless they're going to a frat party, and Frat Row is in the other direction."

His forehead knitted. "I guess I never thought about that. I explored a lot my first year and I guess I never really looked back?"

Wow. They were . . . entirely different creatures. Instead of horrifying her, the thought kind of made Maya more curious. She laughed. "I'm pretty sure I didn't go past first-year dorms last semester."

"Really?" Nishant said, sounding a little shocked.

"Hey," she said. "Be nice."

"No, no, I don't mean it in a mean way," he said. Maya found herself following him over to his DJ booth. "It just doesn't seem like you."

Huh. It wasn't entirely her, if she were being honest. How had he known?

"What do you mean?"

"Maya, you stood up in front of everyone and announced you wanted to revive Holi. Everyone else was terrified, but you weren't," he said, the admiration clear in his voice. Maya flushed at it, surprised that Nishant saw her that way.

She had been trying so hard to please Thomas that she had put aside a lot of things she had wanted to do those months. Mixers, club meetings, parties, even that one early-morning art history class she had wanted to audit. Somehow she had let Thomas convince her it was at a bad time—too early for a good class. More like it had been a bad time for Thomas. Maya was a morning person, a fact that Jana hated, and she probably would have done just fine with an early class. Maybe even thrived in it.

After a slightly too long pause, she said, "You're right. I wasn't really myself first semester." She took a deep breath. "I kind of had a weird boy situation."

That wasn't a good description at all, but it was all she had to give at the moment.

To his credit, Nishant merely shrugged one shoulder and reached for his DJ headphones. "We've all been there. Most of my friends who entered college with a relationship broke up in the first semester. A few stuck it out, though we'll see how that goes."

"How about you?"

"I was the one providing tissues and a shoulder to cry on," he said. It sounded like a hedge, but she gave it to him. Not like she had been super transparent about her thing with Thomas.

"There's more I want to show you, by the way," Nishant said, excitement coating his every word. It was so thick that even Maya's annoyed, cynical brain took notice. Something Nishant Rai was excited about? That piqued her interest. He looked so eager it was almost cute, not that she would ever tell him that. And then she realized he was waiting on her to say yes, which was oddly adorable.

Maya nodded and he nearly bounced off the DJ booth. "I swear, you're going to lose your mind."

"Uh-huh," she said. "You said that when we walked in."

"That was a miscalculation," he said. "I know you better now. I know what you like. You need to see it to feel it."

Maya felt warm at that. That was an accurate depiction of her.

She could be a vision person, but she needed the details to really flesh something out. She needed to know the ingredients before she could see the final version. He had gotten all that from just this conversation?

Maya followed him to the back of the warehouse, past the catering kitchen and through a side door that creaked horribly when Nishant tried to open it.

"Are you sure we're supposed to open this?" Maya asked, looking up the narrow, dusty stairs that the door revealed. "Those don't look particularly safe."

Nishant clambered up a few of the steps and jumped up and down. The stairs held, but Maya could've sworn she heard a low creaking moan again. "It's solid. I've been up them a few times."

Maya hesitated, her eyes darting to the stairs.

Nishant bent over and held out a hand to her. "Trust me," he said. "I've got you."

Well, how was she supposed to say no to that?

She took his hand and let him pull her up the stairs. It was a good thing, too, because the stairs were not as sturdy as Nishant had claimed. They reached the top, and Nishant pushed open the door, helping her through.

The door revealed a wide expanse of rooftop that looked over the college campus and to the mountains beyond. Green and blue extended out in front of them as far as the eye could see. Maya couldn't help but gasp.

"I knew you'd love it," he said. She turned around to see Nishant's smirk and immediately thought about yanking her hand away. It was still enveloped in his, to her surprise.

"And why's that?" Maya said.

"Because you have good taste," he said, in that oh-so-charming and oh-so-annoying tone. Maya narrowed her eyes at that. Was he being real? Or was he just trying to flirt his way into her good graces?

"And even though we've been disagreeing a bit recently—" That was an understatement. Their texts since their first meeting had been a series of debates and counter arguments, peppered by emojis (him) and memes (her). "I knew you'd see the potential here. This is where the cohesion comes. The melding together of our ideas."

Nishant tugged her closer, twirling her around so that she was staring out at the mountains and he was behind her. "Think about it," he whispered, close to her ear. "After a day full of playing Holi, we keep the party going by opening up this warehouse so it's an indoor and outdoor space, bringing in local catering and artisans, and then as the sun is going down, and the stars are coming up, we launch the biggest, best South Asian music festival this school—this county—has ever seen. No one will be able to stop talking about it. And everyone will want to know who planned it." His breath tickled her neck. "Maya Sastry."

Her breath hitched. Damn it, she had been sold when he had mentioned the stars. But that finale?

"You want to be event chair for the HSA, right?" he said. "You mentioned it."

How did he remember that? He was actually listening?

"You are dangerously charming, did you know that?" she said, before thinking. Maya was about to take it back out of sheer embarrassment, when Nishant's face relaxed into a pleased expression. Almost as if that was exactly what he wanted her to say.

"That's a high compliment, coming from you," he said.

"From me?"

He chuckled. He was still next to her, close enough that she could see his lashes flutter. "You're a tough nut to crack. It makes me want to work harder."

Oh. He was trying to convince her so he had turned on the charm. It wasn't about her, not really. Maya didn't know why her stomach dropped at the thought.

"Ha-ha," she said, pulling away from him. Maya pretended to fix her jacket, taking the moment to put space between them and get her mind settled from the charm bomb that stood in front of her. "I'm just trying to do right by this event." She looked out at the mountains and then at him. "But I guess you are, too. This is really good work, Nishant."

Something shifted in Nishant's expression, a flash of surprise across his face, though he hid it quickly. Nishant Rai, big man on campus, seemed pleased? That couldn't be right. He probably got positive feedback all the time, especially being as handsome and charismatic as he was.

"So . . . is that a yes?" he said slowly, an expectant look on his face.

She rolled her eyes. "That's a let's-see-if-we-can-get-this-building-first. But yes, I think I'm beginning to see your vision. Maybe we could pull off a music festival, if we can get permits for a multi-day event. Thursday night, the Holika Dahan, then Friday off for classes until the mela launches in the evening. Saturday, we have the whole day to play Holi and then the mela, which leads up to the music festival. We'll probably need to find an audio system to handle all of that, won't we?"

Nishant let out a whoop that was so joyful, Maya couldn't help but laugh. His smile was radiant, but that bright look on his face? Absolutely contagious.

He glanced back at her, excitedly chattering away, his face lighting up in that particular Nish way that seemed to make her heart squeeze double time.

"Hey," she said as they opened the door. "About my next date? Could you find someone single this time?"

Nishant froze and then thawed, all in the span of a few seconds. If Maya didn't know better, she might think that for a second there, he had been annoyed. He rolled his eyes. "I'm working on it."

CHAPTER 10

Nishant Rai: Update?

Maya Sastry: You won't even believe why this one didn't work out.

Nishant Rai: He fainted at your perfection?

Maya Sastry: . . .

Maya Sastry: Do you have a book of these lines or something?

They were barely five minutes into the HSA leadership meeting, this time held in one of the French classrooms, before Zane stepped forward and declared, "Today is an important meeting, one that could spell life or death for the Hindu Student Association."

This wasn't atypical for a leadership meeting, especially one led by Zane. They had a life-or-death situation every other meeting or so, and Maya had been to at least three now. It was just Zane's style—just like the wire-rimmed glasses and classic loafers he always wore.

But his tone made Maya glance up from her notebook. She had an Econ 102 exam in two days and something about microeconomics made her brain feel like canned soup sloshing around in a bowl.

"And by that I mean our budget," Zane said, raising his hand to the whiteboard that stood at the front of the room. He lifted an eyebrow. "Can we please refrain from studying for exams during our precious time together?"

Maya flushed, straightening her spine and shoving her textbook under her notebook, only to notice about four other people on leadership doing the same thing, which made her feel a bit better. At least she wasn't the only one freaking out about exams. She hadn't taken French since junior year of high school, but something about the French language posters around the classroom were giving her serious AP French flashbacks, which was not a good thing for her stress levels. She had much preferred the chem auditorium meetings, but the Model UN club had snatched those up for the month due to their spring conference.

"This is an all-HSA problem," Zane said. "It's going to affect all of our spring events, so let's put our heads together and see what we can noodle."

A low voice spoke in her ear. "If Zane says *noodle* one more time . . ."

Maya swallowed a snort. "You'll what?"

"Eat my shoe?" Nishant said, leaning over the desk behind her with a cheeky grin. Their détente was complete now, and Maya even found that she didn't mind Nishant's company as much anymore.

"Those shoes? Your nice leather sneakers?" she said, her snort now escaping. "I'd pay to see that."

Nishant's eyes flashed. "I'll buy everyone extra coffee?"

"That's more like it," Maya said. "Though it would be a lot of coffee. I'm pretty sure we're in store for many more *noodles* tonight."

"Excuse me," Zane said, clearing his throat. "Nishant, any reason you keep whispering into Maya's ear?"

"Thinking of ideas to save our event," Nishant said, without missing a beat. "I think a Valentine's Day fundraiser could be great."

Damn it, that was a great idea. Valentine's Day was really popular at Neadham and people got into it, especially as it was right after midterms. Plus, HSA held a Valentine's Day formal every year, dubbed the V-Formal, and it was the talk of the Neadham community.

Payal Grover, town gossip, always wrote an "anonymous" recap of the event in the school newspaper the day after. More than one relationship had been launched off the back of the HSA V-Formal.

Zane looked mollified, nodding along. "That's a solid idea. Let's jump off that. Pooja, I know you've been working on the V-Formal. What do you think?"

"I like it," Pooja said, fluttering her eyelashes at Nishant. "What about a kissing booth? Or a kiss-gram? It would be a great way to make connections." He gave her one of those obnoxious boy head nods.

"Keep it in your pants, DJ Nish," she whispered to Nishant.

He tilted his head at her. "You've been thinking about my pants?"

Maya pretended to gag.

"A little old-fashioned, but I like where we're going," Zane said. "Why would anyone do that now, though, with Meet'em free? Maya, what do you think?"

Maya felt a zing up her arms, as she always did when Meet'em was mentioned. She hadn't forgotten the shame of her account being suspended. There still had been no update on what had happened, though Jana was using the investigation as the driving storyline of her documentary for the Neadham Film Festival. She would often close her door mid–phone call, which meant she was following some lead or another and didn't want Maya to hear.

"Because sometimes people need a way to do something they've wanted to do but are too scared," Maya said, before she could stop herself. Oops.

Zane stroked his chin. "That is a fair point."

"Like the stoplight party that Sigma Chi hosts," Pooja said. "A concept like that lets people let loose, removes the awkward beginning." Her gaze darted toward Nishant.

Pooja had a point. After the string of failed dates from Nishant, maybe she needed to go try things the in-person way again. It was almost as if after Anthony, Nishant was trying to find guys who would be wrong for her. Or maybe she was the problem. Sigh.

Plus, Jana hadn't stopped talking about it and had been trying to convince her to go for a week now. Maya doodled *Stoplight party?* into her planner. The way Jana had been talking about it, there was very little chance she was going to be able to escape it. Stoplight party this, stoplight party that—what exactly was so exciting about this party? Maya hadn't the faintest idea.

"What facilitates easy romantic beginnings?"

"Kiss-gram," Maya said. "You can send someone a kiss anonymously . . . and then maybe we reveal them . . ."

"At V-Formal," Nishant finished, winking at Maya.

She rolled her eyes, though it was a good idea—fun, viral, and a great way of driving sales to V-Formal.

"Yes!" Zane said, jumping up, startling a few of them. "I knew putting you both together was a good idea."

Whoa, that was a stretch. First, he hadn't put them together, and second, Maya still wasn't positive it had been a good idea. They hadn't killed each other yet, and they had kind of succeeded on the whole save-the-date-and-lock-down-an-event-venue thing, but otherwise?

Jury was still out, in her opinion.

But she did like the way Zane was looking at them like they were his golden children. That would make her job showcasing her event chair abilities easier.

Zane clapped his hands. "Let's get into small groups and brainstorm."

"I call partners," Nishant said. He scooted his desk next to her. "How are the dates going, by the way? I know Tyler was a bust, but what about Jorge?"

Jorge had been an okay first date, but he had asked her out for a second date, which had been a coffee hangout he had fled quickly— Maya still didn't know why that had happened. Jana had spent half an hour convincing Maya that it was not, in fact, because of the sweater she had been wearing.

"Yeah, he was lying," Maya said, making a face.

"Maya, I don't think he ran out because he hated your angora sweater," Nishant said. "I have to agree with your roommate on that one. He ran out because he's a jerk who doesn't know how to treat a girl."

"Surprising from you," Maya said. "Since you've never been on a third date."

"That's not the point," Nishant said, shaking his head. "It's bad form to ghost."

"What, you let people down easy or something?" she said.

"Yes, actually. Maybe not easy, but I'm at least clear about it. I take the time to have the conversation, even if it's awkward. Not everyone's a good fit and there's nothing wrong with that," he said, shrugging.

Probably not what the girls who dated Nishant would say. They probably left with their hearts broken while Nishant left with his conscience scot-free. Though she did have to award him a begrudging point on not ghosting and being up-front.

"Uh-huh," Maya said. "So, what you're saying is that even my angora sweater will find its match? Even though it's apparently horribly ugly according to Jana."

Nishant snorted, loud enough that Zane shot them a look. "Sure, we'll go with that." He paused. "Is it really that bad? I need to see a photo."

Maya whipped out her phone and managed to get through three photos before Zane marched over to them. Nishant hid her phone from view, and they quickly shifted to talk about kiss-grams and Valentine's Day as he came into earshot.

Zane paused nearby, his eyes narrowed as he pretended not to listen to them. Finally, he left and Maya giggled.

"He totally knew," Maya whispered.

"That's the fun—" Nishant whispered, stopping short as his phone rang. He glanced down at it. "Be right back."

Maya turned her attention back down to her phone. The sweater really wasn't that bad, but it was *unique*. And Nishant was right— she wanted to find someone who would like her and her sweater. Apparently, that wasn't Jorge.

A few minutes later, Zane called for a break before they were all to present their ideas. Maya ventured out to the hall to stretch her legs for a bit, taking a stroll.

She didn't mean to overhear, but Nishant's voice echoed in the small, narrow hallway.

"Yes, I'm one of the event chairs. For Holi." Beat. "I know you thought I couldn't do it, but—" Nishant was silent for a few moments, though she heard the rustle of shoes on the linoleum floor. "No, Papa, I don't plan on messing it up. I don't mess everything up, even if you think so. Yes, I have a partner. Yes, I'm helping out."

His voice was tight, earnest, in a way that Maya hadn't heard from Nishant. Raw, even. Like the mask he normally wore had been ripped off, exposing the boy underneath.

"Yes, I'm still DJing, but my grades are high and it isn't a distraction— No, I'm not. I'm not doing that." A beat of silence followed. "Of course I'll DJ the Guptas' anniversary party. Oh, so now it's useful? My idea was good! Just because it didn't immediately work—"

Maya stepped away quickly, suddenly. This conversation wasn't for her, and though her curiosity burned at those few whispered words, she didn't want to intrude any more than she had. Already,

Maya had seen a raw side of Nishant that she hadn't before. Unvarnished.

It was clear from the snippet she had heard that she had been wrong. Being a DJ was not some perfect fit with his parents, despite their business. Her heart lurched for him, remembering her own conversations with her parents about her desire to bake, to intern with a nearby wedding planner her junior year instead of their neighbor who was a doctor. But they had got through it. Sort of.

Maya hoped Nishant would find that peace with his parents, too.

She made her way back to the main hallway. Pooja waved at her as she walked toward her. "Hey, is the bathroom—"

"It's out of order," Maya blurted out.

"Ugh," Pooja said, frowning. "I have to go to the third floor now. Tell Zane so he doesn't think I've absconded and lecture us for thirty minutes."

Maya gave her a thumbs-up and then slunk back to the meeting room, Nishant's phone call rattling in her brain. The move to protect him had been instinctive. A good Samaritan. She wasn't changing her stance on Nishant, was she?

Except that maybe she was, especially after what she had heard. The pieces of the puzzle started to slide together in her mind. Why Nishant had been so keen, so desperate even, to partner with her on Holi, why DJ Nish even cared to do it in the first place.

And even though she should have felt annoyed, the overwhelming emotion in her chest was one of understanding. Maya had started to suspect that there was more to Nishant, and this only convinced her of it.

Who was Nishant under the mask? Who was he really?

CHAPTER 11

Maya Sastry: No. Just no.
Nishant Rai: What's wrong with him?
Maya Sastry: Nishant, I said no more hikers!!
Nishant Rai: My bad.

Normally, Maya could count on Jana to be forgetful, whether it was her keys or who left the teakettle on, or any manner of things. Not today. Not on the big stoplight-party day. The day Jana hadn't been able to shut up about since Maya had turned single. Especially after Jana had weaseled a yes out of her, taking advantage of Maya in her post–basketball game haze, when she had said she wanted to experience more of what the Neadham social calendar had to offer.

Jana bounced into her room with a big smile. In her hands were two extremely short dresses in different shades of green. She had been sending her texts with different green outfits for them both to wear for a few weeks now. Maya had been hoping that if she ignored the texts, and ignored the party, it would just go away. Clearly, she had been wrong.

"Pick one," Jana said. "Time to stoplight!"

"Why did I agree to this again?" Maya said, with a slight groan.

"Because you owe it to me?" Jana said.

Maya gave her a look. "I came to your documentary taping yesterday! I provided the cupcakes and signed away my life rights to you, apparently."

"Fair. Because you owe it to yourself?" Jana said.

Ugh, Jana was right. She had bounced home after the V-Formal planning session of the event committee and told Jana that she needed to go out and meet people IRL because Nishant was failing as a date guide and because Maya 2.0 wasn't going to become event chair by staying in her room all the time.

She hated Maya 2.0 right now.

"Ugh," Maya said. "I don't think I'm ready for a frat party. It's going to be pure chaos."

"Exactly!" Jana bounced on the balls of her feet. "That's what's so exciting. It's going to be a good party, especially after another huge basketball win yesterday. Everyone's going to be out."

That's what worried Maya.

"I changed my mind," Maya said. "I think I'm perfectly happy with going through my first year, maybe even all my years, without that experience. I'll meet boys at the coffee shop or in class or—"

"Nuh-uh," Jana said. Her eyes narrowed, emphasizing the cat-eye eyeliner she had on. "Not so fast. I know all your avoidant crap, darling. Get on your feet. This is for event chair, remember? To help you get out of your comfort zone and experience the university?"

Maya groaned again. Jana tapped her foot on the ground. "Up we go."

When Maya hesitated yet again, Jana pulled out the big guns. "I'll let you take me to that new bakery, and I'll taste every single pastry they have with you."

"Fine," Maya said, after a minute of consideration. She had been trying to convince Jana to do a taste testing with her for a few weeks now. And after sitting through the rehearsal of her documentary, where Maya had to answer the same question thirty times, she was definitely going to follow through.

About a half hour later, Maya looked in the mirror and tugged at her dress, wondering why exactly she had given in to Jana.

First of all, the whole concept of a stoplight party seemed to have embarrassment baked into it. Dressing up in red, yellow, or green based on your relationship status? Why did it make her weirdly sad to be wearing this green dress?

At least it wasn't an unfortunate green. Jana had been trying to persuade her to wear this sparkly lime-green halter dress, but Maya had decided on this hunter-green dress instead. Classy, but still tight enough to make Jana happy. Which meant that Maya could already anticipate that this night would be mildly painful, in more ways than one. At least she could keep her white sneakers on. Jana had approved those.

They were out the door shortly after, with Jana steering them toward Frat Row with expert care. Jana had been right—the school was out tonight. People milled around on the main college road and spilled over onto University Drive, all the bars showing impressively long lines. They waved hello to a number of people wearing green and gold, which meant that Maya actually got a couple of cheers and high fives from people who thought she was cheering on the basketball team's victory, which she was totally fine letting them think.

Maya rubbed her arms, fighting back a slight chill as they walked. She could feel her nerves taking over her entire body.

"Question for you—who would actually wear yellow?" Maya said, referring to the stoplight colors. Green was for *go*, yellow for *it's complicated*, red for *I'm taken*. "It feels kind of aggressive, doesn't it?"

Jana chuckled at her. "You would say that. But I agree, it's a choice to wear yellow and anyone who does is looking for trouble, in my opinion. Though that's half the fun!"

"Hmm," Maya said, wondering again what she'd gotten herself into.

"Hey," Jana said, turning to her. She walked backward as she talked to Maya. "Can you try and have some fun tonight?"

Maya grunted something intelligible. Jana squinted at her.

"I'll try, okay?" Maya said finally.

"I'll take it!" Jana said with a whoop.

Maya tried not to make a face; she would rather be home with a good book, a cup of hot chocolate, and a baking competition playing in the background on the TV.

But this was Maya 2.0! She could be that version of Maya any day. And she had boys to meet! A social calendar to fill! Experiences to experience!

And who knows, maybe she would have a great time.

———— ✐ ————

Maya was already not enjoying this party.

The party was in the basement level of an old, somewhat rickety frat house that was already groaning under the weight of twenty boys living in it. The basement was not faring so well, either, with the faint musty smell that seemed to descend from the ceiling, peeling wall paint, and duct-taped windowpanes. But it made for a perfect party situation.

It looked like the entire basement had been cleared out, with couches and tables pushed to the side and a makeshift dance floor in the center, a bright disco ball hanging overhead as the only real light in the space. Which, of course, meant that Maya had tripped over a few things in her first minutes in the basement.

Jana had already found a group of people she knew, all of them in yellow, and Maya had tagged along. She was now playing the plus-one friend, smiling and nodding along to jokes she didn't totally understand. It wasn't like she could hear anything, either, so every time someone tried to talk to her, she had to pretend like she knew what they were saying.

Plus, being the only green in a sea of yellow made her feel like the odd Skittle. Where were all these people finding situations to even complicate?

Even with Nishant as her dating guide, she hadn't quite found anyone that she'd consider, or who would seriously consider her. Sigh. Maya tried to nod along to some joke or another, trying not to worry that any available guy might think she was a yellow by association, too.

Somehow, it seemed like everyone in the entire room was having a better time than her.

Until she turned around and spotted a tall figure with a semi-scowl on his face. Nishant stood in the corner of the room, clad in black clothing that faded into the background, except for a layer of bead necklaces whose color she couldn't quite see. He was talking to a tall girl in a tight green dress. She had somehow managed to drape herself all over his arm, a feat in and of itself, and Nishant looked like he wanted to be anywhere but there. It was probably the first time Maya had ever seen him look less than happy in the presence of someone, especially a girl.

The girl leaned into him and whispered something that immediately caused Nishant to shake his head. The pout she gave him was next level, but after Nishant didn't react, she sighed and left. The moment she left, Nishant seemed to visibly relax and then— the slightest of movements, a small downturn of his mouth that hinted at a frown. She wasn't sure she had ever seen Nishant show any emotion before, other than that winking, charming mask.

It was like seeing a whole new man. Maya found herself walking toward him without thinking.

"Everything okay?" Maya said in greeting.

Nishant turned slowly to her, giving Maya enough time to look him over, taking in his slicked-back hair, the long eyelashes that fluttered as he looked at her. As always, he was dressed impeccably in tailored clothing and sharp lines that flattered his body, a contrast to every other boy around him.

It was a power move, Maya realized. Dressing that well? He must know the air it gave off. Confidence. Charisma. It was a suit of armor that was impenetrable.

"Better now," he said slowly, looking her over, his gaze lingering on her dress's hemline.

Maya rolled her eyes. "Stop."

He grinned at her in a way that made her stomach warm. Betrayal from her body. Ugh. Especially when she realized the bead necklace he was wearing was, in fact, yellow. Double ugh. She thought about leaving, but then realized she had nowhere else to go.

Why was everyone she knew in yellow at this party? It was beginning to make her feel like something was wrong with her.

"What are you doing back here, hiding in the corner? Going for the spy look?" she said, pretending as if she hadn't seen him there with whoever that was. She was aiming for light, and Nishant seemed grateful. His shoulders relaxed a little.

"You found me out," Nishant said. "I was hoping to fade into the background."

That was a surprise. Nishant, fading into the background? She figured it was a joke. This man could never fade into any background, and he must know that. Even now, Maya could see a group of girls whispering and looking over at him in the corner.

"Can I join you?" Maya asked. "In the whole disappearing thing."

"What? You're not having fun?" he said.

She gave him a look. "I'm not *not* having fun. I'm just . . . not as much of a social butterfly as Jana is." He raised an eyebrow at her. "Jana Singh-Kota? She's my roommate."

"She's the one in the middle of that group, I take it?"

Maya nodded.

"You came straight to me instead," he said. "Wise choice, Maya."

"What?" she sputtered. "That's not true."

It was kind of true. He tilted his head at her, giving her that piercing look that made you feel like he knew every single part of your soul.

"Ugh, fine," she said, instead of admitting she had been watching him. "I hate group dances and everyone there is such a yellow, and I saw you, so yes, I guess I escaped to you."

Nishant chuckled. "I'm honored."

She didn't mention that she thought he had been wearing green as well, because that would just be embarrassing.

"What are *you* doing in a corner, anyway?" she said.

"Try to say that with a little less disgust." He laughed.

"It's not disgust, it's just—" She considered her words. "Confusion? Zane has called you a man about town so many times I thought I would see it in action tonight."

"Even I can have my off moments," he said, his eyes darting to the corner of the room. He seemed a little distracted, just enough that it took him a beat to realize what he had just admitted. "I'm surprised to find you here, though. At this party."

A clear change of subject but done with finesse. Maya wasn't sure why she was surprised. Nishant stepped closer to her as a couple jostled down the stairs near him, close enough that she could smell a hint of clove and orange in his aftershave. His fingers brushed across her wrist, and he tugged her to the side, away from the stairs.

"I'm also surprised to find me here, to be honest," Maya said. "But I told Jana I wanted to go to my first—to a frat party, and she is nothing if not determined. My mistake was telling her I wanted to experience more of the Neadham social calendar."

"But now you're here," Nishant said. "What do you want to do?"

"Huh?" she said.

Nishant turned his warm brown eyes squarely on hers. "What do you want to do? You're here now," he repeated. "So let's make the most of it. Why did you want to come out, anyway?"

It was a great question. Maya had wanted to go because it was an experience she hadn't had before, but she didn't feel like sharing that with Nishant at the moment. She didn't think he would make fun of her, but she didn't want Nishant to realize she was so inexperienced in college life, especially given that he was the opposite.

"Jana said everyone would be out tonight and I guess I wanted to meet people?" she said. "How can I be event chair if I don't know anyone?"

Enough of the truth, but not as embarrassing as admitting to her grand plan of Maya 2.0.

"Let's do it, then," he said.

"What?"

"Meet people," he said. "I know most of the people here, even the people I don't want to." He said the last part under his breath, but Maya was shorter than him and she caught it. Interesting. There were layers to Mr. Social. She found herself a little surprised at the hint of annoyance in his voice.

Then what he said hit her.

"No, no, no," she said. "That's totally fine. I appreciate it, but no need to do any of that."

"Come on," he said, waving to her to follow him. When she didn't budge, he gently tugged her elbow. "I promise it won't be that bad. Or it might be, but you'll feel a lot better after."

"I doubt that," Maya muttered.

She gave Nishant a thumbs-up or, well, she was going to, but he had already whisked her through the basement doors over to a group outside on the back lawn.

"Hey, everyone, this is Maya," Nishant said.

She recognized a few of them from HSA—most of them were upperclassmen—and it took every ounce of her rusty social skills to not melt out of anxiety. But to her surprise, it wasn't as bad as she had thought. After a few minutes and quick intros, Maya found herself laughing along to a bad joke from Paul, an upperclassmen econ major, and asking questions to Mirabel, who was a business major with an amazing head of pink hair.

"See? Not so bad," Nishant said, leaning over to whisper in her ear.

Maya did her best not to jump out of her skin. Nishant's breath was soft against her back, her skin exposed under the thin straps of her dress. She could feel his warmth, radiating out.

"No, not so bad," Maya agreed. "They're all really nice."

"They don't bite." He raised an eyebrow.

Maya rolled her eyes. "Okay, calm down, Mr. Social. Number one, I didn't think they would bite." Or at least, not too hard. "And number two, not all of us just find it easy to *meet* people."

"And you think I'm one of those people," he said. Maya tilted her head in acknowledgment. "I see. I feel like I should take that as a compliment, but I'm also not sure with you."

"What?" Maya said, surprised.

He gave her a half smile. "You seem all sweet and cute, but you've got sass to you, Maya Sastry. You've been trying to put me in my place since the day I met you. Don't worry, though, I like it."

Maya flushed to the tips of her fingers, at the compliment and the way he said it. He liked that side of her? "You do bring out something different in me. I really am a perfectly sweet person, usually. I bake people muffins!"

Nishant's laugh was full throated and deep. Maya's skin warmed at the thought that she had caused that laugh from him.

"And you should take it as a compliment. Being able to make friends with anyone is a skill," she admitted.

"And I don't believe that you've lost the ability to make friends," he said, shaking his head. "You seem perfectly socialized to me."

"No, really," she said. "My first semester was not good."

"Really, Maya, I feel like we know two different versions of you. The girl I've come to know is—"

They had somehow separated from the group yet again and had been pushed into the far corner of the dance floor by a group of singing people in shades of yellow, who all seemed to know each other. From here, they could see the whole dance floor in relative darkness. Which is why when Maya shuffled a little to avoid being stepped on by one of the dancers nearby, she nearly jumped out of her skin when she saw who was standing in the doorway.

Shit.

Double shit.

"Oh no," Maya said with a groan. She ducked behind Nishant. "Hide me."

Nishant twisted around, looking at her as if she had grown two heads. Thomas turned, and while she was pretty sure he couldn't see her yet, Maya ducked again. Nishant turned and Maya grabbed on to his shirt, moving with him.

"What. Are. You. Doing?" Nishant asked.

He grabbed her forearms and swung her around to face him. It was a good thing Nishant was taller than her because he still mostly covered her. Maya gave him a nervous smile.

"I'm hiding," she said. "I thought I mentioned that."

"Sure, but from what?" He followed Maya's gaze to the clump of boys that Thomas was standing in. Maya clocked that Thomas was wearing red. She hated the way the realization hit her gut, a soft thud of hurt that melted into resignation. He had already moved on. Was she really that surprised? "Or from who?"

"From who is the right question," Maya said. "Though I hate to admit it."

"Earth to Maya," Nishant said, waving his hand in front of her face. The strobing lights of the disco ball hit his face, highlighting the neon-green paint on his cheekbones, which she hadn't noticed before. Why did that look so good on him?

"Ugh" was all she said.

Maya tugged Nishant into the dark corner. There was a couple making out to their right, and Nishant glanced over at them and back at Maya. Normally, Maya would overexplain herself, but she was on heightened alert with the whole ex-is-thirty-feet-away situation.

Nishant stepped closer, as if he could sense her distress.

She took a deep breath. "It's my ex. You know, the one who potentially got me kicked off the Meet'em app? He's standing over there and I've somehow managed to avoid him since our breakup and I really would love to keep that streak going. Forever."

Nishant nodded. "This is a pretty big place. We can lose him."

"Wait, you're going to help me?" Maya blinked at him.

"Am I supposed to leave you here? Looking the way you do?"

"How do I look?"

Nishant bit his lip, like he was holding back from saying something. When he spoke, he said, "You look like you might jump out the window if you needed to."

Was there a window she could jump out of? That would solve her problem. She looked around only to remember that no, they were in a basement and the door was all the way on the other side. Plus, Thomas was standing right by it.

"The door is too far away," Maya said as more of an afterthought.

Nishant shook his head. He gently turned her around while still covering her. "Okay, who exactly is this villain we're talking about?"

Maya let out a deep sigh. "There, in the back. In the red button-down. Slight curl to his hair?"

Nishant tilted his head and scanned the room. Maya could see the moment he caught sight of Thomas. It was instantaneous, the change. Nishant's brow furrowed and his jaw tightened.

"That guy?" he said, sounding incredulous.

"Yeah," Maya said, cringing. "Wait, do you know him?"

Nishant shook his head. "I can't believe— Honestly, Maya, you have the worst taste in men."

"Hey! I liked the last boy you set me up with, kind of, so what does that say about you, since they're your friends?" Maya said.

"I'm *friendly* with them," Nishant said, crossing his arms. "That's entirely different from being actual friends. And that just means I have unimpeachably good taste."

Maya rolled her eyes. The ego on this man.

"But Thomas?" Nishant said.

"What do you have against him?"

Nishant didn't hear her, or he ignored her. "His brother is the biggest jerk on campus," he continued, looking legitimately annoyed. Maya wasn't sure she had ever seen him so frazzled. "And you were dating him? He's the boy trouble you mentioned?"

"Yeah, well, it was a good lesson," she said. "But really, how do you know Thomas?"

"I don't know him well. But I did have one run-in with him. It wasn't pleasant. Let's leave it at that," Nishant said.

"That sounds so ominous." Maya gnawed on the side of her lip.

Nishant's body language relaxed. "Nothing ominous, just glad you got out of it. You're smart but considerate, passionate yet focused, and he's, well, he's none of those things. You can do so much better."

Maya's face flushed at his words. Did he really think that of her, or was it just a part of his charm offensive? Her heart fluttered heavily, but her brain told her to rein it in. He was right, though, she could do better, which she knew. Didn't mean it wasn't nice to hear it from Nishant.

Plus, somewhere along this partnership, she had started to maybe, almost, kind of respect his opinion? Granted, he still had a lot of stupid ideas, but he wasn't all that bad.

Weird.

Nishant stepped closer, like he was about to say something, when someone waved at him from down the hallway. He made to move toward them, and Maya started to freak out, looking around for exit options.

He held out a hand to her, and she did a double take. Wait, he wasn't leaving? "I'm just going to go say hi. We used to DJ together in high school," Nishant said. "Come with me."

"Huh?"

Nishant tugged her closer so that a group of three could dance past them. "Come with me. He's a cool guy. And he's in the opposite direction of Thomas."

Maya still didn't get it. Why was he trying to save her? He could just as easily dump her here and go about his life. Was he secretly planning a way to undermine her later and that's why he was playing so nice? That seemed too devious for him, but you never knew with a boy like Nishant.

Nishant's arm curled around her, and she realized it was still there, warm and comforting.

"Okay," she said. "Thanks."

He tugged her behind him, and they waded through a sea of people dressed in yellow dancing with one another. Complicated, indeed. Nishant's friend waved them over into a corner and they half shouted greetings at one another. Maya felt an initial burst of awkwardness, but it quickly went away. Nishant's friend, Immanuel, was loud and fun, and she started to hit it off with the girl he was with, Annie.

Nishant didn't leave her side the entire time, even as other people he knew came and went.

"You don't have to stay," she said, yelling over the music. "Or be, like, my bodyguard. I'm okay."

"Like you were okay when you saw him?" he said, laughing.

"Hey," Maya said. "That was a surprise. You try running into one of your exes."

Nishant's eyebrow rose just as Maya turned red. Okay, he probably ran into one of his exes every time he turned a corner, so not the best analogy.

"You're not going to say it?" he said.

"I'm already thinking it, and it still feels pretty good," she said. Her mouth quirked upward, but she managed to hold herself back, which she thought she deserved a medal for doing.

Nishant held her gaze through it all, his eyebrow rising higher and higher. "Strong self-control. But yes, I do know what it's like to run into an ex."

"Does two dates count as an ex?"

"Apparently," he said, his tone so dry that Maya couldn't help but laugh. There was no annoyance or ridicule in his voice, though, only something that sounded a little bit like resignation.

Nishant Rai, the riddle. Was it bad that she wanted to solve him? Ever since she had overheard that conversation with his parents, Maya couldn't help but wonder if she had gotten him wrong, had placed him into a category too quickly.

"I do appreciate the help," she said. "But I could've handled myself. Eventually."

"My first reaction wouldn't be to duck," he said. "But I do agree with you. You could've handled yourself."

His voice was sincere, and its warmth crept up Maya's spine. The music thudded against the walls around them, pushing them to stand even closer together.

"Oh?"

"You're pretty fierce, Maya. I'm not sure you know it," he said, grinning. "I was nervous that day, when you said you didn't want to partner together."

"I was pretty set on that," Maya said, rubbing the side of her face. "Sorry."

"Don't apologize for having convictions," he said. His cheeks dimpled into a smile. "And anyway, I won you over, didn't I? With my charm and persuasion and good—"

Maya pushed a hand against his chest. "Stop there. You are so full of yourself."

They were inches apart, so close that Maya had to will herself to remember that he was just this close to prevent hearing loss. It didn't mean anything.

Nishant grabbed the hand that rested on his chest, looking down at her with a mischievous expression. "Ever thought it was for good reason?"

She had never realized how good a boy could look with face paint, though Nishant looked good in just about anything. If she wasn't careful, she could find herself falling into the depths of those eyes and never coming out. But would that be such a bad thing?

"Maya?"

Both of their heads swiveled to the intruder.

Thomas's curly hair gleamed in the strobing lights, highlighting the red of his shirt and the odd expression on his face. Maya jumped away from Nishant, her body immediately going into flight or fight mode, mostly flight in that moment. The only thing that held her there was Nishant, and the slight pressure he kept on her hand.

"This is what you've been doing?" Thomas said, his face contorting.

"What?" Maya said.

She shook her head. Did he really think— Yes, he did. Thomas was glaring at Nishant as if he had personally taken away his favorite stuffed animal. Yet he was wearing red, and she was wearing green. It had only been a month since their breakup. What a hypocrite.

"You broke up with me for him?" Thomas spat the words out. "I listened to you talk about baking and musicals for hours for this?"

"No, it's not like—"

"I didn't know you were so shallow."

Nishant didn't visibly react, but she knew him well enough to see the way he tensed, the set of his jaw. Almost like this wasn't the first time he had heard those words. What she hadn't expected was the way his eyes narrowed, his warm brown eyes growing cold and assessing.

"Hello, Thomas," Nishant said. "Nice to see you again. How's your brother doing?" His voice was perfectly pleasant, but there was an edge to it.

"Stop pretending to care, dude," Thomas said. He looked at Maya, dragging his eyes up and down her outfit. "You really think you're going to get him to want a relationship? It's like aiming for the major leagues when you wiped out in the minors. You couldn't even convince me—what makes you think *this* will be different? Face it, Maya. He's never going to be interested in you that way. You're just not that type of girl. "

His words were like a slap across the face, a sharpened dagger to the last vestiges of her confidence. It wasn't like she had a ton of it anyway, but she felt herself tugging at her dress without realizing. She wasn't an idiot. She knew she wasn't the most beautiful or the most interesting or the coolest, and she knew Nishant didn't want a girlfriend, she hadn't even tried to— Wait, how had she let Thomas get into her mind like that?

This wasn't about Nishant, this was about Thomas being a jerk.

"Step away, man," Nishant said.

Maya couldn't help but stare at Nishant. She thought he would immediately deny such a ludicrous notion and claim they were just friends, washing his hands of the whole thing. It was what most guys would do.

But Nishant stood by her side, giving Thomas a hard look. Anyone else might think to back away. Maya revised her opinion of Nishant. There were shades to the man—he chose to be the nice, sociable, shameless flirt everyone saw, but there was more to him. There was steel under the mask. What else would she find?

"You couldn't leave the normal girls for us?" Thomas said. His cheeks were flushed and red. He glanced back at the group of boys he had come with and then stepped toward Nishant.

Ouch. Maya knew she shouldn't take what Thomas was saying to heart, but that had been another direct hit. Was that why he had been with her this whole time? Because he thought she was boring, normal, easy to get? Easy to keep without much maintenance? Would always stick around just for scraps of a relationship?

Nishant placed a warm, reassuring hand on her back. Maya broke out of her thoughts and glanced up at him, trying to hide what she had been feeling. And failed. Nishant could clearly see she was bothered by Thomas's words.

His eyes narrowed at Nishant, but there was a flicker of triumph when he looked at Maya. Nishant met his step with one of his own.

"She chose to not be with you, and given what you just said to her, I'm not sure she should have ever been," he said, his voice taut, low. "And I feel bad for whoever you've managed to catch in your web."

He looked like he meant it, his eyes flashing a fire she hadn't seen in him before. Nishant was defending her. And somehow, his belief in her sparked her own belief in herself.

Maya finally found the words to stand up for herself, or try to.

"Thomas, just stop," she said. "We're not together, but even if we were, it would be none of your business. I never asked you for much before, so no need to start pretending to care now." Maya could hear her voice rising. "You don't need to concern yourself with my life at all. Please leave me alone."

Thomas reached out to her, but Nishant stepped in between them. "She asked you to leave her alone," he said, loud enough that his voice carried when the song ended.

A few people turned around, whispering. Maya normally would have cowered away from it all, but she found that she didn't care anymore. Let them talk.

Maybe it would be a good thing for other people to hear this. Because for the first time, Maya was seeing Toxic Thomas in real life, and she wondered if maybe Jana's theory had been right. There had been a part of her willing to give him the benefit of the doubt, but the veil had lifted.

When Thomas looked around, and clearly couldn't find a friendly face in the crowd, he finally backed away with a sneer.

"Whatever, dude," Thomas said. He turned to Maya, lowering his voice. "Don't say I didn't warn you. You really think he's going to help you bake and stay at home with you on a Friday night? Just because you're here doesn't change who you really are, Maya. Maybe you should stop pretending."

When he finally disappeared from view, Maya realized she was shaking. Nishant stepped in and rubbed her shoulders lightly. He had noticed her shaking, too. Embarrassing, but she also was super grateful in that moment for the connection, for the tactile feel of his fingers bringing her emotions down.

"That sucked," she said finally, after a few beats. "Thanks, Nishant."

"Nish," he said. "After that, you can definitely call me Nish."

"I'm sorry," Maya said. "He's a—"

"Complete jerk?" Nishant said. "I hope that's what you were about to say."

Maya gave him a half smile. "Basically. More so because he took his anger at me out on you."

Nishant shrugged. "Not anything I haven't heard before." The words were spoken with a certain amount of resignation.

She was about to ask him more, tell him that he didn't deserve any of it, but instead he said, "And you're not normal. I hope you know that."

The intensity with which he looked at her when he said it—it nearly took her breath away. "Oh" was all she could say.

She stepped closer to him, losing herself in the warmth of his touch on her back. His eyelashes fluttered as he looked down at her.

"Thanks again—"

"Stop," he said. "We're partners, right? Got to look out for each other."

Oh yes. They were partners. He was right, so then what was that sinking feeling in her chest? Partners. Obviously. Nishant, despite all the bluster and the persona he seemed to don, was a good guy underneath.

A good friend.

Maya mustered up a smile. "I guess so."

Nishant cocked his head toward the door, and Maya followed his gaze. His buddy from before, Immanuel, was waving at him, swaying a little as he stood with an empty cup in his hand.

"Oh no," Nishant said. "That doesn't look good. I'll be right back. Meet you at the door—"

Immanuel pitched over and Nishant shot her an apologetic look before sprinting toward him. Leaving her alone. Maya rubbed her arms, trying not to feel self-conscious as she stepped back and attempted to fade into the shadows, trying to forget everything

Thomas had said. She considered leaving when Jana's head popped up out of the crowd, a scowl the size of Arizona on her face.

"What happened?" Jana said. "Angelo sent me a text that there was a fight and that you were in it."

"Run-in with Thomas," Maya said. Jana's face started to turn purple. "But I handled it, and Nishant was there, too. He helped."

"Really?" Jana said, a curious look on her face. She took in Maya's state, a frown forming on her face. "How bad was it?"

"Bad" was all Maya said.

"And where is your knight in shining armor now?" Jana said, peering around.

"Gone off to save someone else," she said. "I think we can go."

"Enough said." Jana nodded decisively. "Let's get out of here. Get some pizza, extra cheesy the way you like. On me."

"Let's do it," Maya said. She waved goodbye to Paul and Mirabel, the two new friends she had made, thanks to Nishant.

Jana demanded a play-by-play of what she had missed as they left the basement and walked out into the cool, crisp air. People had spilled out onto the lawn outside. Maya couldn't help but look back at the basement once more, glancing over to where Nishant stood with his friend, who looked pretty green and was hovering near a bush. Immanuel was not going to feel well tomorrow.

"I'm assuming your silence means I have tacit approval to put cockroaches in Thomas's dorm room as a way to suss out if he was the one to get you kicked off and to add to the drama of my short film," Jana said.

"Huh, what?" Maya said, yanking her attention away from Nishant. "No. No, please don't."

Jana made an exasperated face. "Fine, if you insist. But . . ." She continued her tirade until they made it to University Drive and the lights of the late-night restaurants were in sight.

Thomas was wrong. She wasn't trying to change Nishant or become his next two-date wonder, but she was starting to realize there was a lot more to DJ Nish than he let on.

And to her surprise, she wanted to know more.

But would he want to know her?

CHAPTER 12

Nishant Rai: Have you been to that bakery on Main and First?

Maya Sastry: Is that a serious question.

Nishant Rai: Their croissants are pretty good.

Maya Sastry: Their croissants are frozen and have no flake.

Nishant Rai: So we shouldn't go there for our next meeting?

Maya Sastry: I'm not answering that.

Maya waited for Nishant outside the main steps of Lewis Hall, standing at the halfway point between their morning classes that they had designated their spot. She basically had his class schedule memorized by now, which was a fact that she would keep closely guarded for fear of ridicule from Jana.

Plus, it wasn't on purpose. Try coordinating schedules with a popular upperclassman, and you'd have to learn a few things as well, even if you didn't want to. Though if Maya were being honest to herself, she might even admit that she had started looking forward to their meetings, had maybe even started dressing up a little nicer for them.

Not that she would admit it to anyone, and especially not to him. Probably would only feed that ego of his and make him even more of a menace to society. She didn't have a crush or something ridiculous, but Nishant always dressed nice, so she started to up her own game.

"We've got a problem," Maya said in greeting to Nishant, her notebook in her hand. He had ambled over from Harrison Hall, where most of the upperclassmen math and econ classes took place.

"You mean other than the massive surprise exam Professor Mueller threw our way for Calculus 302?" Nishant said, striding up to where she sat on the steps.

He looked put-together for a Thursday morning, which was usually the day that Maya started to give up a little. Instead, Nishant wore a sleek bomber jacket over a perfectly coordinated beige sweater and light denim combo.

"Good thing I'm not in Calculus." Maya eyed the second coffee in his hands. "Is that for me?"

"Maybe," he said. "If you're nice."

"I am. Very nice," she said. "So nice you'll want to give me your sweet, sweet caffeine."

"You're kind of an addict, aren't you?" Nishant said, handing the coffee over to her.

"Not at all," she said. "I'm a normal college student." Maya inhaled the scent. Black with a hint of milk, exactly the way she liked. Good job, Nishant. He *had* meant it for her. Why did that make her feel all warm and fuzzy inside? "Jana's the addict."

"Jana Singh-Kota?" he said.

"Do you call everyone by their full names?" she said.

"Nope," Nishant said. "Case in point." He gestured to her.

"Mmm," she said, sipping the coffee. The bitter and sweet notes mixed together as they hit her tongue, and even though she knew it was impossible, she immediately felt the caffeine coursing through her veins. "Okay, the problem." Maya took a huge gulp of her coffee to fortify her, even though it burned a little on the way down. "We got rejected for the warehouse, which means we have to find a backup now. At the last minute."

"What?" Nishant said, his mouth dropping open. "I had an in."

"You *had* an in. *Had* is the key word. But the art school put the venue booking through the Activities Office, and event spaces are run by Mrs. Porter."

Nishant groaned into his hands. "No, not Mrs. Porter. She's hated me ever since I DJ'ed for the Hanukkah Ball and accidentally blew a fuse in the audio system. I swear, it was not my fault. But if the vice president pours a drink onto a speaker . . . well, you can imagine."

She could, and she felt maybe a little bad for him, but they had a bigger issue on their hands.

"Well, that explains why we got rejected," Maya said. "I should've left your name off the application."

"Hey," he said. Then he slumped a little. "That's fair. If I had known, I would've recommended that as well. She may be the one person who dislikes me on campus."

"Only one?" Maya said. "What about the trail of broken hearts you've left?"

Nishant's face shuttered close with a surprising speed. "That's not fair. I don't make any promises."

His tone was on the edge of icy, a decided contrast to the hot cup of coffee he had gotten particularly for her. Maya winced, feeling a little bad. They were getting along, and she wasn't trying to antagonize him, at least not on purpose. She hadn't realized it would be such a sore point, and he knew what people said, didn't he? Why did it seem to bother him today of all days?

"Okay, sure," she said.

"No, really," he insisted, turning to face her full-on. There was something earnest in his expression, like he wanted her to believe it, though she had no idea why he cared what she thought. Maybe the girl from the party was working out? Ugh. The thought made Maya's stomach drop, hard. "I'm up-front. It's just a date."

"Or two?" she said, unable to help herself.

His eyes narrowed at her. "Or two. But I don't lead them on."

While Maya would say a few girls on campus might disagree, he did have a point. She didn't know if it was the caffeine or the way he kept glancing at her, but she considered his case.

Was it fair to Nishant if he was up-front about what he wanted? It didn't change the fact that anyone who wanted something serious should probably stay away from him, but maybe she had been a little bit harsh in her assessment. At least he was clear about it, unlike some people she had known.

Unlike Ari, who had strung her along for the better part of a year. Better to know you would never get that third date than to keep trying to attain it. Better to know that Nishant would never be interested in you so you could nurse your little crush until it, hopefully, vanished one day. Not that that was a thing she was experiencing or anything.

Still, Maya couldn't completely let it go.

"But why even go on a second date?" she blurted out. "That's already giving someone the idea that there could be more."

"Because maybe I want to see if it could be more? Maybe I don't magically know after one date?" Nishant said. "Had you considered that? That I might be looking for something in particular?"

No, she hadn't. Because it didn't make sense.

"I don't believe you. If that were true, then you'd have found someone you liked by now," she said.

Nishant crossed his arms. "Is that so? And what about you? Found your soulmate yet?"

"I don't actually believe in soulmates," Maya said. "But, no. I haven't. I'm trying, though. By the way, where's my next date?"

Nishant frowned briefly, but then his face slid back into neutral.

"Not everyone wants to jump into a relationship, Maya," he said. The way he said it wasn't unkind, but it cut across Maya regardless. She could tell he wasn't trying to be cruel, especially since he didn't know her background. But the *everyone* he was referring to? That was her, wasn't it? "Some of us enjoy dating, getting to know people. And I'm working on your next one."

"Sure," Maya said, mostly because she could sense she had touched something sensitive, maybe a little raw. She wouldn't have thought it before knowing him, but it was possible Nishant didn't enjoy the rumors about him. The reputation he had fairly or unfairly gotten.

That was the thing with Nishant, wasn't it? Sometimes it was hard to tell who was the real Nishant—DJ Nish or the boy she was slowly starting to know. He looked at her suspiciously, but she dodged his look.

"It never seemed to bother you before," she said. Maybe the extra boost of caffeine was jet fuel, because her mouth kept running on its own.

"What?"

"What people say. The two-date thing," she said. "Unless you didn't know, and I was the first one to tell you before, and then I'm going to shut my mouth and we'll pretend none of this ever happened."

A slew of emotions crossed Nishant's face, each one too fast for Maya to pin down.

"I wasn't unaware," he said. "But maybe I just don't want *you* to think that of me."

Huh. Why? Did he actually care what she thought about him? And why would he, DJ Nish, all-around man-about-town, care what she thought?

"You are my partner, after all, and I think we're making a pretty decent team," he continued.

His words were an instant cold bucket of water. Of course. He cared because they were partners. Made sense. Logical.

"And I want my friends to know me," he said. "The real me."

Friends was good. Friends was fine. Friends was the best-case scenario when you were stuck working with someone else. Right?

Unbidden, Thomas's words came back to her.

You really think you're going to get him to want a relationship?

Well, she wasn't trying to make Nishant want anything. Feelings, what feelings?

"Oh, we're friends now?" she said, swallowing her thoughts.

"We're not enemies, are we?" he said. When she didn't respond, he nudged her. "Are we?"

Maya made an *ehhh* noise, and he rolled his eyes at her.

"This is what I get for bringing you coffee?" he said.

"Fine, that was pretty cool of you," she said. "Though Jana would tell you I'm probably too friendly with my enemies."

"I could see that," he said, shaking his head. "You're too kind for your own good. Don't think I didn't notice how you helped Pooja with her budget proposal for the HSA Valentine's formal even though she's definitely late on it."

Maya flushed. It hadn't been that big of a deal. Pooja had been stressing in the lobby of Lewis Hall, and Maya had happened to run into her on her way to help Jana with her short film. The distraction had been welcome.

She had agreed to be the subject of Jana's film, but she hadn't realized it would require so much of her when she was already busy juggling school and Holi planning—plus with the documentary being an investigation of her Meet'em debacle it meant she had to relive it every week. But she had agreed and she couldn't back out now.

Still, Nishant didn't need to know all that.

"So, Mrs. Porter. What are we going to do about it?" she said, suddenly desperate to talk about something else, something that was not her.

Not her best segue, but good enough to get the job done. Nishant pursed his lips. "We'll find another way. That venue is too perfect for us to give up on so easily." A look of determination crossed his face. "You said we were rejected by the Activities Office. What if we went around them?"

"Is that allowed?"

He smiled at her. "Does it matter? All's fair in love and event planning."

"Is it, though?" Maya said. Working with Nishant had done a lot to push her outside her normal thought or planning process, but she was still a rule follower at her heart. She squirmed a little at the thought of breaking one, let alone more than one.

"It is," he said firmly. "Don't worry, I'm not saying we do anything that gets us in trouble. But if we got rejected, someone else must have applied, too, right? If we can find out which club tried to reserve the spot the same weekend . . ."

"We might be able to convince them to swap spots with us?" Maya finished. "Okay, still kind of devious, and still unlikely it will work, but I don't have any other ideas. Other than giving up and going back to the soccer field."

"Not an option," Nishant said. "Especially since it will be after marching band practice. It'll be just mud and dirt. We need a lawn and a space that can be outdoor/indoor for the rest of the event. You know I'm trying to get my audio system approved, but it's slow going. Plus, the warehouse and the lawn have all the electrical outlets."

"Okay, okay," Maya said, taking another deep gulp of her coffee. "I hear you. And I might have an idea of how we can figure out who applied for the warehouse."

Nishant cocked his head at her to go on, but Maya only smiled. "Follow me."

—— 🖋 ——

"There," Maya said. "That's the recycling for the Activities Office." She pointed at the large blue cart that stood by its lonesome in the corner of the hallway. "One thing I noticed about Mrs. Porter is that she is big on the whales, if all those photos in her office and on her social media are any proof. She's definitely a recycler."

"Isn't everyone these days?" Nishant said, peering around the corner.

"You'd think so," Maya said, a little darkly. "But you'd be surprised."

"To be clear, you're saying we should rifle through the recycling to—"

"Find the other application," Maya said, nodding.

"Hm," he said. "I assumed that stealing was not your style, but I guess I was wrong."

Maya made a face. "I'm not a totally bland vanilla blob." She said it a little more forcefully than she had meant to, probably because she could still hear the echo of Thomas's words from the party. "And anyway, we're not stealing anything. It's already off in the recycling cart, which means it was discarded. Plus, I'm not doing anything. *You* are." She smiled sweetly at him. "Mrs. Porter already hates you, so if you do get caught, it won't matter. I need to keep my pristine reputation. For Holi, of course."

"Of course," Nishant murmured, a hint of mirth dancing in his eyes. "I'll throw myself on the dagger for you."

"For us," Maya said.

Nishant rolled his eyes, but he started to inch toward the recycling cart. "Cover me."

Maya did as he said, arranging herself on a bench nearby with her textbooks. She had a perfect line of sight to the only entrance here. A little shiver of excitement trickled down her spine as she watched Nishant tiptoe over to the recycling cart out of the corner of her eye. Stealing was not her style, but she found she was enjoying a tiny bit of subterfuge in order to get what they needed. Old Maya would have had the idea but been too scared.

It helped that she had a partner willing to consider her ideas. Nishant made his way to the bin and started to rummage around, moving the mounds of paper with an alarming speed.

"You're missing one," Maya shout-whispered. "Check that other stack over there."

"Stop back-seat stealing."

"We're not stealing," she whispered back.

A few minutes later, Nishant emerged triumphant with a proposal in his hand. He was looking at it strangely and Maya didn't understand why until he walked over to her.

"First of all, I can't believe your plan actually worked," he said. "And second of all—"

"Oh no," Maya said, catching the names on the proposal. "We're going up against the entrepreneurship club. Only one of the most focused and hustle-culture clubs at Neadham."

They walked out of the Activities Office, after turning it back to rights, and into the fading sunlight of the late afternoon. Spring was hinting at its arrival with small flowers starting to bud on the side of the lawn, but otherwise, it was cool outside. Maya pulled her cardigan tighter against her and frowned down at the proposal.

"We'll have to find them," she said slowly. "They meet—"

"On Mondays, but we can't wait that long," Nishant said. He took out his phone and tapped quickly on it. Maya tried to peer over only to realize that attempting to look was futile, given their height difference. His phone pinged and he smiled wide. "Great. We're heading to Lewis Dining Hall."

It took Maya a few seconds to catch up to Nishant's stride. "Um, why?"

"Because I happen to know the president of the entrepreneurship club."

"Wait, explain. You can't just—"

"We need to catch her," Nishant said, tugging Maya along beside him. He grabbed her bag, seeming to think it was slowing her down. "Pauline is at the dining hall now and then she's in a pitch coaching session for the rest of the night, so this is our best time to get in front of her."

"But—"

"Let's go!"

Nishant walked fast—too fast, Maya decided. She could feel herself breaking out into a light sweat, and Lewis Dining Hall wasn't even that far away, maybe a quarter mile? A few minutes of huffing later and they made their way into the hall, which was teeming with hungry students.

"There," Nishant said, pointing at a girl with a wild riot of brown curls in a creamy-white trench coat and heeled boots. On a Thursday! Damn it, why couldn't Maya be one of those girls who dressed to the nines on a Thursday? "Pauline."

Maya walked forward with Nishant, but he held up a hand and

pushed her back into the seat he had pulled out from a table nearby.

"Let me run point," he said. "Pauline and I go back."

She raised an eyebrow at Nishant. "Do I want to know what that means?"

"It's not what you think," he said, giving her a slow, sure grin, which didn't convince her that it wasn't what she thought. "We were both on the same hall freshman year, and I think she's always had a crush on me. Which I may be able to use to our advantage."

Why was that somewhat sexy? The *our*, not the potentially going on a date with another girl.

"You're honey trapping for our venue?" she said.

"Are you surprised?"

"Not at all," Maya said, shaking her head.

There was a flash of emotion across Nishant's face, quick and fierce, almost as if he had wanted her to say no. But how could she with DJ Nish on grand display for all? He was using it for good, but he was using it.

Somehow, Maya didn't think Nishant would appreciate that.

"Good luck, Godspeed, and please get us the warehouse," Maya said.

Nishant gave her a short salute, which caused a snort to erupt rather noisily from her and made a few of their dining hall neighbors turn around. Maya ducked her head to avoid being caught and to get a better view of Nishant's game playing out in front of her eyes.

Pauline jumped to her feet and wrapped her arms around Nishant's neck. Okay, so she was definitely into Nishant, and it was obvious that the years hadn't faded anything.

Nishant leaned in, mimicking Pauline's body language. Pawn

to bishop, knight to D4, his moves were expert and calculated. It didn't seem like Nishant, not the one she had started to get to know. How had she never noticed that before? That he was almost playing a role? It seemed to come naturally to him, but that didn't make it any less of an act.

Still, Maya had to admire the dance. It was like watching a synchronized mating ballet, one which she had *not* bought tickets to. Pauline grinned at him and tossed her hair, saying something in a low voice that made Nishant laugh. Maya sharply glanced away, trying to ignore the roil of emotions in her gut.

She reminded herself she had no reason to feel the way she was feeling. That she had no right to. Nishant was enjoying college, the way she should have been and maybe would be. If Nishant was using his infinite charm and that smile of his to help them achieve their goal in a relatively harmless way, what was it to her? Everyone got what they wanted.

Maya tried not to watch too much, checking her grades on her latest problem set on her laptop instead. Finally, she heard a peal of laughter and an "Oh, Nishant!" and then Pauline took her leave.

"So?" she said as Nishan sauntered over.

"Success," he said. "Apparently, they got approved for the warehouse, but they hadn't put in the deposit. And if they say no, we'll get it by default." Nishant stepped closer to her and lowered his voice. "They weren't sold on the warehouse anyway, but once I casually mentioned that Baja Lounge on University Drive had an already set-up sound system and in-house catering, she started to really see my points. She's sending Mrs. Porter an email as we speak."

Maya's brow knitted. "I'll be honest, I wasn't convinced you could do it, not because it was you, but because it's a killer venue that anyone would want—"

"That I found."

She rolled her eyes. "Yes. I was there. But nice work. I'm impressed. I thought you might have to give a kidney or promise her lifetime coffee or something. The entrepreneurship club are no slouches."

"Agreed," Nishant said. "Which is probably why they realized they couldn't hold their first venture-capital-investment event at an untested venue. And why she drove such a hard bargain." He winced. "I'm going to have to skip on our meeting tomorrow. I have a date with Pauline—to the business school formal."

"Tomorrow?" she said before she could help herself.

"I know, but we could meet up the day after?" he said.

"Um, yeah," she said. Maya bit back her initial surge of jealousy. Because of Nishant, they now had a venue. And more importantly, they were just friends.

Even though he had said they were going to spend the night together researching vendors to go visit the day after, and he had mentioned that he wanted to try her latest baking creation.

It was fine. She had no reason to feel jealous, which is what she kept telling herself.

"Try not to look so miserable," she said. "I hear it's a fun time."

"True," he said. "But I'd much rather be spending the night going over our event budget with you." He batted his eyelashes at her playfully, and Maya ignored the resulting flutters in her stomach.

"Oh, shut up," she said, half-heartedly. "No, you wouldn't."

He caught her wrist as she moved away. "You don't know that."

She laughed and tugged her arm away. He was such a flirt he almost didn't know how to help himself, did he? "Thanks for saving our venue, Nishant. Now, how about I go show you what a good croissant looks like?"

CHAPTER 13

Maya Sastry: How was the formal?

Nishant Rai: Good.

Nishant Rai: Actually, kind of fun.

Maya Sastry: 👀

Maya Sastry: Is it fair that you're going on more dates than me right now?

Nishant Rai: OK, OK, hint taken. I'm working on it.

Maya found Nishant in the library for their next meeting, which was surprising in and of itself. She wasn't sure she had ever seen him there before, but granted, she never studied on the main floor or anywhere she could be distracted by actual people. Usually she sequestered herself in the darkness of the basement study rooms, where the fluorescent lights only seemed to add to the dim atmosphere.

It was perfect for her and helped her focus. Jana called it her study prison.

Nishant was a main hall person, obviously, one of those social butterflies who shone in the bright lights of the atrium. To her surprise, he seemed to actually be studying and the main hall wasn't packed to the brim. There was just a scattering of people around on the couches and posted up on the long tables. Nishant had gotten one to himself and had spread out over three seats. Boys.

She tapped him on the shoulder. "Any of these seats available or are they all for you?"

Nishant looked confused for a second, clearly deep into whatever he was studying. Maya noted that Nishant actually looked good in sweats, which was slightly annoying. She wasn't sure she had ever seen him not look good, whereas she often looked like a gremlin who had crawled out of the nearest storm drain when she came to the library.

He removed his headphones and Maya took a breath, ready to repeat herself.

"Actually, I'm reserving all of them," Nishant said, surprising her.

"Too bad," she said. Maya pulled out the chair one down from him, just as Nishant moved his stuff. He motioned at the chair next to him. Maya hesitated.

"Scared?" he asked.

She huffed and took the seat. "By the way, just because I don't want to do exactly what you think doesn't make me scared."

"That's not why I think you're scared," he said. He leaned back in his chair, observing her, which only made her feel more flustered.

"You're so annoying. Come on, we need to finalize this vendor list before V-Formal next week," she said. "Or Zane is going to have our heads."

Nishant made a noise in the back of his throat. "We're only a little behind," he said. "February just started."

"And we're a little over four weeks out now," she said. "After we get these vendors locked into contracts we can then worry about performers. You said you had something? Did you actually put it in list form this time, or were you going to text it to me one at a time?"

"I only did that once!" he said.

"Uh-huh."

Nishant looked as if he were about to come back with another one of his quips, but then the expression on his face changed rapidly. He shifted in his seat, looking down at his computer and then back at her with a hint of hesitation, almost like he was trying to come to a decision. He rubbed the edge of his cheek, unable to hold her gaze, a move that was strangely endearing.

"It's sort of perfect timing, because there was something I wanted to share with you," he said.

Curiosity spiked within Maya. He wanted to share something with her?

"Let's hear it."

"Well, that's exactly it," he said. "I've been brushing up on my Hindi music, especially some of the old classics, and seeing how I can remix them together. Particularly the Holi repertoire, which is so classic we can't ignore it."

"We can't?" Maya said.

"Of course not," Nishant said, clearly not realizing that a few weeks ago, this would have been another fight. Maya supposed they were rubbing off on each other, and then immediately proceeded to shut down that trail of thinking when the image started to become a little more than friendly.

"I've been working on this one remix, if you want to hear?" Nishant glanced at her, an almost nervous look on his face. Maya was sure he had no idea, but he looked like a very expectant puppy dog. How could she say no? "I hope you like it."

"Of course," she said, realizing she meant it. She was curious to hear what he'd been working on. DJ Nish was known for his modern, synth-focused mixes, and he often used Indian music, particularly bhangra, but old Hindi classics? That made her curious.

He grinned at her, that ridiculous grin that made her stomach flip. Probably the extra seltzer she'd had earlier. That had to be it. Maya closed her own laptop and pushed it away, only to knock elbows with Nish. He didn't seem to notice, too occupied by pulling up his files and figuring out the mess of earbud wires he had.

"Crap," he said. "I don't have my extra headphones. Would you mind going old-school? Sharing?" He held out one of the wired earbuds after wiping it down. "Don't want to wake up the three people who are in the library. I'm already on thin ice with the librarian after that time I left my coffee behind."

Maya nodded, putting the earbud in. "You left your food behind? Isn't that the one rule of the library? Clean up after yourself?"

"It was an empty coffee cup," Nishant said. "And I had just pulled an all-nighter, so I was not in my best state of mind. But yes, I'm now on the librarian's naughty list."

Maya couldn't help but laugh at that, and it came out as a short bark. She clapped her hand over her mouth.

"Be careful or you're going to be on it, too," he said, waggling his finger at her.

She rolled her eyes and gestured at his laptop. "Only because I'll be guilty by association with you. I should leave."

"You that worried about being seen with me?"

Maya gave him her best *Shut up* look. "Come on, play this thing for me before I grow white hair."

"You know, I found a white hair two weeks ago," Nishant said conversationally.

"Now I just think you're stalling," she said, raising an eyebrow.

Nishant smiled at her. "What if I am?"

Was he nervous? Maya looked a little closer, noticing the tightness in his jaw, the way he was looking around. It was sort of comforting to know that even Nishant still got nervous sharing his music.

She nudged him and pointed at the laptop. "I'm waiting. You've been going on about this for a full five minutes now. Play it for me."

Nishant put his headphone in and leaned over to open the file. The earbud wire didn't stretch very far, so Maya found she had to scoot over, close enough that her thigh was pressed against his. So close that she could smell the soft hint of aftershave that he wore.

"Here we go," Nishant said.

The song started to play, and Maya got swept up into it. Nishant sat back, stretching his arms out around both of their chairs and draping it over the end of hers. But the song was captivating enough that it distracted Maya from Nishant's too-big physical presence, sweeping her away into a thudding beat and soaring lyrics.

Maya heard a voice she didn't recognize threading through the mix. DJ Nish had a signature musical style, and it didn't usually have male vocals in it, or new vocals at all. This was a little different from that. In this song, DJ Nish was acting more like a producer in some ways, especially with the vocals that he had threaded through the background.

Damn. He was talented. DJ Nish was good. Nishant was good.

The song came to an end and Maya sat back.

"What do you think?" he asked, his hands folded together. There was a nervous energy on his face.

"This is fire," she said. "Really. And those vocals? What did you sample that from? I can't place it, but it makes the entire song." Maya could feel herself get excited. "If you release that before Holi, it would be a huge hit. Every dance team on the eastern seaboard would be dancing to that in their competition mixes. We could use it as marketing for our event."

"You like the song?" There was something hesitant in Nishant's voice, like he didn't believe her.

"Honestly . . ." His face dropped a little. "I love it. But seriously, those vocals. We should reach out to them to headline or do a set at Holi!"

Nishant had an expression on his face that Maya couldn't quite decipher. Had she said something wrong? Maybe Nishant didn't want to mix his DJ world with Holi, but they were too far gone for that now.

"What, did you steal the sample or something?" Maya joked. Nishant shook his head, the movement tight. "What's the problem, then? Who are they?"

"Just a friend," he said.

"Can we get them?" Maya bounced in her seat. "This is exactly the type of fusion you were talking about, and wow, that voice. We need to get this person to perform at Holi, they're clearly classically trained, and it'll bring that old-school element." She had a sudden thought. "Wait, you're friends? Or friendly?"

"We're friendly," he admitted. "I'm not sure we can get them."

"Well, try," she said. "I'm surprised you know someone like that, given the whole EDM DJ thing."

"Hey," he said, tilting his head. "I know all sorts of people. It's part of my charm."

"You have charm?" she said, cocking an eyebrow at him.

He let out a laugh loud enough that a few people turned around and stared at them. One of them shot them a dirty look.

"Shhh," Maya said. "I don't want to be on the librarian's naughty list as well."

"That's the goal," Nishant said, leaning in. They were still connected by the earbuds, and Maya found that somehow they had ended up facing each other. The earbud wires had wound their way around them so that when Maya tried to move away it only dragged her closer to Nishant. She glanced up to see him watching her.

There. That glimmer in his eyes, it hinted at deeper waters, at a wide expanse of ocean that she didn't know—and wanted to explore.

"Nish—" she started.

"I don't think you've ever called me that," he said. His eyes darkened and he moved an inch closer. It felt like a mile. "I like it."

Damn it, he had beautiful eyes. And lips, and . . . She needed to stop staring. What was she thinking?

"Then I should stop, shouldn't I?" Maya said. "Don't want to give you any ideas."

"Oh, Maya, I don't think you want to know the ideas I've had," he said, letting out a loud laugh.

Maya's face flushed. What did that mean?

This time, the librarian swiveled around, glaring at the two of them. The main library was scarier than Maya had remembered, or maybe it was just because she was with Nish, library miscreant.

"I think we need to go," Maya whispered.

"I think you're right," he whispered back. "I have a huge midterm in two weeks, and I'd like to be let back in."

"Let's make moves," Maya said. "We can continue our meeting at the café, I think they have an after-hours menu on Thursday nights."

Nishant nodded. "I did make a list of performers to reach out to, if you liked that sample. I'm thinking we have a full three-hour set for the evening. And then for the afternoon we do local performers like you had mentioned."

"Zane mentioned we should hold tryouts for Neadham students and clubs."

They both quickly packed up their belongings and crept out of the hall when the librarian's back was turned, breaking into a quick half jog as soon as he turned around.

"I just realized I left another coffee cup," Nishant said over his shoulder. "Run!"

"What?!"

Maya struggled to keep up with his long legs as he pushed through the doors and outside. She tugged on his backpack to stop. He slowed down.

"So? What does it feel like to be guilty by association now?" he said, his eyes twinkling.

"You are a menace," Maya said. She stopped and heaved a huge breath. Wow, she was out of shape.

"Music to my ears," he countered.

They grinned at each other. The courtyard was mostly empty, except for a few people milling about on the benches. Somewhere in the time she had been in the library, night had fallen. That was one thing she loved about Neadham—you could see the stars here, cast across the sky, outlined by the Blue Ridge Mountains in the back. The suburbs she grew up in had never had such clear skies.

Nishant turned to her, his profile a silhouette in the night sky. "You have to admit, we're actually pretty damn good partners."

"Pretty damn good?"

"Great."

"Now, that's a stretch," Maya said. "We've managed to not murder each other but—"

Nishant looked at her in mock shock. "You thought we were going to murder each other? Or you've been planning to—which one is it? I knew I should have been more scared of you."

"The first," Maya said. "And I would've progressed to planning to, if need be. And you should be scared of me." She blinked. "Wait, why would you be scared of me? Other than the fake murder bit."

"I thought your beauty might kill me," he said, looking deep into her eyes. Then he blinked and she saw the smile at the edges of his mouth.

He almost had her. If anyone was dangerous, it was Nishant Rai. Maya shook her head. "You've got some lines on you."

"Who says it was a line?" She crossed her arms and stared him down. "Okay, fine, it was a line, but who says it can't be true?"

He bumped her shoulder with his own. They had taken to slowly walking the long way out of the courtyard. Neither of them mentioned that there was a shorter, faster route; instead they both took the path to the right together. The other path was always crowded anyway, or so she told herself.

"If it's a line, it's something that can be used for anyone," she said. "I'm sure you've tried that one out on a few girls already. How would I know you're being serious if you're saying the same to multiple girls? How would I know you were trying to court me?"

She tried not to look directly at him and instead stepped away. He caught her by the wrist, his hand warm on her skin in the cold February air. Maya glanced at his hand, and then up at him. The intensity in his gaze made her heart stutter.

"Oh, you would know if I was trying to court you," Nishant said, his voice a shade deeper than before. Warmer.

Their eyes briefly met in the darkness, and it felt like a jolt, a live spark between them.

Maya looked away, and Nishant cleared his throat. "I can't believe you got me to say *court*. Does anyone say that anymore?"

"Well, I just did, so people do say it." Maya tilted her head. "But okay, fine, I'll admit to watching too many period romance films."

Period romances made her think of Imogen, and Imogen reminded her of the string of broken hearts the boy in front of her had left. She straightened her spine on principle. Still, it was getting harder to reconcile that boy with the one she was getting to know.

"I knew it," Nishant said, like he had just uncovered the greatest held secret of all time. "You seem the type."

"Oh?"

"The type to believe in true love, romance, all of that," he said.

"You mean normal, adult love things?" she said. "I'll give you the true-love thing does seem a little far-fetched in this day and age, but love does exist. Why are you so against relationships, anyway?" Maya said. She turned around and walked backward in front of Nishant.

"I think most people value being in a relationship more than being with the right person, but I'm not against relationships exactly," he said, after a beat. "I've been in one or two before."

"One? Or two?"

"One," he admitted. "It didn't end well."

Maya sensed that this wasn't something she could, or should, push on. She let the moment sit there in case he wanted to open up, but he remained tight-lipped.

"Well, you know how my last situationship went, so I can say with full confidence that I understand," she said.

"I still can't believe you dated Thomas," he said, shaking his head. He stuck his hands deeper into his pockets.

"Not my finest moment," Maya said. "To be honest, I don't think I've always made the best choices romantically. I've made my fair share of mistakes."

Nishant let out a dry laugh. "Same here."

"Not as bad as me," Maya challenged. "I spent my entire senior year of high school thinking that I was with a boy who was just leading me on. Lying to me. I found out right before prom that he had been seeing my friend the whole time. Apparently, he had been seeing us both and I wasn't the one he chose."

"He sounds like a—"

"Jerk?" Maya said. "Yeah, he was. But I also didn't know any better."

"I was going to say *selfish ass*, but that works, too," he said. "He sounds horrible. And then Thomas? Come on, Maya." He bumped into her on purpose when her mouth started to slide into a frown. "Kidding. I'm sorry, that sounds pretty rough. But you're not the problem there."

"I guess so," Maya said, shrugging. "Still made me feel horrible. Took me a while to get over that, and maybe that's why I so desperately wanted Thomas to call me his girlfriend. Just so I knew it was real."

They walked together in silence for a few beats, except for the faint crinkling of the grass beneath them.

Nishant hesitated for a minute, looking away and then back at her. He set his jaw. "That one relationship I mentioned? I went into it because my family wanted me to, even though I knew from the beginning that it probably wouldn't work. But I wanted to make my dad happy, so I said yes to a few dates with the daughter of someone my dad knew."

"And?"

"And then it went up in flames, like, literally." Nishant shook his head.

"What?" she said.

"We broke up at a summer barbecue. There was a fight and there was a grill and yeah, well, you can imagine the rest."

Um, no, she couldn't, but Maya nodded along. At least she wasn't the only person with some major relationship fails in her past. It made her feel a certain kinship with Nishant in the moment.

"That's why you don't do a third date?" she said, laughing.

Nishant shrugged. "It's not that I'm against a third date. I just haven't found the right person yet."

"You sure it's not because you're scared of another relationship?"

she teased. Maya knew she'd hit the mark when his brow furrowed. She couldn't keep her mouth from twitching, though, and he noticed.

"Ha-ha," he said. "Trying to turn the tables back on me? Use my own tactics against me?"

"Possibly. But I'm also curious," she said. "Once burned, twice shy?"

Nishant considered her question for a moment. "I guess I just don't see what the point is, you know? If I can tell it's not right by the second date, the relationship isn't going to last. And anyway, who wants to produce the same beats for every song, you know?"

"Huh?" Maya said. "Wait, are you comparing being in a relationship to that?"

Nishant gave her a half nod. "Sure. Not my best analogy, but yeah."

"Well, there's a reason why people have favorite songs. Or why they keep remixing things," Maya said. "It's the same in a relationship."

"If it's the right person." Nishant shrugged. "And counterpoint, there's a reason why the Grammys has a Best New Artist award."

"Okay, fair. But real talk, if you never let anyone get a third date, are you really getting to know anyone? Or are you just deciding they're boring before they have a real chance to become your favorite?" she said.

Nishant pressed a hand to his heart, like he had been shot. "Ouch, you got me. I'm just looking for the worst in people." He gave her a sardonic look and she couldn't help but roll her eyes. "Or maybe . . . we're just not a good fit. It's not that deep, Maya. I'm just waiting for the right person."

She had thought she was getting somewhere with him, but it was clear she had hit a dead end, as clear as it was that there was more than Nishant was letting on. He may not think it was that deep, but she wasn't so sure. Waiting for the right person? Sounded like an excuse to never take a risk on anyone, to never get too vulnerable.

Nishant stood silhouetted against the night sky, soft moonlight shining around them, and when he caught her looking at him, he immediately smirked, turning on that classic Nishant charm.

And as she watched him shift back into the mask he wore, she wondered.

Nishant knew everyone on campus, but did anyone really know him?

CHAPTER 14

Maya Sastry: Send me luck.

Nishant Rai: Why? Are you trying to contact Paneer Pete's again?

Maya Sastry: Ugh, no.

Maya Sastry: I'm finally getting to the bottom of my Meet'em ban. I hope.

Nishant Rai: You trying to replace me?

Maya Sastry: When's my next date?

Nishant Rai: Econometrics is killing me. I'm working on it.

Maya took a deep breath before walking through the door of the small coffee shop. She had thought she had found all the coffee shops on campus, but Suki had asked to meet here, and Maya had been surprised to learn of it. Now that she was here, Maya understood why she hadn't been so far. It was right near the engineering hall, which she had been astutely avoiding this semester due to Thomas.

And last semester, well, the less said about that the better.

"Remember when Thomas said he didn't like coffee?" Jana said from her right as they both stepped to the back of the long line. "And then you never drank coffee around him?" She held a thermos in one mittened hand, her first caffeinated beverage for the day. Jana typically had at least three, which Maya kept trying to tell her was probably not very good for her sleep schedule.

"Ugh, don't remind me," Maya said. "I was actually just thinking about that."

Jana pointed between them. "Bestie mind meld, at your service."

Maya snorted. "Sometimes I could do without it."

"Take that back," Jana said, with a mock gasp. "Banish that thought from your mind."

"Someone is quite dramatic today, despite only one coffee," Maya said.

"It's a double shot."

Ah, it all made sense now. Maya had been wondering why Jana had seemed particularly chipper that morning, especially when Maya was a ball of nerves. Suki had sent a message to Jana saying that she wanted to discuss Maya's appeal to rejoin Meet'em. She didn't know exactly why she felt nervous, only that it felt like the morning before an exam, maybe because of their history.

It wasn't that Suki was mean or even unkind before, but she had been firm on not being able to help them until Thomas's claim had been fully investigated. Maya appreciated her thoroughness and dedication to her app, but it still felt supremely unfair, even when Jana had found the connection between Thomas and Meet'em a few days ago and reported it. He had coded the entire backend! As Jana said, he had a clear motive, and his work on Meet'em showed that he had means as well.

The line moved up a little and Jana turned to her. "You don't need this. Remember that."

"I don't need this," Maya repeated. "But do I?"

Jana made a noise in her throat. "You have a deal with the most social guy on campus."

"True," she said. "Though he has yet to send me my next date. He's been shirking his duties since the stoplight party. I bet it's econometrics. Though I do have to say, they haven't been that great recently. Some of it isn't his fault but . . ."

Jana gave her a look like *What did you expect from DJ Nish?* Maya didn't think that was particularly fair.

"Anyway," Maya said, sighing.

"Just a reminder, you don't need this," Jana said. She tucked a short lock of her hair behind her ear. "I'm actually still kind of mad at Suki for not hearing you out earlier. But, um, I also found out that she dated Thomas for a bit right after your breakup. I think it's over now, which would explain the outreach."

Maya did a double take. "That must have been why Thomas was wearing red at the party."

Jana nodded. "And how does that make you feel?"

Maya took a deep breath and let it go. "Okay? I feel kinda bad for her, I think."

"Right answer," Jana said.

Maya stepped closer to Jana to let someone with huge headphones slide past her. She wasn't sure if it was because the coffee was that good, or that the vibe was that good, but the coffee shop was packed.

"You know, regardless of the dating-Thomas thing, Suki was in the right initially. She has to take all claims of community regulation violations seriously. I mean it's crappy, but she did the right thing for the community," Maya said. "And I can respect that."

"You sure I can't put a hit out on Thomas still?" Jana said, a little too loud. One of the girls at a table nearby looked up and between them. "I got you motive and means."

"No, Jana," Maya said. "No hit. Though I highly doubt you'd be able to even do that."

Jana shrugged. "I know my way around Reddit."

They had reached the front of the line, and both of them quickly ordered their go-to drinks. Jana handed over her thermos to the barista. "You can put it in there."

"Isn't that supposed to be full?" Maya said.

"That was ten minutes ago," Jana said primly.

Maya shook her head. She checked her watch as they waited for their drinks. She had a few minutes till she had to meet Suki on the upper level of the café, and Jana had to go meet her study group for Psych 102.

"Maybe it happened for a good reason," Jana mused out loud. "You never would've made that deal with Nishant otherwise."

"I thought you were anti-Nish," Maya said.

"When did you start calling him Nish?" Jana countered.

Maya frowned. She wasn't sure, actually.

Jana looked at her phone. "Crap, my study group is already here." She glanced up at her. "Catch you after? We can do dinner at Lewis

Hall, they put in a new dumpling cart there I've been dying to try."

"Yes, dumplings sound amazing," Maya said. She waved bye and trudged up the stairs to the second level. "And I can help you with that assignment for Bollywood 101."

"Ugh, that class is the bane of my existence," Jana groaned, giving her an air kiss. "Later."

Suki was sitting in the back corner, and she waved at Maya. She looked friendly—a positive sign. Maya really had no idea what to expect from this meeting, which was exactly the type of meeting she hated. She took a deep glug of her coffee, letting the taste envelop her mouth. Mmm. Smooth and full-bodied. The coffee was good, and the vibe was good. A true find—and she hadn't been here because of some misplaced fear of her ex.

The thought shot a burst of self-righteous anger into Maya. He had taken enough from her. Maya marched over to Suki and slid into the seat opposite her, exchanging quick pleasantries.

"Sorry to make you wait so long," Suki said. "But we had a few bugs and iOS updates we had to handle before we could tackle this. But we've done an investigation, and it seems like your account was sending some unsavory messages." Suki blushed a little.

"What?" Maya said, sitting up straight. She had been wondering how exactly Thomas had gotten her account suspended, and now she finally had the answer. He hadn't just gotten her account suspended; he had potentially ruined any of the connections she had made by misrepresenting her. What an absolute jerk-faced jerk.

Suki looked a little surprised by her reaction. She recovered quickly. "I was surprised, too; the messages don't really sound like you, especially the way Jana talked about you. Also, I checked your messages before—" She winced and mouthed *Sorry*. "Just to see the continuity. It's a clear difference."

"Because it wasn't me," Maya said. "I was excited to be on Meet'em. Thomas and I had just broken up and I was having fun and meeting new people."

"Jana mentioned that," Suki said. "Look, I believe you. But I just need proof."

"Let me see those messages," Maya said. Suki looked uncertain, but Maya pressed again. "I can't defend myself if I don't know what was said."

That should've been enough to convince Suki, but Maya did actually understand the need for proof. And she was sure she could provide it.

Suki let out a breath. "Okay, but if anyone asks, I didn't do this." Maya nodded quickly, and Suki turned her laptop around to show her the messages that had been allegedly sent by Maya. They were not her at all. It was language that Maya would never use, but how could she prove that she would never have sent these horrible things? People regularly said worse things on Reddit and TikTok comments, even on Neadham's public gossip site.

Maya racked her brain. She reread a line of the text, zeroing in on a phrase. It sounded so familiar. And then it hit her. She whipped out her phone and went back to some of the first messages Thomas had sent her, back when he had been trying to be flirty and sexy (both things which he had failed at, a clear warning sign she had obviously missed), and one of those lines had stood out.

She turned her phone around and pointed out the line to Suki. "See here? These messages don't sound like me, but they do sound like Thomas." Maya scrolled down to more of their messages, fighting back the embarrassed blush that threatened to take over her face. She was a private person normally, but not if it meant defending herself from clear injustice. "Run these against his other messages in Meet'em, see if they have similarities."

"I don't have a way to do that." Suki paused, her mouth quivering. "Wait, actually I might. Let me see."

Suki's fingers flew across her keyboard, and her brow furrowed in concentration. She glanced up once at Maya, who smiled back at her.

"You're right," she said, sitting back with a sigh. "I should've noticed Thomas had made those up. But as I'm sure Jana told you, we dated for a little bit and he helped build the backend of this app. I just couldn't believe it was him," Suki said. "He must have really liked you."

It didn't pass Maya's notice that it was in past tense. The idea didn't bother Maya one ounce. Not anymore.

Maya shook her head. "No, he just didn't like being shown up. Being broken up with by someone. If he really liked me, as you said, if he had cared, he would've tried to at least talk to me. See how to improve our relationship and if we could try again."

Suki's eyes widened. "You've got a point. And, well, you're right. I ended things pretty quickly once I started to investigate and things came up suspicious." She sounded a little contrite.

"It's okay," Maya said. "You didn't know, and Thomas can be very convincing."

"Yeah. Well, let me be the one to welcome you back to Meet'em," Suki said. She tapped Maya's phone. "I've even given you a few extra credits, on the house. As an apology for getting it wrong."

"I appreciate that," Maya said. She swiped to her Meet'em app and opened it. Lo and behold, it worked this time, the silver-and-blue screen flashing and fading into a new photo for her to like or dislike.

She was back.

"And for what it's worth," Suki said, "I hope my app can help you find someone—who doesn't have vengeful-ex tendencies. Maybe I should build an AI detector for that." Her eyes lit up. "Think you could help me with that? We could use keywords."

Maya smiled at the excitement on her face. "I'm not sure how helpful I'll be with that."

"But think of what—" Suki went on, turning into a full-on ramble.

Maya looked down at the Meet'em screen and the photos that awaited her. Instead of that initial frisson of excitement she had felt before, Maya felt only a mild disinterest.

Meet'em was like a carousel of photos of her to prejudge, all at her disposal, but what exactly did those photos really reveal about a person? Only that they knew how to pose decently well and compose a few sentences that projected the person they wanted to be. The mask they wanted the world to see. She was learning that there was so much more to a person.

She found herself closing out of the app without swiping.

"And I'm realizing I'm talking your ear off," Suki finished.

"No worries," Maya said. "Actually, if you're going to work on a feature like that, I'd love to help. Let me know what I can do."

Suki's face lit up. "Really? Thank you! This is huge. We can give you credits, or think of something else for your time."

Maya waved her away. "Of course." She lifted up her mug. "And no need for that. Just help me fuel my caffeine addiction a few times and we're golden."

Suki sat back in her chair and tilted her head at Maya. "Thomas is an idiot."

Maya grinned and raised her cup in the air. "I'll toast to that," she said as they clinked their cups together.

CHAPTER 15

Maya Sastry: Hey, wanna introduce me to that singer?
Nishant Rai: Later.
Nishant Rai: I might have a date for you.
Maya Sastry: I'll believe it when I see it.

After the conversation with Suki, Maya felt particularly emboldened, like a supercharged version of New Maya, ready to conquer the world and find the best performers for the Holi festival. They had the date and venue locked down now, as well as the audio system. But if she wanted to hit that target ticket-sales number, they needed something unique. Something significant.

She had contacted a list of local vendors and artisans from all over Virginia, and Nishant was in the process of sourcing potential musical acts and artists for the music festival. But he was behind on his list due to econometrics, so she had decided to take things into her own hands and go to local events and open mics that week. Tonight was the one at Sleepy Rose, the new café downtown. And to her surprise, Omniscient, the singer on Nishant's sample, was going to be performing. She considered texting Nishant, before deciding against it. He might not have wanted to introduce her to yet another one of his friends, but if she ran into them, that was different, right?

Maya took the free bus from university grounds to the downtown area of Lewiston. It wasn't a very large area, though when she had first arrived at Neadham, the downtown had felt huge and unwieldy. Now she could see that it wasn't that vast. She wasn't sure if that said more about her new comfort with Neadham and the town, or if it merely pointed out the difference in her headspace since first semester. Moments after leaving the bus, she found her way to the coffee shop via the large semi-neon sign outside.

She let herself in and found her way to the back. The event space was minuscule. But somehow, the owners had managed to squeeze in almost fifty people, each of whom were laughing, talking, and nibbling at the food that had been laid out on the plastic side tables.

Normally, Maya would bring a friend to something like this, where she knew she wouldn't know anyone and would be in a new environment, but being here alone this time felt okay. Even comfortable. She didn't need to have anyone else there as her security blanket anymore, which seemed like progress. Very un-old Maya.

People milled about the tiny room as best as they could, laughing and nudging past one another as they found seats. The performers seemed to be mingling with everyone else, lending to a casual vibe. Omniscient could be anywhere here, Maya realized.

Maya went to the table and grabbed herself a plate full of food, including the habanero guacamole that she might regret tomorrow morning. A tall, rangy young man with a high fade and an ear piercing walked up to the mic and tapped on it, causing a slight screech of feedback that made everyone yelp. "Sorry," he said into the mic. "But welcome to Open Mic Night. We'll be getting started in the next few minutes, so please take a second to find a seat, or a perch, or whatever floats your boat."

Maya looked for a seat and spotted one in the corner, swooping in quickly and settling in. The lights dimmed and the first performer came on, with a powerful spoken-word poem that had Maya sitting forward in her seat. After that followed a woman with an operatic voice and a guy who tried out a stand-up routine that only half landed, probably because, for some reason, his jokes were mostly about clowns.

When was Omniscient coming on? Maya checked the small flyer that had been on her seat, checking that Omniscient was, in fact, on the performers list. There, in thick black letters, was his name, confirming his performance.

And then out of the corner of her eye, she saw a head of hair that she recognized, one that was hard to forget.

Nishant was pacing back and forth to the left of the makeshift stage.

Oh crap, had he found out she had come here without telling him? How had she not considered the fact that he might be here himself, supporting his friend? Maya had never seen him look so nervous—well, really, look anything but perfectly poised and all smirk-y (which she knew wasn't a word).

Maya whipped out her phone, thinking through what she should text him to head off any potential confusion, when she noticed that Nishant was holding a guitar.

Wait, what was he doing holding a guitar?

"And next, we're lucky to be graced by the tunes of . . . Omniscient."

Then Nishant came onstage. He walked out with his guitar in his hand, blinking into the lights as he leaned into the microphone.

"Hey, everyone," he said, glancing around the room, face going a little pale. "Uh . . . Today I'm here to play—I mean, I'm playing something I composed myself or, well, kind of composed. I took inspiration from one of my favorite songwriters and tweaked one of their— Well, I didn't take it or anything." He stopped and seemed to take a huge, slow breath. "I'm not doing a very good job of introducing myself or this song, am I?" A smatter of laughs went across the crowd, and it seemed to embolden him. "What I'm trying to say is that this was inspired by one of my favorite songs, but this is my own take on it. A little Omniscient perspective."

What the hell. Nishant was Omniscient?

Omniscient. Ohm-Nish-int.

Oh my god.

Pieces began to snap into place, his hesitation to play the sample for her, the earnest way he had spoken about the mix, the caginess when she asked him for an intro. DJ Nish sang? She couldn't understand why he would hide something like that, especially when he was clearly so talented.

Nishant settled onto the stool and started tentatively, strumming a chord on his guitar. When he started to sing, the entire room fell into a hush. The acoustic song he had written was a perfect vehicle for his voice, mixing modern American songwriting with classical Hindustani scales. She had never given DJ Nish a fair shake, but it was clear he had a perspective on music, one where he kept pushing it to the next level.

Innovation becoming a beautiful tribute to the past.

Sort of like the Holi Mela they were planning together. How had she missed that? Maya couldn't believe that she had seen that desire to create as arrogance, that push to elevate as spitting on the past. There was beauty in the fusion of the past and the future, and she hadn't seen it before Nishant.

When he finished, there was a hush of silence. No one moved or even dared to breathe. Nishant looked up from his guitar, worry flashing across his face.

Maya was the first one to start clapping, but then the crowd was thunderous. She wasn't the only one whooping. Even her neighbor, who had been pretty sparse with his applause, was clapping loudly and nodding along.

Nishant tried to hide his smile without much success. He rose to his feet and bowed, before speaking into the mic. His normal DJ Nish mask was back on, the charm turned on full blast.

"Like I said, I wrote this myself, and I've got a number of other songs I'm working on that you can find online—"

That only served to make the crowd go wilder.

Maya sat back in her chair as the next person came onstage, feeling bad that they had to follow Nishant. He had been amazing, powerful, transformative. She found herself more surprised than she had the right to be.

And properly chastised.

She got up and caught Nishant as he came off the stage.

"Nishant. Nish!" she said.

He turned, his entire body tensing as he caught sight of her, like a deer ready to flee.

"Maya? What are you doing— Don't tell me—" He paled and quickly tugged her to the side. "You can't tell anyone."

"Wait, what?" she said. That wasn't what she had been expecting.

"Did you bring anyone else?" he said, his eyes shifting around the room.

"No," she said. "Why are you being like this? I mean, sure, it's surprising that you sing, but it's not that weird."

Nishant stopped glancing around the room and faced her fully, her words seeming to calm him down. "Really?"

"It's a little surprising, sure."

"I know, seems unlikely," he said, with a wry twist of his mouth. The sharpness of that motion, like he was used to this, like he had heard this before, stopped her.

"Maybe a little," she admitted. "But only because you're a DJ. Though I guess there's no rule that DJs can't be super-talented singers."

His eyebrow rose. "Super-talented singers?"

"Above-average singers," she said.

"I got demoted? In less than thirty seconds?" he said, sounding mock outraged.

"That's a consequence of being annoying," she said. "All jokes aside, Nish, you've got an incredible voice. Can I ask, why don't you sing on your own tracks more often?"

His face shuttered a little, his lips forming a tight line that looked like a mask. One that he was used to wearing. Nishant moved away jerkily, like he wanted to flee.

Instead, Maya took his hand and pulled him to a table at the corner of the room. She motioned for him to sit, and he did.

She tilted her head at him. "Spill."

"I love music," he said slowly. He let out a deep sigh like he had made a decision he was coming to terms with. "Always have. I started DJing on the side for our family's event planning business and I guess it stuck. Plus, it's not a waste of time, according to my dad."

"And singing is?" she said.

"Well, both are," he said, his voice tense. He put down his guitar and leaned in, dropping his voice as the next act started. "My dad brought over the family trade from India, and he's the type of man who wakes up and goes to bed thinking of business. My mom was the artistic side to our family business, and when I first started to dabble in music, it was useful to my dad, so he tolerated it. I made the mistake of singing at one of the events I was DJing and, well, shit hit the fan. The client wasn't happy at my improvisations, and my dad said it made the family look bad, especially since I'm to take over the business, and that I shouldn't be pushing my ideas on clients. Like I was the problem, instead of the one trying to bring our business into the twenty-first century and try new things—" He blew a frustrated breath out. "I'm sorry, it's a . . ."

"Sore subject?" Maya said. "I can tell. For what it's worth, my parents don't get my baking, either. Or that I want to go into event planning. Apparently, spending fifty hours a week in a cubicle has more prestige. And is somehow a better way of living my life."

Nishant chuckled. "It sounds like you've told them off. I wish I could have seen that."

"I haven't actually," Maya said, shaking her head. "They still think I might take my business degree and go into consulting or finance. And maybe I will do that initially, but I also want to take these four years to really try event planning out, you know? So that . . . maybe I don't have to go down the expected path?" Maya rubbed her temple. "I don't know. It sounds ridiculous, but—"

"I get it." The words were said simply, straight. A lifetime of understanding.

"Anyway, we were talking about you being a singer and somehow it became about me," she said. It was her way of giving him an out, if he needed one.

Not for the first time, Maya saw that there was more to Nishant Rai than he was willing to show, more that she desperately wanted to see. But it also wasn't her place to force it out of him. Even if she could tell that part of her could fall for the boy she was finally seeing behind the mask.

Even if that was the exactly wrong thing for her to do.

Nishant ran a hand through his hair, doing that lip-bite thing again. "Our family business," he said. "My dad expects me, and my brother, to keep it going."

He looked as if he wanted to say more but wasn't sure.

"And that's why you wanted to plan Holi?" Maya said.

"No. Well, yes. Kind of," he said. He sighed, rubbing his nose. "We had a fight over winter break, and I wanted to prove to my dad that he was wrong about what he said about me, that I could do this, but with my ideas. I wanted to prove him wrong so much. He never would have approved of something like a music festival, and I wanted to show . . ."

"I think I get it," Maya said. "You wanted to plan Holi to show your family you could do it, even if you did it your way. I wanted to show myself I could."

"I'm sorry, it sounds stupid—" He stopped, grimacing. "And I really do care about Holi. I do want it to be a success, I'm not . . ."

"Nish, I think you've proven that by now." Maya nudged his elbow. "Also, that sounds like a lot to put on someone. To keep the family business going no matter what, and to keep it going the same way."

"I know I sound ungrateful," he said slowly. "And I do appreciate that I even have the opportunity to question it. I don't think my father did, or his father before him."

Maya rested a hand on top of his. "I get it," she said, echoing his words from before. "You were amazing. Where have you been hiding those pipes? And did you compose that yourself? Or arrange it? Whatever the term is?"

"Whoa, lots of questions," Nishant said, though he sounded a little pleased. "I did arrange it myself. I'm glad you noticed."

"I'm not the only one," Maya said. "Everyone loved it. You're going to be a hit at Holi."

Nishant frowned. "You think so? Wait. What?"

"I think you have to do it. You have to perform," Maya said. "Omniscient has to perform. You know we're still looking to round out the musical artist set."

"Yes . . ."

"And you'd be perfect. We don't have to get the list in until the week after, so you can think about it if you need to."

"I don't know," he said, his mouth quirking to the side. "I'm not sure anyone would be interested in yet another DJ who's a wannabe singer." He laughed at his own joke. "That's just the truth."

It was the most self-deprecating thing Nishant had ever said, and it surprised her. Was that really how he saw himself?

"That's a little mean to you," she said.

Nishant looked away and then back. "My ex may have said something like that. And my dad."

"Wow," Maya said. "That's horrible." She couldn't imagine having your ex, then girlfriend, side with your family over you. Or say something so harsh.

He shrugged a shoulder, as if he didn't believe her.

"No, really, that's really horrible," she said again. She wrapped her hand around his forearm, squeezing it lightly. "Seriously."

There it was again, that little shrug. But it seemed a little less sharp, a little less hurt. "If you say so." He shifted his position, suddenly looking uncomfortable. "I tried to keep it up, you know. My singing. But it became a secret from my family, something I had to do on the sly because of all the comments. And when I got to college, well, I thought it might be easier to be who everyone else thought I was. Who my dad thought I was."

"You think people want DJ Nish and not Nishant?" Maya said.

He stayed silent for a moment. "Apparently."

Nishant didn't have to say the rest, Maya could see it on his face. Hadn't she done the same thing? Look at the face he presented to the world and decide that was all he was, all he could be? Her cheeks burned as she considered how wrong she had been.

"All the more reason for you to sing at Holi, show everyone how wrong they are," Maya said.

Some of the wry humor dropped from Nishant's face, turning it into an icy mask. "I don't think it's a good idea."

"Why?" she said. "You are clearly—"

"Just no, okay?" Nishant's voice was knife sharp.

Maya tried to swallow the hurt that rose up. She was only trying to be encouraging. Show him that she saw all of him, wanted to see all of him.

"Sorry, that came out harsh," he said, sighing. "I appreciate you asking, but no. It's too soon. This open mic was my first performance in a while, and I'm not ready. I can't risk my parents finding out and making another example of me, or worse, deciding I'm unfit for the company. I want to take over our family business, just in my own way." His voice softened. "And if I'm being honest. I'm not ready for everyone else to see this side of me."

"But, Nish—"

"I'm sorry, Maya," he said. There was a resoluteness on his face, one that Maya knew would be hard to budge.

Clearly, she had hit a very raw spot.

She used to think DJ Nish, Nishant, was one of those people who walked through life untouched by other people's opinions, the bright light in every room. But really, he cared. He cared deeply. Why else would he go through all the trouble to prove his parents wrong? To hide his beautiful voice.

Maya wished he could see the boy she saw.

"All right," Maya said. "Since you kicked up such a fuss—"

"Did not."

"Who are we going to get to headline, then?" Maya asked. "Have any of the artists you reached out to bit yet?"

"Four have," Nish said. "Topaz Smoke, DJ Jai Ho, Shakti Power, and Amit Sehgal."

"Wait," Maya said. "I love him! He's that guy who started making YouTube a cappella videos, right?"

"Yup," Nishant said. "I'm waiting on a fifth, I'll keep you updated. If the tryouts tomorrow are good, we may not even need them."

There was a part of Maya that was worried no one would show up. Planning had taken so much of their attention that they hadn't been able to market the tryouts as much as they wanted. Would people be interested in Holi anymore? That was one thing she hadn't considered when she had volunteered to plan it. They'd find out tomorrow.

The coffee shop was closing up soon, so Nishant grabbed a quick bite from the food table as they helped stack the rest of the chairs before leaving. Night had fallen quickly, and the stars twinkled in the sky outside, winking down at them.

She and Nishant chatted about the other performances on their way back on the bus, a little respite from their constant Holi planning. Maya could tell that they both needed a night off. He insisted on walking her back to the dorm, despite it not even being very late. It was a kind offer, though, so she took him up on it, not only because part of her didn't want their time together to end.

Cold air pricked her skin as they walked back to the dorms from the bus stop, passing by students on their way to a night study session at Calhoun, or dance team members on their way to the gym for their evening practices. Nishant waved to a few people as they passed, and stopped to talk to one guy who was wearing a Bhangra Blaze T-shirt, whom Maya had seen around HSA.

"What's going through that brain of yours?" Nishant said as they approached her dorm building. It was on the border of the main quad area, built more recently than the other buildings. They arrived at her building and came to a natural stop.

"I had a really nice time," she said. "And I heard this really great singer, Omniscient. Have you heard of him?"

"I might have," he said. "And he might be willing to do a private concert or two. For a good friend." He nudged her arm, and she ignored the way it made her stomach flip.

Maya realized they were both standing there, smiling at each other like idiots. She had gotten a glimpse of the real Nishant tonight, and she had found she liked it. He deserved to know that, too, and maybe she would wake up and think it was a mistake tomorrow, but she had to say it.

Even if it meant that she could no longer keep him in the box she had before, the one designated for friends, because the one thing tonight had also revealed was that she was undeniably drawn to the boy standing across from her, to all the sides of him—DJ Nish, Omniscient, and Nishant.

"By the way," Maya said, turning to Nishant, "I know you said no, and I respect that, but I think you're wrong. I think you've been told that you should only be one thing, but you can be so much more if you let yourself."

Nishant didn't say anything, his expression inscrutable. Maya stood on her tiptoes and gave Nishant a kiss on the cheek before she lost her nerve.

"Good night, Nishant. Thanks for walking me home."

And for the first time since she had met him, Maya left Nishant Rai speechless.

CHAPTER 16

Maya Sastry: Where's my date??
Nishant Rai: Wow, you are impatient.
Nishant Rai: Fine. I'm setting you up tonight.

Maya sighed as she looked in the mirror. She had another date tonight, one she hadn't been able to stop thinking about for the past few days, even through a particularly brutal problem set for Calc 102.

Nishant had started out strong, but clearly he had been distracted by all his planning for Holi, or whatever, because the dates he had sent her on post–Anthony and Jorge and had been an utter failure, like walk-in-the-door-and-she-knew-something-was-wrong. She had poked Nishant a few times since the stoplight party, and he had kept telling her that good things took time, which only made her think that he was bailing on their deal and that maybe it was getting too hard for him to find any boys that would be a good match for her.

Because there was something wrong with her. The resulting spiral from that thought lasted two days.

After the previous failures, Maya decided not to waste her time getting *too* ready for this one. She put away the sparkly dress and went with something a bit more casual. Her fingers brushed against the hunter-green dress she had worn at the stoplight party two weeks ago.

She hadn't seen Nishant at the last HSA meeting or the informal coffee hangout the club had later that week. It wasn't like queen bee Nish to miss out on social events.

Speak of the devil . . . her phone buzzed and *Nishant* flashed across the screen.

Nishant: This one is a good one. Godspeed.

Maya snorted.

Maya: You said that about the last one. He ordered a salad without dressing or nuts or fruit or veggies. Surprise, that's just lettuce. He said he "doesn't believe in sugar." You know I'm a baker.

Those three little bubbles popped up and then disappeared.

Nishant: OK, I'll admit, not my finest. This guy is it though.

Maya: We'll see.

The way Nishant had been avoiding sending her dates had made her question if maybe, even, he might possibly just show up himself? It was ridiculous, but what else was a girl to think? Nope, nope. Definitely ridiculous. Just her mind dreaming up unrealistic fantasies.

One last look in the mirror and Maya was ready. She hadn't bothered with heels or curling irons, but she had kept her trademark kohl cat eye. At the last second, she grabbed her fancier wool coat instead of her puffer as she closed the door behind her.

Fifteen minutes later, she found herself in the warmth of Vincento's. A cozy fire was crackling in a brick fireplace, tables lined the tall windows looking out over the main street, and a low cello lilted throughout the room. At least this man had taste.

Maya had been dying to go to Vincento's since she had walked by it her first week. There was something so adult, so romantic about the interior, with all the brick and wooden beams, the dim lighting and soft music. She had tried to hint—and then directly asked—Thomas to go a number of times, but he always ended up making some excuse.

But she was here now. Maya took a second to bask in the ambiance, soak it all up like a sponge cake in lemon syrup.

"Maya?"

She turned around, a laugh on her lips, and immediately froze. "Dev?"

"That's my name," he said, grinning.

Maya had not been expecting Dev to be so handsome. Strong-jaw-straight-nose type of handsome. He wasn't particularly tall, but taller than her 5'5", which was all that mattered to her, and he was well dressed for a college boy, gray slacks under a dark sweater and a long driving coat. He looked promising, but then again so had many of Nishant's other dates.

Still, she couldn't help but feel like she should've changed.

Maya tugged her coat closer together, glad that her frigid veins had made her grab the warmer, and much nicer, option. Otherwise she would be standing here in jeans and an oversize puffer. Maya mentally kicked herself for not expecting something like this to happen. How was she supposed to know, though? She reached a hand up to her hair to smooth it down and instead somehow managed to get her fingers caught in the tangles at the end.

Thankfully, Dev didn't seem to notice. Or he was just a naturally smiley person. Maya was really fine with either, especially when the smiles were as good as his.

He stepped up to the host table. "We have a reservation. Dev Shankar."

Swoon. He had made a reservation. It didn't seem like a huge thing, but when you were going out on dates with college boys, Maya had realized it was—her last date, lettuce guy, had them go to three restaurants before they could find something that had an opening for them. Not only had Dev thought of a restaurant that would be romantic, but he had taken the trouble to make the reservation beforehand. Jana would say that wasn't a particularly high bar, but after Thomas and her other dates, it was still one Maya was happy to have cleared.

The host nodded and led them to their table, which happened to be right by the window. Maya shivered a little as they sat down.

"Are you cold?" Dev asked.

Maya began to shake her head, but Dev had already turned around and flagged the waiter. He leaned in to talk to them and pointed to the empty table near the fireplace. The waiter shook their head.

"They're booked for the night," Dev said as he turned back to her, looking a little unhappy at the idea. "Are you sure you'll be okay?"

Not even ten minutes in and he was already looking out for her, and he had taken initiative to fix a problem. Granted, she hadn't actually said she was cold, but still.

"Yes, it's okay. I have my coat," Maya said.

Actually, it worked out well because she now did not want to take off her coat and reveal the outfit underneath. She fixed her hair in the window when Dev looked down at the menu, smoothing out her flyaways as quickly as she could.

"I wanted to let you know," Dev said, "I'm really glad Nishant connected us. It's been a little hard meeting people at Neadham, and first semester was a little rougher than I thought it would be." He looked nervous, which only made him look cuter.

"You're a freshman?" she said.

He gave her a half nod. "I'm a sophomore, but I transferred in from out of state."

"Oh," Maya said. "That must have been really hard. First semester was rough waters for me, too, and I didn't even have the excuse of transferring."

"Misery loves company, eh?" Dev winced. "Not that you were miserable, or that I was, or that—"

"It's cool, I get it," Maya said with a laugh.

What a nugget. The date had just started, and they already were bonding over their shared experiences, which Maya saw as a very positive sign. Plus, seeing him a little flustered, well, it made her feel more at ease.

"Where did you transfer in from?" she asked.

"Eastern State University," he said. "Over on the coast. The undergrad business school here at Neadham is just too good to pass, especially since it took the number two spot in US rankings."

"I'm a business major, too," Maya said, smiling wide. She didn't mention that she had also come to Neadham after seeing them climb the charts for their undergrad business program. Two peas in a pod, weren't they? "Next you're going to tell me you love baking and know how to make a mean shortbread. Which I've been struggling with, so if you have any tips, I'm all ears."

Dev let out a loud laugh. "No, no, I'm not much of a baker myself, but I do love shortbread and I've recently started getting into this TV show, *The Great British*—"

"Oh my god, *Bake Off*, really?" Maya said, nearly jumping out of her seat. "I love that show."

"It's so calming, isn't it?" he said. "It even convinced me I might have some baking talent, and I tried to make an ill-advised batch of scones."

They continued chatting, their conversation flowing easily, like she was talking to a best friend—or herself. Which is more than she could say about most of the first dates she had been on recently. There was something about Dev. He fit everything she was looking for, that she could see easily, and there was a sweetness and an eagerness to him.

Or maybe it was just that he seemed so similar to her, which was a refreshing change of pace.

Maya was unable to hold back the bright smile that appeared on her face as Dev started to speak about his love of Indian festivals and how he was even planning a spring break trip back to see his parents right after Holi, which just happened to be one of his favorite festivals. Like her.

Nishant had been right—Dev definitely seemed like he could be it. Compatible, polite, and best of all, he clearly wanted a relationship. So what if she didn't necessarily feel those butterflies in her stomach. Her head told her that he could be a great match.

And that's all that mattered.

CHAPTER 17

Nishant Rai: Paneer Pete is the worst.

Maya Sastry: Tell him we have another potential vendor for lunch if he wants to keep being annoying. I talked to one yesterday.

Nishant Rai: Ooh, hard-ass Maya. I like it.

Maya Sastry: 😐

Apparently, word had gotten around about the Holi festival performance tryouts.

"Looks like people are excited," Jana said as she followed Maya into the university gym.

The rough cut of Jana's documentary (even with Maya starring in it) had gotten rave reviews at her class midterm, and her professor had convinced her to send it off to a film festival in New York City.

Maya had even baked a special batch of cookies designed to look like video cameras to go along with Jana's application, since it had worked so well for her. Unfortunately, Jana wouldn't hear back for a few weeks, which meant that all of Jana's energy had turned her into a nervous ball, to the point where Maya had started giving her random Holi-related tasks to distract her.

Surprisingly, Jana had taken to them with aplomb, and within a week she had fifty ticket sales from the engineering frat alone and was now working on a plan with Maya to advertise Holi at the next film studies movie night. That combined with Nishant's efforts on reaching upperclassmen meant that Maya's anxieties were mildly more manageable. They were inching ever closer to the thousand ticket number and her hopeful shot at event chair.

They were on the lower floor of the university gym where the entire level was mirrored dance-studio spaces, each one sectioned off with glass. Most of the dance teams practiced here, and the upper level was used for conditioning. Maya had booked the space early, which was a good thing—they were going to need all of it.

Groups of people huddled together in a makeshift line that was out to the staircase. Maya and Jana threaded their way through to get to the top. Jana waved their HSA folder like an FBI badge whenever someone complained, which normally would have made Maya laugh, but today all she felt was a wave of stress.

When had Holi become this huge thing? Look at where they were now. On one hand, it felt great to be a part of something so big, something that got to showcase their culture to everyone. On the other hand . . . it was exhausting carrying the weight of all those expectations.

Nishant was running a little late due to one of their caterers, who wanted to renegotiate their contract for the second time. Maya had sent him to figure it out, mainly because she couldn't stand the vendor. An idea hit her as she took the seat behind the table the HSA had set up. Zane was walking over, and she threw him a wave.

Zane slid into a chair next to her, glancing at Jana as he sat. Actually, more like doing a double take, his mouth parting a little in surprise. Jana, of course, was totally oblivious as she chatted away with another one of the HSA members.

"That's my roommate, Jana," Maya whispered to Zane. "She's single."

Zane shut his mouth. "What? Oh. I'm not sure why you're telling me."

"Uh-huh."

"Anyway," he said, clearing his throat. "This is an incredible turnout. You really blew this out of the water. I wasn't completely convinced about having student and local community performances initially—"

"You're the one who told me we should go for it!" Maya said, unable to hide her alarm.

"But I'm sold now," Zane finished.

"You're the worst," Maya said, shaking her head with a sigh. "I don't mean that literally, but—"

"I get it." Zane shrugged, adjusting his glasses. "I think it's part of my charm."

They looked at each other and Maya chuckled. It was true, the more she had gotten to know Zane, the more she realized that his stressed-out gopher act wasn't an act, and he became a little more lovable.

Zane stood up and clapped his hands. "Time to get started. Can the first set of performers enter?"

"Phew," Jana said, after the last performer had finished. "That was . . . a lot. Great, but a lot. I don't envy you two for making the decision."

Nishant had arrived halfway through the first performers' act, sliding into the seat next to Maya after confirming that her negotiation tactic had worked. He tapped his pen on his notebook, squinting at the list he had made, a small crease in between his brows. It was kind of cute, a thought that Maya tried to immediately squash.

"You starred everyone but two acts," Maya said. "How exactly is that making a list?"

"It's a process," Nishant said. "You wouldn't understand."

Jana leaned over. "Yeah. You even starred the duo who did improv. Bless their hearts, but that's not going to fly."

"I kind of liked them," Zane said, a little defensively. Jana looked at him as if he had said that he believed that unicorns were real.

"Are you serious?" Jana said, her eyebrows shooting to her hairline. "You liked them?"

"Um, yes," Zane said, showing more backbone than Maya had seen anyone show in front of Jana before. "Yes, I think they had potential."

The university gym receptionist came in, telling them they had to turn the room over. They all got up and started to help put the chairs and tables away. Jana stuck to Zane, peppering him with more questions about why exactly he had such horrible taste, which he took well. It almost sounded like Jana had finally met someone who could hold up against her barrage.

Maya hid her grin as she watched them. That was going to be interesting. Her pocket vibrated and she pulled out her phone to see a text from Dev.

> **Dev Shankar:** Hey! Hope the tryouts are going well. I tried that recipe you sent me for lemon lavender short-bread. Maybe we can talk about it over a cup of coffee? Or dinner?

Maya couldn't help the little smile that took over her face.

> **Dev Shankar:** To be clear, that's me asking you to go on a second date. If you want to?

Nishant bumped into her as he closed the legs on the foldable table and moved it to the side wall.

"Any reason why you're smiling?" Nishant said, leaning in. His hand brushed against her waist, and Maya tried not to jump away.

It's not like she had a problem being near him, not really, but putting distance between them wouldn't be a bad thing. For her sake. She could admit she had a little crush now, even if it was very inconvenient. She hoped that admitting it would make her heart shut up, especially because Nishant was like a piece of double fudge chocolate cheesecake—delicious, until you woke up with a stomachache and a sugar hangover.

Maya pushed the thought away. She didn't need to repeat the mistakes of her past, and Nishant might be a good partner, even a good friend, but that didn't change the fact that he was a two-date wonder.

"No reason," she said, glancing down at her phone screen and the message from Dev.

Maya wanted a real boyfriend, a nice, safe one, who wouldn't hurt her. Who wouldn't waste her entire semester or break her heart.

And she had Dev now, didn't she? Well, she didn't have him, but she thought the date had gone pretty well and he had texted for a second date and—

Wow. Maya reeled herself in. Dating was confusing.

"So? How was the date?" Nishant asked.

Maya blinked, wondering if Nishant could read her thoughts or something. "You were right, he was a good one. The best one so far, actually."

Nishant looked satisfied, but there was something else in his expression, too. Something Maya couldn't entirely place. Probably trying not to look too pleased with himself.

"I'm glad," he said, sounding not very glad. "Dev's a good guy. He's very you."

"What is that supposed to mean? Don't tell me you're going to call him a dadi, too," Maya said, arching an eyebrow. Was she imagining it or did she sound a little annoyed?

"I'm not saying it as a bad thing," he said, throwing his hands up. "Just that he's very similar to you."

"Oh," Maya said, her mouth twisting. "That is true."

Dev had been totally on her wavelength, from the way he dressed to his tastes. A complete match. Game and set.

"He was really nice," Maya said.

"I came through for you, didn't I?" Nishant said.

Maya rolled her eyes and poked his shoulder. "Don't get a big head about it. We'll wait till the second date."

"There's going to be a second date?"

Maya ducked her head. "I think so."

"He'd be stupid not to," Nishant said. He leaned in and gave her a lazy smile. "Now tell me how amazing I am."

"Nope, I'm not doing that. This was a simple deal. You're holding up your end." She pointed at him. "You don't get extra praise for doing what you said you were going to do."

"I'm doing more than that. I just delivered your perfect man, apparently. What do I get in return?" Nishant blinked down at her with those stupidly dreamy eyes of his. Normal eyes of his, she corrected. Exceedingly normal.

"Nothing," she said. "Except for my top-notch partnership and some mild friendship. I'll even throw in a kind ear after your next econometrics exam, since you talked about it for half of our last meeting."

"Not true," Nishant said, looking mildly offended. Still, there was a laugh forming at the edges of his mouth.

It never ceased to amaze her that she somehow made Nishant laugh, just by being her unvarnished self. By being the Maya she had always felt she was but was never able to show around boys.

"True," she said. "But I'll grant you one econometrics-level-friendship event. And actually, here's one."

Maya pulled a paper out of her bag and handed it to Nishant.

"I did it," she said. "I may have exaggerated a little about how involved the club is, but I think we can bring them in more, especially for marketing, but I used the idea anyway and I channeled you and—"

"Whoa," Nishant said. "What exactly is this?"

Maya wasn't sure where to start, wasn't sure how to tell him that she had worked some New Maya magic.

"Remember we talked about audio? This is another thousand-tickets-level win." She tapped the authorization form she had gotten signed before and pushed it over to him. "We're locked in for audio for the weekend. Actually, we can have a music festival all weekend if we really wanted. I went back to see Mrs. Catcher."

"You what?" Nishant looked shocked.

"I went back to the Activities Office with my latest batch of lemon bars and did a little song-and-dance routine about how excited we were to bring Holi to the town and the whole county, you know, the whole razzle-dazzle pitch as you said." Maya did mini jazz hands. "I petitioned to have full use of the audio system for the entire weekend. You worked so hard to get all those musical artists, I figure let's showcase them properly."

Nishant scanned the paper, skipping to the next section. "You got them to agree to let us use the amphitheater speakers? Maya, you're . . ."

"Hardworking? Far thinking? A great event planner?"

"Incredible," he said, a hint of awe in his voice.

Maya flushed at the way he was looking at her.

"This goes beyond what I was thinking. I was going to ask a friend of a friend for a hookup and hope the administration didn't get too bad, and you just steamrolled your way through all that red tape," he continued.

"I didn't—"

"I mean that in the best way." Nishant shook his head again. "This is a game changer. I know you didn't really believe in bringing a music festival to Holi at first, but this is going to make the event. We could even advertise this to get more artists to perform. Thank you."

Maya felt heat rising to her face. "Yeah, no problem."

No problem? What sort of a response was that? It clearly undercut the depth of feelings she had before about all of this. She waited for him to ask what had changed, waited to see if she would have to find some way to scramble and cover up the fact that he had changed her.

But he didn't ask; he kept staring at the form in awe.

"So, I did good?" she said, raising an eyebrow.

"Yeah, Maya," he said, grinning at her in a way that made her entire chest squeeze. "You did real good."

And for the first time since she had agreed to plan, Maya finally felt like they might actually pull this thing off.

Maya hated being late. She ran across the road, avoided nearly getting hit by a car, and swerved into Umbra Coffee.

She skidded to a stop in front of a very long line and then noticed the new sign plastered on the wall advertising a Valentine's Day latte-and-doughnut combo. She glanced around the crowd, and Dev waved to her from across the room.

She rushed over. "I'm so, so sorry," she said. "My statistics office hours ran over because our TA speaks at turtle speed, and we have this huge exam—"

"I get it," Dev said, with that easy smile of his. "I got you something."

"Oh—"

He handed her the coffee cup and looked at her expectantly, so she took a sip. Good thing she had practice controlling her expression because the hit of sugar almost bowled her over.

It was one of the seasonal lattes that Umbra always had, the kind that tried to mimic Starbucks but with a spin. It wasn't bad, but it wasn't really to Maya's taste, though. But how would he know? They had only been on one date, and she had never told him that she was more of a pour-over girl, that sugary-sweet lattes were only her I've-had-a-horrible-day drink.

Maya made an *mmm* noise paired with a smile. He seemed to buy it. "Thanks, Dev. This is really thoughtful."

He flushed a little at that. "No problem. I remember statistics, and it was not fun."

"You had to take stats?" Maya said, leaning in. "You never mentioned that."

"Probably selective memory. My brain trying to save me from having to relive that trauma," he said. "I ate way too many croissants during that period."

Maya laughed so loud that the couple nearby looked over at them. He smiled back at her, clearly pleased at having elicited such a response.

"How was your sister's trip to India, by the way?" she asked, remembering a detail he had shared at their first date. "I bet your parents were so happy to see her after moving back. It's been a few months, right? She probably had a blast."

"She did," Dev said. "Bought way too many clothes, according to my parents. But she couldn't stay too long because her college's spring break isn't that long." He glanced up at her. "Any plans for spring break?"

Maya sighed. "Jana wants to do something big and fun, and since it's after Holi, I might be able to swing it, but we haven't been able to decide on anything. Which means no plans at the moment."

Dev nodded. Their conversation flowed from there, though Maya noted that Dev kept asking her about her planning schedule for the Holi Mela. Not in a weird way, like he was annoyed by it, but like he was trying to guess her schedule.

Which was oddly cute. She had never had a boy who was romantically interested in her care about her schedule. Or respect that she had one.

She also noticed he was a bit more fidgety than normal. Maya wasn't sure she had ever seen Nishant fidget or look anything but cool and collected. Well, except anytime he got one of those phone calls from his parents. He transformed into an entirely different person then, but only she seemed to have noticed that, mostly because she seemed to notice a lot about her partner.

Maya willed her brain to shut off and focus on the cute boy in front of her. One who actually wanted to be there and to date her.

Finally, after twenty minutes, Dev sighed. "I suck at this. Maya, I know it might be a little rushed," he said. "But will you be my valentine?"

Dev pulled out a red rose and handed it to her.

Oh wow. His question took her a little bit by surprise. None of her other dates had progressed this quickly. She was so surprised that she found herself unable to speak.

Dev glanced down at the rose and then her. "I know Valentine's is in a few days, and I was going to ask you to the V-Formal first, but I found out I won't be able to go. I wanted you to know I'll be thinking of you."

"Oh," she said, surprised by the sweet gesture.

He looked at her expectantly, and she realized he wanted an answer.

What was there to think through? Dev wanted her, and he asked. He clearly was planning ahead for them, possibly even for a relationship, and wasn't that a good thing?

"Yes," she said, reaching across and taking the rose. "I'd love to be your valentine."

"Fantastic," he said, trying and failing to hide his wide grin, which was endearing in the sweetest of ways.

So why did she keep thinking about her next meeting with Nishant? Or if he was going to receive any kiss-grams at V-Formal?

Maya reminded herself of the red rose for the rest of their date, and she kept looking at it even when her attention drifted away a little or she felt herself getting a little tired of having the same conversation about their business major classes.

She glanced down at the red rose again, taking in the creamy shell of the petal, the fragrance. Thomas had never done anything like this for her. No one had, really. Maya hadn't received a romantic gesture from just about any boy in her life.

Dev was nice, reliable, didn't seem to have any weird predilections, plus he actually left the house frequently. He listened to her and didn't just talk about himself, and they shared a lot of the same interests. And he was serious about love, and from the looks of it, he was serious about her. He would keep her heart safe.

That's what mattered, wasn't it?

CHAPTER 18

Nishant Rai: We just hit 500 ticket sales.
Maya Sastry: !! Really??
Nishant Rai: Yes, I'm surprised you didn't know.
Maya Sastry: Oh, that's what those seven missed calls from Zane were about.

Maya had always loved paneer, the delicious, chewy Indian cheese she had grown up on, until this exact moment. Paneer Pete's, the premier Indian fusion food truck in Lewiston, was delicious. Paneer Pete himself was a pain in her ass.

"And the Holi Mela is going to be one of the biggest events at Neadham this spring. We're updating the classic Neadham Holi to become more modern. We know college students are your primary demographic, and as a gold sponsor we can get you in front of an even larger audience. Not just HSA students, but also presidents of other clubs who are looking to find hot and trendy catering for their events. We've already sold five hundred tickets."

"An interesting premise," Pete said with a sniff. "But I've been negotiating with Nishant and I expected to see him here."

Maya hid her frustration. Pete had gone out of his way since day one to work only with Nishant, continually making it clear that he thought Nishant was the leader. They were partners, sure, but Maya had been handed the reins of Holi first. Jana told her to tell him off, but Maya didn't really have the energy to spare on a man who couldn't handle a woman in charge. She chalked it up to a good learning experience for her future career. There would always be people who underestimated her.

"I don't have all day," he said, tapping his foot, his arms crossed to show off the large gold watch he wore. Pete himself was a middle-aged Indian man with a penchant for gold jewelry and a low amount of patience.

"I know," Maya said. "And I'm sure my partner will be here any minute."

She tried to sneak a look at her watch, wondering herself where he was. A tall figure turned the corner and Pete glanced over.

"Maya. Pete. My apologies," Nishant said.

Maya turned to give him a decidedly annoyed look, and almost doubled back when she caught sight of him.

Nishant was disheveled . . . well, for him. The left side of his hair was sticking up in the back, and a corner of his button-down was untucked. He kept tapping his fingers on the glass of his phone screen, which was a nervous tic of his when it came to things that stressed him out—Econ 302, away basketball games, and his parents.

Maya didn't bother to ask herself why she knew so much about Nishant Rai because it was just a fact now.

Nishant took a deep breath. "Pete," he said, turning to him. "Gold sponsor is made for you. We're exceeding our ticket sales goals, and people from all over the university will be attending. This is your time to build awareness for your brand."

"She mentioned that," Pete said. Maya tried not to bristle. *She* had a name. "Five hundred tickets, you say?"

"Five hundred seventy-five as of this morning," Nishant said. "We just got the entirety of Sigma Chi to buy tickets."

Pete looked impressed, and Maya had to admit she was as well, even if she was still annoyed that her partner had come so late.

"Nice work, my man," Pete said, slapping Nishant on the back.

"Actually, it was Maya who made that happen," Nishant said, throwing her a covert wink.

"Only because—" she started.

"She's the mastermind," Nishant finished.

Pete looked between them, eyes narrowing, unsure if he was being chided. "Well, it must have been because of your leadership."

"Not really," Nishant said.

Maya mouthed *Don't bother* at Nishant. Nishant mouthed back *You sure?* and she nodded. They weren't going to change Pete, but they could nail this sponsorship.

Thirty minutes later they had gotten a tentative signature for gold sponsorship from Paneer Pete's, and Maya was munching on one of his delicious rolls. The food was good, very good, and once they left, the roll in her hand was the only reason she didn't immediately jump down Nishant's throat for arriving late and almost ruining their negotiations, plus the fact that he had tried to stand up for her.

Her instincts told her this was a moment for Old Maya. When they came to the crosswalk, Maya stopped Nishant.

"By the way, care to explain?" she said.

"What?"

"Spill it," Maya said, sighing. She threw her wrapper away in a nearby trash can. "I can tell from the way you're gritting your teeth that something happened today. Would've appreciated the heads-up, by the way, especially since we're in crunch time for Holi. A surprise econometrics exam again?"

Nishant grimaced. "No. It's worse."

Okay, well, that wasn't good. Maya pulled him over to the side of the lawn and pointed at a wooden bench.

Nishant slumped into the wooden bench in a very un-Nishant-like way.

"My parents decided to surprise me with a visit right before Holi, like I really needed that. Apparently, they're excited to check in on their son now that they think he's doing something worthwhile," he said, his voice dripping with bitterness. He shook his head, shaking away some of the cloud hanging above his head. "I'll need to spend time keeping them happy, since they've decided to grace me with their presence at the most inconvenient time," he added. "I could drop them off in Calhoun Hall and lock the door, pretend a fire alarm was pulled?"

"Okay, buddy," Maya said. "How about we take a beat. How much did you sleep last night?"

"Between the prep for the event, my exam, and this? Not much."

Maya nodded and promptly handed him her coffee thermos. "Please drink."

"Is it Irish coffee?" he said. "I could use some right now."

"No, it's just regular cold brew," Maya said. "But—"

Nishant had already downed half of it. He blinked at her owlishly, color slowly returning to his face.

"Better now?" Maya sighed, looking mournfully at her thermos.

"Better," Nishant confirmed. His expression shifted. He bit his lip and looked away for a second before looking back at her. "Remember that one relationship I was in? That my family wanted? What I didn't tell you is that everyone blamed me for the breakup. It was right after the singing incident and, well, surprise, the client was her dad. She took her dad's side, and when I pushed her on it, that's when the fight and breakup happened. A very public one. My dad had to work overtime to repair that business relationship. The shame of that, and everything else, was too much for my family." He made a face. "I became the screwup after that, and the singing didn't help. I've realized I can't make them happy, but—"

"There's a part of you that wants to," Maya finished. "I get it."

"I knew you would," he said softly. "You always seem to get me, even when no one else tries."

Did he not believe that people wanted Nishant only? How could he when his ex hadn't even stood up for him? Or his family?

Maya's heart was weighed down by a feeling of sadness for Nishant. Her parents couldn't visit that often, but if they were driving in, she would be excited. Not trying to run away from them or worried about which version of herself to be. Even if they didn't quite get her career aspirations, she had never felt like they didn't understand her or love her for who she was.

She reached over and squeezed his hand.

"Now, about your parents," she said. "Let's just send them on one of the campus tours? That will get them out of your hair for the day. Tell them it's usually sold out, but you somehow managed to get them tickets."

Nishant's face shifted into a thoughtful expression. "That could work. Very devious, Maya." He gave her an appraising look.

"It's clever," she said, a hint of objection in her tone. No one had ever called her devious before, but when she really thought about it, she wasn't sure she hated it. "I'm looking out for my own interests, really. I need you to be fully on your A game. Why exactly did they pick the week of Holi?"

"To torture me," Nishant muttered. He sighed. "I think they're just excited. Ugh, they'll want to have a meal together," he said, shaking his head. "My mom will probably want to have dinner at some place off campus and inconvenient to get to."

"Which you'll go to with a smile," Maya said. "And you'll see them, and it will be fine. If you need to escape, you can always text me and use Holi as an excuse."

"True." Nishant had calmed down now, and he looked at her like she was the sun and he was the earth rotating around her. "You're quite good at this whole crisis-planning thing."

Maya flushed. "Well, yeah. Try not to let this get to you, okay? You can spend the whole time telling them about Holi and what we created together. There's no way they won't be impressed."

Nishant didn't look very convinced, but he gave her a slow nod.

"It's just annoying," he said. "Their surprise visit, as if they actually care— Sorry. I'm just really not looking forward to this. It's the worst timing. Imagine if I were performing as Omniscient." He shuddered.

She bumped his shoulder. "It'll be fine," she said. "Or at least, you'll get through it fine."

They were sitting close on the bench, their thighs touching, their elbows knocking together. His voice grew soft. "Thanks, Maya. You're—"

"The best?" she said.

"That and some more."

His chocolate eyes turned warmer. How had she never noticed the flecks of hazel in his eyes? The soft way his mouth curved when he smiled?

A Frisbee whistled through the air and they both ducked. It hit the tree behind them.

"Time to move, I think," Nishant said, glowering in the direction of the Frisbee team in neon-yellow visors.

She paused. "If you need to take time off to see your parents, it's totally fine. It's inconvenient that they're showing up two days before Holi, but I can understand. I'll cover your work for the night."

"Really? Not going to accuse me of shirking my duties?" he said.

"As long as you don't," she said. "Plus, I'm going to make you deal with the vendors, anyway. I can handle the volunteer meeting before Holi and all the last-minute things."

"I'm glad I chose you to be my partner," Nishant said, so sincerely that it made Maya glance over at him in surprise.

"You chose me?" she said. "Is that how it went?"

"Yup," he said. "I could've worked with Pooja, but somehow I knew that you would be my match. I'm glad the universe threw us together."

Whether it was his warm eyes or the way he stepped closer to her, the breeze that lifted up her coat or the fresh smell of flowers in the air, Maya felt *something* between them.

Maya noticed he was leaning in, his head dipping toward her as if they were in their own little bubble. She leaned in, too.

"Me too. Plus, I couldn't have done the date—"

Another Frisbee whizzed toward them, taking a nosedive arc right to where they were standing. Nishant grabbed her aside just as it rammed into the tree behind them. They only got a weak "Sorry" from the Frisbee guy, despite Nishant glaring at him.

Maya steadied herself for the second time. There was only one solution to this. "Pizza? Before we actually get hit?"

"You read my mind," Nishant said. "And I can tell you all about how we're going to leverage those photos from the HSA formal to build us some extra buzz."

"Sounds good," Maya said.

And as they walked toward the corner pizza shop Maya did her best to not think about what might have happened if the Frisbee hadn't nosedived toward them.

CHAPTER 19

Maya Sastry: Should I wear these shoes Jana picked out for me?

Nishant Rai: I'm going to say no? Though Jana does have good taste.

Maya Sastry: I'm going to tell her that.

Nishant Rai: Do you think it'll make her like me?

Maya Sastry: No.

The worst part of going to a college formal was realizing that you would have to walk across the quad in the cold—and in heels.

Maya, Jana, and Imogen were halfway across the quad when they realized this. Imogen insisted they flag down the university bus, and Jana stepped in front of the next one so it would stop out of schedule for them, which almost caused a traffic incident.

They clambered onto the bus, shivering, only to be immediately surrounded by throngs of other cold students on their way to V-Formal. The excitement was palpable, and everyone was talking about the kiss-grams—who sent one, who might have sent one, who was going to receive the most.

"Next time," Maya said, "we plan better. Maybe Lyft?"

"Definitely," the other two agreed.

They arrived at the venue quickly, a boutique hotel in the downtown area with a stunning lobby bar and ballroom, which the HSA had rented out for their annual dance. It had been put together after students had complained that they had no event to get dressed up for, unlike the sororities and fraternities. This was the HSA's solution, a formal dance for any and all people who usually came to the HSA's events. Tickets had become a hot commodity.

Maya had been looking forward to it, especially because Nishant had been hyping it up for a while.

They walked into the hotel lobby and were immediately greeted by a throng of students. Hindi music blasted through, loud enough they could hear it in the lobby. Imogen wandered off to find the boy she had been talking to recently.

"You made it," a deep voice said. Maya shivered at the smoke in it, so familiar to her now. Maya looked up to see Nishant standing there in a tux, looking like a movie star. She wasn't the only one who noticed.

"Hey," she said. "You clean up well."

"Surprised?" he said, grinning at her. "You look . . ." His eyes trailed her gown up and down, his gaze heating her up from the inside.

"Why, hello, Jana. You look great, Jana," Jana said.

Nishant and Maya broke away, looking over at her. "Hello, Jana Singh-Kota. You look great, Jana Singh-Kota."

Jana tilted her head at him, like an empress acknowledging a peasant. She turned to Maya. "I'm going to put our coats away." She gave Maya a pointed look that Maya promptly ignored.

"So—" she started.

"Oh my god, Nishant!" Two girls had sidled up to Nishant, ignoring Maya. Going by the look he gave them, he hadn't met them before, but he looked at ease, like this happened all the time. It probably did. "The Holi Mela looks like it's going to be so amazing. We're so excited to go! We're doing an article for the local community journal."

It was like Nishant's charm light instantly went on.

"Couldn't have done it at all without the expert leadership of my partner in crime, Maya," he said. They nodded brightly, their eyes only briefly shooting over to Maya.

"You're DJing, right?"

He nodded. "I am probably going to do a set. But don't tell anyone," he said, winking at them.

The two girls nearly swooned, and Maya had to hold back an eye roll, despite truly, utterly getting their reaction to him. He was swoon-y, wasn't he? Especially with his slicked-back hair and sparkling eyes. The way he spoke to you as if you were the only person in the room, let alone the entire world. Add in that tailored tux that highlighted his shoulders, and he was a walking problem.

"Can we get a photo?" one of them asked. He nodded. "Perfect, we'll send our photographer over."

Maya stepped back as a young man with a digital camera around his neck came into view.

"Where are you going?" Nishant said.

"They're not interested in a photo of me, Nish," she said.

"I doubt that," he said. "Plus, who cares what they want? If they're doing an article, you need to be in it."

Nishant reached out a hand to her, and when Maya hesitated, he tugged her into him. She let herself go with it, even when he wrapped an arm around her waist.

It was just for the photo. It didn't mean anything else.

His hand tightened around her waist, the warmth of his skin radiating through the thin material of her dress.

Nishant turned to her and whispered, "Smile, Maya."

Maya put on her best smile and let the photographer do his job. After a few snaps, she found herself relaxing into it. She wasn't accustomed to this kind of attention. Maya was used to being in the back, hidden away as someone else took the spotlight, but Nishant wouldn't seem to allow that.

No one else had pushed her like this, and she found herself grateful. He seemed determined to tell everyone that this Holi Mela was both of theirs. It shouldn't have surprised her so much after getting to know him, but it still did, in a small part of her heart that assumed no man would ever truly see her—or appreciate her.

So when the photographer asked her for individual photos, Maya didn't hesitate before saying yes, and she tried not to blush as Nishant wolf-whistled from the side as the photographer guided her through different poses. It was all for show, but that kind of attention could still go to a girl's head.

Afterward, before anyone else could spot them, Nishant grabbed her and tugged her to the side. For now, it was blissfully theirs, with no one else around.

"Does that happen a lot to you?" Maya said, leaning against a barstool.

"Being photographed? I know you think I'm spectacularly handsome, but surprisingly, no, that doesn't happen often."

She swatted his arm. "No, the being approached by random girls."

He leaned in, close enough that his warm scent enveloped her. His gaze darkened. "Why? Does it bother you? That I'm popular." Maya started to shake her head. "I'm with you, though, aren't I?"

He was, wasn't he? Maya should be reminding herself of Dev—Dev who wanted to ask her to this formal, Dev who asked her to be his valentine and yet . . .

"That's because I'm witty and wonderful to be around," Maya said, tossing her hair back.

She expected a quip or retort back, but Nishant only held her gaze. "You are. I'm surprised Dev isn't here with you," he said casually. A little too casually.

"He said he was going to ask me," she said. "But I'm dateless tonight because he had a prior event."

Nishant stepped closer, close enough that their hips brushed as they stood next to each other and she could smell his cologne, musky and strong. "Then his loss is my gain."

Maya gulped, her throat suddenly dry.

"You're such a flirt," she blurted out. "It's hard to know when you're being serious sometimes."

Maya noticed a slight wince from Nishant, a tension in his jaw. "That's me. Can't believe anything I say."

"That's not what I meant," Maya said, frowning. "At all."

Nishant looked away and then looked back to her, his mask in place. "I know. Sorry."

"Really, I didn't mean that," Maya said.

He traced a pattern on the velvet fabric of one of the barstools, and then nodded.

Maya relaxed a little. He had unsettled her with that comment, and it wasn't that she didn't trust him or didn't take him seriously. But how could she when he flirted with everything?

"You're not playing tonight?"

Nishant shook his head. "Even I take a night off every once in a while."

Suddenly, his face lit up with a look that Maya could only describe as mischievous.

Nishant leaned in, a lock of his hair falling onto his forehead in perfect old-Hollywood-star style. "Let's dance," he said, an undertone to his voice that Maya couldn't identify.

"Dance?"

"Heard of it before?" He gave a jerky motion. "It's when two people move their limbs around in a—"

"Okay, smart-ass, I get it." Maya glanced around. The dance floor wasn't filled up yet, but there was a small contingent of people in the middle. Enough to make it feel less awkward. It didn't escape her notice that most of the people there now looked like couples, and she and Nishant were not.

Nishant tilted his head at her, waiting. He got to his feet and held out a hand.

"Fine," she said, taking his hand.

She let him tug her to her feet, swaying a little unsteadily on her heels. Nishant held her steady until she collected herself, muttering something about borrowing Jana's shoes.

"Is that why they're so tall?" he asked.

"What, I don't look like a four-inch-heels type of girl?"

Nishant snickered a little and she couldn't help but grin back. "Not exactly the Maya I've come to know."

"Well, maybe you're meeting a New Maya," she said. He might not even realize how true that was.

He led her toward the dance floor and whispers followed them, especially because Nishant hadn't let go of her hand. His hand was large as it enveloped hers, his skin warm and a little rough to the touch.

People milled around the edges of the dance floor, some dancing, others in loud, chatting groups. Nishant pulled her straight into the center, and Maya followed him as he started to sway to the music. She had heard he was a good dancer, and the artistic DJ/singer thing hinted at it, but it was a different thing to watch him move.

He swayed to the music like it was imprinted on him, and Maya couldn't help but be taken along for the ride, despite not being as good of a dancer. She could move her hips and follow choreography, but there was none of that instinct in her movements, and she knew it.

Still, Nishant didn't let her feel left behind at all. He pulled her toward him, twirling her around and matching her movements. He went slow when she went slow, and sped up when she did. It was how she found herself screaming lyrics alongside him a few songs later as they danced their hearts out.

There was something about the way he matched her, the way he looked at her, that made her feel like the whole world could fall apart around them and she wouldn't care. Nishant saw her, and it was all that mattered.

Maya couldn't remember the last time she'd had this much fun with a boy. Or felt so free. Guilt immediately washed over her. What if Dev had been able to come? Would she have had the same experience tonight?

Nishant caught her look and raised an eyebrow. He nudged her shoulder.

"What are you thinking about so hard over there?" he said.

"Nothing!"

"Liar."

Nishant twirled her around and dipped her back in one swift motion. The dance floor was beginning to fill and people were in full-on party mode. The DJ was getting really into his set as well, which even DJ Nish acknowledged "wasn't bad, so far."

A fast and very popular song started to play, and the dance floor was flooded. They were pushed together, and instead of stepping back, Nishant moved in closer, his arm tightening around her waist.

"Got to keep you upright on those heels, don't we?" he whispered in her ear. There was another cheer off to the side as people started singing along.

"Ha-ha," Maya said, her voice catching in her throat. Nishant really didn't need to be that close to her right now or maybe ever, especially if the result was those weird flutters she was feeling low in her core. "I'll be okay."

"You sure? Jana's shoes are merciless," he said.

"You don't have to do that," she said, giving him a wry grin.

"Do what?" Nishant tilted his head at her.

"All of that," she said. "The attention, the fawning. The way you act around all the other girls."

"Oh, so you've noticed how I act around other girls?" he said.

What was she supposed to say to that? "Maybe a little bit."

"How about this? I want to act this way. I enjoy spending time with you. I told you that before. Do you want me to go dance with someone else?" he said, close to her ear.

"No."

She kind of hated herself for the instant reaction, but she couldn't deny it. She swallowed roughly. Sure, she knew nothing should ever happen between them, but her body apparently didn't.

"Good."

That one word sent a shiver down her spine. Maya didn't want him to leave. Or this little moment to end. Even if it was all a lie. But was it? Their conversation earlier, and the way he looked at her, and the way he trailed his hand down her back as they danced, it was all confusing.

Maya's heart flew into her throat, and she stumbled. Nishant's hand on her waist prevented her from falling down.

"Whoa," he said. "You okay? How are your feet?" He tugged her to the side. "Let's take a break."

Maya nodded, not trusting herself to talk with the groundswell of emotion in her chest.

"So? Having fun? Or should I go find another dance partner?" he asked, tilting his head at her, the sardonic expression on his face making it clear that he was joking.

It was exactly what she needed to shake her out of her mood.

"You could," she said. "But no one else is going to match. Good luck finding a better partner."

Nishant's smile was warm, his eyes even warmer as he considered her. "If that isn't the truth."

Maya tried not to notice the way his expression shifted, how his smile brightened. And tried to keep herself from losing her heart a little bit more.

"You know technically, if this counted as a date, we'd have been on more dates than anyone you've been with before," she said, glancing out at the crowd. She had meant it as a joke, but she saw in the way Nishant's jaw clenched that it had hit home. And not in a good way.

"Ha-ha," he said.

"Nish—"

The music ended and a loud voice announced that the kiss-grams were going out. Maya whipped around. She had totally forgotten about them.

Nishant seemed to have as well, a frown spreading across his face. Before she could say anything, two HSA committee members approached them, cupid wings on their backs.

"One for you," the boy said, passing Maya three long-stemmed red roses with a small box attached, before leaning forward and kissing her cheek. "Someone went all out."

"And multiple for you," the girl said, leaning flirtatiously into Nishant. She handed him a pile of notes and then without warning, planted a kiss on him.

Maya couldn't help the surge of green that flooded her veins. She had no right to feel jealous, not while holding her own kiss-gram, but wow, that girl was going in. Nishant broke away from her first, and while it had been only a few seconds in reality, an eternity had passed for Maya.

Nishant winked at the kiss-gram girl and waved goodbye at her as they left for the next set of kiss-grams.

"Wow," Maya said, unable to help herself.

Nishant turned to her with a sheepish grin, shrugging his shoulders. "I did not ask for that."

"You didn't really turn it down, either," Maya muttered.

"Huh?" Nishant said. "Are you mad?"

"What? No," she said. She hugged her roses a little closer. "No, not mad at all."

But it had been a good reminder, a strong stop sign at the crossroads that told her not to swerve off a cliff.

"Okay," he said. Nishant leaned in, giving her roses an appraising look. "Because you totally got a kiss, too."

"On the cheek," she said. "How many do you have?"

"Do you want me to count?" he asked.

No, she did not want that.

"I'll be right back," she said, rising from their seat. "I need some water."

"I can come," he said, following her out. He kept close to her with a hand to the small of her back, and she both never wanted him to let go and wanted to throw it off and flee the event like Cinderella.

She didn't understand. Why would he want to be attached to her when women literally threw themselves in front of him? Thomas hadn't even wanted to be official with her when they were exclusive, and Ari was even worse, lying to her the whole time.

Maya had been living in a fantasy world for a second there on the dance floor, which she did quite often, but it didn't usually hurt this much. Not that she had any real reason to feel hurt. But seeing Nishant flitting about here like the social butterfly he was, like the charismatic bachelor he was, she wondered what place she had in the image.

Which is why the little crush that had started to spark in her chest when she thought of Nishant? It had to be squashed.

Nishant had proven that he was a good friend tonight. And that's all he would ever be, if she wanted to save herself. Tonight proved that.

Friends. That was it.

Nishant passed her a water when they reached the bar, which she took gratefully. "I'm parched," she said. "And you're right, I'm glad I came."

Nishant nudged her. "By the way, thanks again for helping me with the parents thing."

Even though he was leaning in and looking at her in that warm, cozy way that made her want to melt, she knew she had to keep it professional between them. Keep it casual. So when he looked at her like that, she knew there was only one answer.

"Of course. We're friends."

Maya tried not to notice the way his expression faltered, how his smile dimmed a little. It didn't mean anything.

Nishat Rai wasn't for her, and tonight had been a good reminder.

She just had to keep telling herself that.

CHAPTER 20

Nishant Rai: Hey, get pumped, we're close to nailing down a ticket buy from the Entrepreneurship Club. That'll get us close to 700.
Maya Sastry: The finance bros want to party??
Maya Sastry: Wait, duh, of course they do.
Nishant Rai: Apparently, I made a good impression that night with Pauline. 😉 You free tonight to work?
Nishant Rai: Hello?

aya was getting her weekly post–Accounting 102 coffee, which was necessary since it was the most mind-numbingly boring and complex class she had ever taken. Who was the human who came up with the acronym GAAP and the torturous curriculum of Accounting 102? Maya wondered how much hate mail they got on a regular basis from undergrad business majors.

"Your order?" the barista said.

Maya snapped out of it and recited her order, a latte with their medium roast beans and two pumps of their delectable cinnamon syrup, a concoction she had tried for the first time one late night studying. Something about accounting made her want to collapse into a puddle of existential goo that only sugar could solve. Umbra Coffee at least made their syrups fresh, so there was no artificial flavor.

The barista winked at her, writing her name on the cup. She had seen him a few times but hadn't gotten his name, and unfortunately, he wasn't wearing a name tag. "A bad exam?" he asked.

Maya sighed. "No, just accounting."

He gave her a look of sympathy. "Had to take that my first year, too. Chin up, it gets better after the midterm."

"Really?" Maya leaned forward. "Any tips?"

"Read the appendix of the textbook, actually. Professor Chatham likes to pull questions from there. And know your GAAP well."

Maya groaned. "GAAP is the bane of my existence."

The barista nodded and handed her latte to her. "Hopefully this helps."

Maya took a sip and sighed in pleasure. Caffeine. The nectar of the gods. She eyed the small case of baked goods they had and pointed at one in the far corner. "Is that any good?"

"Nah," he said. "I prefer our maple banana bread."

"I'll do that, then. Thank you—"

"James," he said, smiling at her. It was a very nice smile.

And look at that, she had a perfectly nice conversation with a man, and he had offered up his own name. Thank you, New Maya.

Maya could say with a sense of surety that this wasn't something that would've happened a few months ago.

"Maya," she said.

"I remember," he said. Maya mentally slapped her forehead. Duh. He had written her name down on her cup. "Let me get that banana bread for you."

Maya stood to the side as a few people got in line, glancing around the coffee shop. They could do an open mic night here, too, if they wanted. The space wasn't that much smaller than that café from a few nights before, and with a little bit of furniture reorganization, they could create a small events area. It was something she had been doing often these days, she had noticed—planning for future events around Neadham.

Maybe it was too soon, but she couldn't help but dream of what it might be like to be event chair. Even if she didn't get it this year.

Nope. She was not going to pre-disqualify herself. That was not who she was anymore. But yes, even if she didn't get it this year, Maya now knew she wanted to be doing this, to be someone who dreamed of and brought to life events that made people smile.

She only had to pull off the Holi Mela first. No sweat.

Everything seemed to accelerate after V-Formal—ticket sales, vendor negotiations, performer practices—and now, the nerves were hitting her full force. The ticket numbers were almost at their goal, and she had been racking her brain all day for something to push them over the edge with little luck. Just over ten days to the event, she knew they had to get a big win. But what?

Suki had stepped in to help her build an interactive email to the club LISTSERV a few weeks ago, and then they'd done flyering the week after that, and there was the sponsorship spot at the spring opening of the Drama Department musical.

Zane seemed happy with their ticket numbers, but there was a fire in Maya that wanted to get to the stretch goal he had set, the one that had seemed a little impossible before. One thousand tickets.

Maybe she could brainstorm with Nishant, because clearly her brain had taken spring break a little early. True, she had been mildly avoiding him since the V-Formal, but that was just because she had needed some time to get her head on straight. Dev had returned, and they had gotten a quick coffee and pastry catch-up yesterday, which was good because he was the one she should be focusing on anyway.

James came back with her bread, a newspaper in his other hand as he pushed the plate to her across the counter. "This you? I didn't know you were famous."

Maya looked down at the newspaper in confusion. The headline "Holi Mania at Neadham" was emblazoned across the top, and there was a photo from their packed tryouts below it. And then she saw her face below, with Nishant's next to it.

Wow. Nishant had told her he was going to pitch to the newspapers, but she had thought that it was a long shot. He had come through. The idea shouldn't surprise her anymore, but sometimes she wondered if he even realized how impressive he could be.

"That's me," Maya said. "But I'm definitely not famous. We're just planning a big club festival for next week. Holi, if you've heard of it."

"Super cool," James said. "I read a little bit about it. I'll be there, maybe bring some friends?" He looked at her for confirmation.

"Oh yeah!" Maya nodded quickly. "More the merrier." She rattled off the festival website and some more details. "Tickets are selling like hotcakes, so I'd suggest getting them ASAP."

James nodded eagerly. "If you need any catering for caffeine, we do big orders, you know," he said.

"I actually didn't know that," Maya said, thinking fast. They were always in need of backup food vendors—she was realizing that the small mom-and-pop shops around town might not necessarily have the ability to accommodate the numbers they were now expecting for Holi. And it was never bad to start up a new relationship with a vendor. "I'll follow up on that with you, actually; that's really good to know. Could I get your number?"

James nodded and rattled it off. Maya tapped it into her phone, reveling in the fact that she hadn't tripped over her words at all.

"Feel free to hit me up. For whatever," he said, leaning forward, his blue eyes twinkling.

Unexpected. But it felt good, it felt full circle. Sure, she was seeing Dev and it was going well, but the ego boost of a cute boy giving her his number didn't hurt. Especially after V-Formal.

Maya didn't try to hide her smile as she nodded. "Sure!"

She grabbed her banana bread and the newspaper and scampered out of there before anything happened to ruin the moment. Maya found a booth and settled into it, taking a huge breath. The corner of the newspaper peeked out from underneath her bag, and she picked it up again.

"Holy crap," Maya breathed.

This wasn't the college newspaper, as she had thought. They were in the *county* newspaper, which covered the entire range from the Blue Ridge Mountains to here. And the feature was smack-you-in-the-face obvious, right there on the front of the newspaper. Good thing Nishant had gotten them to take those photos at the formal—they both looked professional and glamorous, and nothing like the scared college kid she felt like.

She looked official. There was something in the eyes of photo Maya that she never felt like she really saw in the mirror. Photo Maya looked strong, confident, like she could take on the world. Real Maya usually just wanted to get back in bed and eat muffins most days.

A dread rose up her torso, one that had been threatening all week as the event drew closer. What if they couldn't pull this off? What if it was a huge, utter, monstrous failure and everyone who came absolutely hated what they had put together—even with the massive ticket sales?

What if even Maya 2.0 couldn't pull this off?

Suddenly, her thoughts careened into a ravine. What had made her even raise her hand during that HSA meeting in the first place? This was why she went safe and steady, because the alternative was huge and scary.

Maya took a deep breath, trying to calm herself down. She wasn't alone, she had Nishant as a partner, and the entire HSA community was invested in Holi now.

A ping came in on her phone.

Nishant Rai: Did you see the cover?

And then a few seconds later.

Nishant Rai: We look good. This is fantastic marketing,

if I can pat my own back. Tickets are going to fly off the shelves.

Maya turned back to the newspaper and inspected their photos again. They did look good together, like a team.

> **Maya Sastry:** Tickets can't fly off the shelves.
> **Nishant Rai:** 🙄
> **Maya Sastry:** But I get your point. And you did really well with this article.
> **Nishant Rai:** 😃
> **Maya Sastry:** We can pull this off . . . right?

Not even a few seconds passed before he responded, but Maya's chest had already squeezed into knots.

> **Nishant Rai:** Without a doubt.

The knots in her chest began to loosen, but still, Maya knew this wouldn't be over until every last vendor had arrived, until the last performance. Until Holi was a big smashing success.

No pressure, right?

CHAPTER 21

Nishant Rai: Kill me. I cannot deal with the volunteer committee.

Maya Sastry: They're so great! I'll trade you the audio-visual tech crew.

Nishant Rai: Gladly.

Nishant Rai: Wait, can we actually switch?

Maya loved the feel of spring in the air, from the faint warmth to the horde of students poking their heads outside. Well, she could probably do without the latter since she was now having a particularly hard time getting through the crowds on University Drive that night. It wasn't even that late, it just seemed like everyone wanted to be out.

She didn't fully begrudge them, but she did a little, mainly because she had spent the nice weather of the week cooped up indoors, hunched over her computer or yelling on the phone at someone, all thanks to Holi Mela hell week.

Maya had been part of a musical once in high school, and that hell week had been fun. This one was not. She couldn't remember the last time she'd had a hot coffee (mostly because she kept getting distracted), and she had to have Jana remind her to shower (more than once).

Maya turned the corner, dodging another group of hollering students who seemed to have started their night early, her dinner in tow. Jana had convinced her to leave the house and pick up some of her favorite noodles from Galangal Villa before she exploded (Jana's words, not hers), which is why she was here. She took a sharp turn onto a back road to cut across the corner and avoid those masses of people, when she saw a familiar head of hair bobbing around in the crowd.

Nishant came into view, trailing behind a few other people. They all looked dressed up and he did as well. In fact, he looked very, very good. Crisp-button-down-and-dark-jeans good. Maya flushed, trying to hide her reaction.

Wait, it was Wednesday.

"Nishant?" she said.

He turned around and blinked at her for a few seconds before throwing his arms wide. "Maya! Just the person I wanted to see," he said. Nishant tugged her over to his other friends and began introducing them, and Maya gave them tepid smiles.

Once he had finished, she pulled him closer to her.

"Nishant, it's Wednesday," she said, lowering her voice. "The

Wednesday before the Holika Dahan. You know, the first event of our Mela?"

"Yes," he said, nodding sagely. "It is."

"Aren't you supposed to be at a dinner right now?" she asked pointedly. "With your parents? You know that big dinner you were really worried about?"

"Oh, that." Nishant waved his hand, looking unconcerned, but Maya noticed that his posture was laced with tension, like a puppet being held up. Despite the casual expression he had on his face, it was pretty clear Nishant was not okay.

"Nishant," she said, glancing down at her watch. "If you leave now, you can be only slightly late."

"Eh, I'm not worried." At her raised eyebrow, he shrugged. "I dunno, maybe I won't go."

She gave him a stern look. "Nishant, seriously? You're going to stand up your parents? That doesn't really seem like you."

"Well, maybe you don't really know me that well," he said mutinously.

Maya resisted the urge to rub her temples. Unfortunately, she did know Nishant. They were partners, they were *friends*. If nothing else, she needed him to be on point for the next few days, and seeing him like this wasn't very reassuring. Standing his parents up? Even less so.

"Why are you out here all DJ Nish-ing it up, Nishant? As your friend, I have to ask."

Nishant shook his head. "That's not even a term. I just—" He stopped and took a deep breath. "I'm still freaking out. I can't do it." He shook his head. "They're going to know I did the open mic and then we're going to fight and it's going to be a whole, long thing and I just can't. Usually my brother is there, but when it's just us three . . . things get bad. Yelling, fighting, crying, the whole thing."

"Okay," she said calmly. "That does sound hard. But they're your parents, and don't you think avoiding them is only going to make it worse? Didn't you start this whole Holi thing because you wanted to prove to them that they were wrong?"

"I mean it started that way," he said, flinching.

Maya switched her takeout to her other hand and reached over to Nishant, squeezing his arm in a way that she hoped was supportive. "You can do this. But you really should leave now. You'll definitely start an argument if you're super late."

Emotions flashed across Nishant's face as he came to terms with what she said. Maya could almost see the moment he realized how late he was, and how much crap he was going to be in for it. What she didn't foresee was what he said next.

"You have to come with me." Nishant grabbed her hands. "Please?" He gave her the biggest puppy-dog eyes.

"Uh. . ." Maya said. "I have plans. Tonight."

"You clearly just picked up dinner at Galangal Villa," he said, pointing at her takeout. "You're not a very good liar. You're just going to go home and watch *Bake Off* before you stay up for another few hours working."

True. But he didn't have to read her so hard.

"Which sounds infinitely preferable to having dinner with your parents. They want to see you. Just suck it up and go," she said.

"They'll be on better behavior if you're there. Please come. Please be my backup?" Nishant pleaded. "I can't do this without you."

"Uh-uh," Maya said. She looked out into the crowd to see if there was a way to make a quick exit. "I've got a pile of work to do because I was covering for *you*. I don't have time to babysit as well!"

"Really, I mean it," he said. "What if I handle all the paperwork for the rest of the planning?"

"Our event literally starts tomorrow," Maya said. "Not much of an incentive there."

"I'll deal with all the caterers!" he said. "Including Paneer Pete."

Maya pursed her lips. "Okay, now that's tempting."

"Please?" he said, his eyes warm and his voice soft and insistent. "I need you."

How was she supposed to say no to that?

Maya decided to work on her ability to say no later, because she realized the puppy eyes had gotten her. Plus, she could never say no to helping someone.

"Okay, fine," she said, sighing. "If I do this, we'll get straight to work for the rest of the night? No distractions?"

Nishant nodded his head quickly. "Promise."

"Anything I should know?" Maya said. "Skeletons? Obsessive phases in middle school? Actually, what do they think you're majoring in here?"

"They know I'm an econ major," he said. "And obviously, they know about the DJing."

"Got it," she said. "Fine. I'll be a great wingwoman, if only because I've got a reputation to uphold." Maya pointed a finger at him. "Parents love me. No, really, don't give me that look, they do."

They bickered the whole way to the restaurant, which was an upscale French place a few streets over from University Drive. It shouldn't have surprised Maya that Nishant's parents had picked the nicest restaurant in town.

"Rai? Party of—" Nishant said to the host.

The host smiled at him. "They're already here. Right this way."

Nishant exchanged a look with Maya, who shrugged.

Oh crap, she still had her takeout. "I'll be right back," she said to Nishant. "And it'll be good for you to prep them on why you showed up with someone they've never met before."

She left a protesting Nishant to find the host and the coatroom, where she tucked away her noodles.

The waiter led her to a table in the back where two polished, impeccably dressed adults sat alongside Nishant.

"I hope it's not taking away from your studies. You're still an econ major, aren't you? Or is your lateness another sign of—" his dad was saying, his voice carrying.

"Maya!" Nishant's mom stood and came over to her, wrapping her in a warm hug. "We're so excited to have you here."

"Oh, thank you," she said, a little surprised.

His dad stood as well, nodding at her. "Hello."

Nishant's mom had the same warmth and twinkling eyes that Nishant did. Her hair was a dark raven black, thick and lustrous, and her entire presence radiated put-together. This was a woman with grace, and Maya understood where Nishant had gotten a lot of his charm.

It wasn't from his dad, who looked like a stern general. His eyes kept darting around the restaurant. Not a man who understood how to relax. That, Maya could call from a mile away.

"It's such a pleasure to meet you both, Mr. and Mrs. Rai."

"None of that nonsense," his mom said. "Sheila Auntie and Mahesh Uncle. Please."

"Mr. Rai is also fine," his dad said, ignoring the look from Nishant's mom.

Maya nodded, offering a small smile as she took the seat next to Nishant. She was not wading into that.

"How's it been going?" she whispered.

Nishant whispered back. "The question barrage has already started."

Maya winced. "That bad?"

Sheila Auntie threw them a curious look. "What are you two chatting about?" she said. She looked between the two of them with a curious expression.

"The Holi Mela," Maya said, before Nishant could. She was here to help, wasn't she? "I was just catching Nishant up with the vendor arrival times and the bonfire schedule tomorrow. He put everything into place, you know. Couldn't have done it without him. That econ major really helped—I'm a business major myself, but Nishant's experience was so valuable."

Sheila Auntie smiled, and even Mahesh Uncle gave Nishant a considering look.

Nishant relaxed at her side. Underneath the table, he squeezed her hand in quiet thanks. She squeezed back.

Maya hadn't lied before; she had always been great with parents.

"Oh, well, of course. Nishant has always been like that. That's why we want him at the business," Mahesh Uncle said. "Maybe you can help him see that. Get him focused, leave behind all this music nonsense. Though DJing has been an appropriate hobby, it can't go on when he joins the business. We have a reputation to uphold."

"Of course you would want him at the business," Maya said. "I'm sure you love how full of ideas Nishant is. The only reason we got the press we did was because of Nishant's DJ background. It was his idea to have an EDM festival at Holi. Now we're in the newspaper!"

"Really?" Mahesh Uncle said, looking intrigued.

"Oh yeah," she said. "It was all over the regional newspaper. Nishant didn't show you?"

Sheila Auntie frowned. "Nishant, what is this about?"

"Thanks, Maya," Nishant said dryly, with just enough of a smile to know that he was joking. "You blew up my spot."

"Nishant," his mom said. "You must send us this article immediately."

"Is it like the coverage your brother got for winning the Innovation Cup at Grantchester?" his dad asked, perusing the menu. "We had three top-tier startup events come in after that."

Maya could feel Nishant tensing up next to her. "You'd have to tell me."

Thankfully, the waiter arrived just then to take their orders.

"Corporate events are our bread and butter," Sheila Auntie said in explanation to Maya once the waiter had left.

"Makes sense," Maya said. "That's a hard market to corner in your industry."

"Indeed," Mahesh Uncle said, giving her an assessing look. "And we've maintained our relationships with our clients for many years. That is our secret sauce."

"I'd love to hear more about that, Mr. Rai. . . ."

The rest of the night went smoother, with Maya helping Nishant navigate the conversation with his dad and piping up where she could to compliment him. Make him look good.

It was surprisingly easy, and throughout the dinner, Maya began to realize just how much she herself had undervalued Nishant in the beginning, thinking that he was just a DJ. Just a two-date wonder. Maybe he hadn't fit her initial criteria for traditional success, but she had been an idiot to not see that he was so much more.

Maya excused herself to the bathroom right before the entrees came. She checked her lipstick as she washed her hands. So far, so good. This new brand Imogen had suggested was really working. Her phone pinged as she dried her hands.

Dev Gupta: Got any spring break plans yet?

Maya Sastry: Nothing concrete still, despite Jana's efforts.

Dev Gupta: Would you maybe be interested in doing something with me?

Dev Gupta: Only if you want to.

His texts stopped Maya cold as she walked out from the bathroom. Would she like to do something with Dev? Was he asking her to get more serious, even though they had only been on three dates? Was this some form of boy code? He wouldn't be asking about spring break plans if he wasn't thinking about next steps, right?

This was supposed to be exciting, but all Maya could think about was the boy outside, the one whose parents she had just met. In any other world, that would mean something, wouldn't it?

But it didn't in Nishant's world.

A tall woman came out of the bathroom and nearly barreled into Maya, and she came back into her body. She sent a quick text off to

Jana and then took a deep breath. Tonight was for helping Nishant, who was a good friend and for—

"You okay?" Their waiter appeared in front of her.

"Yes, yes," Maya said. "Just taking a second."

The waiter nodded at her. "You're the girlfriend, aren't you? First time meeting the family?"

"What? No," Maya said. "I'm not the girlfriend."

The waiter shrugged. "Well, none of my business. But the dad seems to like you, and he doesn't seem very friendly."

That was a bit of an understatement. Wait, if they thought she was his girlfriend . . .

Nishant caught her eye across the restaurant and gave her the head tilt, their *Save me* signal. She nodded and walked back to the table.

The waiter's words hit her as she slid back into her seat. What would it be like to really be Nishant's girlfriend? She had immediately denied it, but here she was, playing the girlfriend, wasn't she? She had spent the evening talking Nishant up, supporting him, making jokes and charming the parents.

Maya smiled and inserted herself seamlessly back into the conversation. "Oh, did I tell you all about how Nishant found us a beautiful event venue?"

That captured their interest and led them into more talk of the Holi Mela, which both Maya and Nishant could relax into—they were used to talking about the planning and all the events, especially with the extensive marketing they had to do recently.

The rest of the dinner passed relatively easily enough, except for an incident with the lasagna Nishant's dad ordered. Maya was just glad to see that Nishant had gone from a greenish color to a normal human pink color, which meant she was making progress in her newfound job as wingwoman. She had even managed to get his parents to forget that Nishant had been late.

All in all, a success.

And even though none of this had started out as her problem, a sense of accomplishment washed over her. Another event managed.

Nishant and Maya walked with his parents to their car after the bill was paid, weaving through the students who packed the sidewalks of University Drive or lined up outside of Bill's for Wednesday night shenanigans.

Mahesh Uncle looked around, serious eyes under his thick eyebrows. "What a great environment to make connections," he said, surprising Maya. "I hope you're taking advantage of it."

Nishant didn't look very surprised and gave his dad a weak smile. "I am."

"He's underplaying it," Maya piped in. "He's been invaluable in our marketing efforts—he knows everyone. He's created a brand for himself as DJ Nish. Everyone wants him at their party, and after the Holi Mela, everyone will want to work with him on their events as well. Devious, if I may say."

"Hmm," his dad said, looking a little impressed despite himself. He clapped Nishant on the back, which made Nishant turn bright red, before nodding at his wife. They said their goodbyes and left quickly after.

Maya and Nishant waved his parents off and then turned to each other.

"Phew," Maya said. "That wasn't so bad." Nishant's eyebrow rose a teensy bit. "I said not that bad. But I get your stories now. Though, Nishant, they do love you."

Nishant looked down at his shoes, his hands in his pockets. "I know," he said. "I sometimes wish that love would look a little different, but I know."

"I think that's very normal," Maya said.

Nishant nodded slowly. "I think they had fun?" he said in wonder. "And by all standards, my dad seemed pleased."

"Not with the lasagna," Maya said.

"Nope, that lasagna was never going to survive my dad's standards, or withering glare."

"I felt bad for the waiter."

"I felt bad for us," Nishant said.

Maya laughed at that.

"I can't believe we did it," Nishant said. His eyes were wide, and there was an excited smile curling across his lips. "A dinner without my brother that had no fighting or tears."

"We're great partners," Maya said. "Oil and water make a great vinaigrette."

Nishant burst out laughing at that, a deep, full-throated laugh. It was so infectious that Maya found herself smiling.

"You're amazing," he said.

"I am," Maya agreed.

"Pizza?" he said.

"How can you eat after that dinner?" Maya said, shaking her head, wondering when pizza with Nishant had become a regular, normal thing.

"Maybe because I was so nervous I barely ate anything? And my dad was right, the lasagna was not that good."

Maya snorted at that. "Fine, pizza it is." She looked at the line that was curling out of Jeff's Eatery with growing concern. "Though we're going to have to make moves."

Nishant's phone rang and he looked down at his phone. "Sorry, I've got to take this, it's the parents."

Maya released a deep breath when he walked away, letting the night air envelop her. The weather was warming with just a hint of humidity in the air. And the forecast was even better for this weekend. Maya hoped it held, especially with all the outdoor events and the food stalls they had planned.

Yeah, she had made sure they had put aside yards of tarp, but no one wanted to celebrate Holi under smelly tarps. If this could hold for just a few more days, it would be perfect.

Part of her couldn't believe that tomorrow was the Holika Dahan, that tomorrow everything they had painstakingly stitched together would finally be finished. A frisson of excitement zinged through her, and she tried to catch it, hold on to it, before it fled and the worry returned.

Tomorrow, everything would come together. Just like she and Nishant had come together. She had to believe that. Maya spotted Nishant's figure pacing near the edge of the road. Who would have thought she would have gone to dinner with his parents two months ago? Or that she would swoop in to help him?

Definitely not her.

When Nishant walked back, Maya could tell something had happened. The easy Nishant from a few moments ago was gone. There was a tension in his body, a shiftiness in his posture. What had that call been about?

"Ready to go?" Maya said. "I think Jeff's Eatery is going to be a no-go, but we could try Corner Slice."

"Mhm," he said. He shifted on his feet, looking like he wanted to leave. "Maybe we should leave the pizza for another night. Not feeling it anymore."

What? He had just asked her. "You just said—"

"I dunno, I changed my mind," he said.

All right, it had been a long night, and even she felt it. Being your best, most sparkly self was tiring in its own way. The night was probably finally getting to him.

"Level with me," she said. Despite logically understanding that Nishant was probably tired, she could smell the weird vibes from him. Something was off. "Did I mess up? Did I break my parents-love-me streak?"

Nishant shook his head. "What are you talking about? My parents loved you," he said.

"Wait, really? Then why are you acting so weird?" she said. "Have I somehow failed in my mission to be your wingwoman? Did your parents say something? Is that what the phone call was about?"

Nishant shook his head. "No, you were great."

"Then why do you look like you swallowed a frog?" Maya said, trying to keep it light. There was a tension in Nishant's jaw that she had only seen a few times before but never directed at her. And the sudden coldness that had frosted his tone, it was alarming.

"I'm not acting weird," he said, ignoring her question. He angled away from her. "I was just thinking. You did me a solid tonight, but

I don't want you to get the wrong impression." Maya blinked at him like he was an alien. What? Did she just hear that right? "We've had some good moments, but I want to be clear."

"What are you trying to say?"

"We're better off as friends," he said. "And you don't want to have to deal with this all the time, anyway, do you?" He tried to smile at her, but it felt off. Wrong.

"Huh?"

"Look, I'm trying to be nice, but you're not my girlfriend, okay?" Nishant said. "You don't need to, like, take care of me. Anymore."

Maya was so shocked that for a few seconds, no sound left her lips. And then the anger rushed in, hot and fiery.

"Um, okay, I never said I was. *You* asked me to be here," she said, her cheeks getting hot. "I reminded you that you should probably show up to dinner with your parents, and *you* begged me to go with you. And now you're rewriting history."

"I didn't beg you," he said, a little coldly.

Maya was already over it. Especially because she could feel her heart squeezing tight in her chest, memories flooding her system from senior year and another conversation like this.

"You were the one to suggest pizza," she said. Maya stepped away from him, putting space in between them.

A beat of silence passed between them.

"Yeah, yeah, I did," he said. Nishant rubbed his jaw. "I don't think pizza is a good idea. Anymore." His gaze moved away and then back to her, but he didn't make a move to bridge the gap between them.

Something had shifted here, a tidal wave engulfing them. She could try to cross it, but instead, Maya grabbed her bag tighter to her.

"No problem. I'll see you tomorrow," she said. "Please show up to that, at least."

She turned on her heel and walked away from Nishant.

CHAPTER 22

NO NEW MESSAGES

The next morning brought Maya a pounding headache and a heavy emotional hangover. Though that was possibly from the tub of chocolate chip cookie dough she had eaten the night before. Jana hadn't been home, which meant Maya had time to stew, and stew, and stew a little bit more over her fight with Nishant.

The anger had been strong, and Maya could still feel it pounding through her veins, but something else had gotten lodged along the way as well. A small kernel of hurt, just large enough to bother her.

Just large enough to make her eat that entire tub as she ruminated over everything that had happened. As she replayed her conversation with Nishant over and over, comparing it to the heartbreaking one after senior prom, when Ari had told her that he would never want a relationship—with her. That he had found someone else, had been lying to her the whole time, too.

She had walked right into it all over again. Worse, she hadn't even been "seeing" Nishant. But there had been something between them.

Something she should have shut down long ago. Maybe she should go on spring break with Dev just to get away from it all.

Thankfully, she had fallen asleep before she had found where Jana had stashed the second tub of cookie dough. But she was paying with a major sugar hangover now.

Maya glanced down at her watch with bleary eyes. Damn her for setting her alarm so early for today, though an early rise would give her some time to snap out of this funk she was in.

And get her head straight. She turned on some music and chugged two glasses of water before getting ready. Her texts were zooming in as vendors and others started to confirm the timings for the day.

Thirty minutes later, Maya was dressed, pressed, and had her head on straight. No boy was going to ruin her day today, and if he showed up having woken up on the wrong side of the bed again, she would show him exactly who he was dealing with.

A text pinged in her inbox.

Nishant Rai: I'll check in with the vendors and confirm that the stage is being set up on the field for tomorrow.

Maya should have been glad that Nishant was being professional, but she couldn't help the slight sinking feeling in her chest. But this was good, right? Today, the goal was to make the bonfire go off without a hitch.

> **Maya Sastry:** Great. I'll be briefing the volunteer committee until then.
> **Nishant Rai:** I'll meet you there. We can go to the bonfire together after.

Maya rewrote her reply about three times, waffling between a thumbs-up emoji and something sharper, when she finally decided to just not reply.

Even if it was petty.

Maya was going over the details of the bonfire with the volunteer committee one last time on the field when she saw Nishant from the corner of her eye. He stood on the edges of the field, giving attendees directions and handing out the little pieces of paper they would need later.

When had he arrived? And why did he have to look so good?

"And that's it, folks," Maya said. "Take one of the turtle brownies, no nuts because I know Molly and Keith are allergic. Traverse the field, make sure everything stays safe, and remind people that the big event starts tomorrow. If they haven't bought a ticket, tell them they can pay in cash, and if they don't seem interested, mention that we have over twenty-five local vendors and artisans coming, including musical acts."

Maya took a deep breath. "Let's do this."

A cheer went up from the volunteer committee, and Maya let herself cheer with them. They dispersed quickly, especially as people began to stream in, and when she turned around, Nishant was by her side.

Twinkle lights were spread around the border of the lawn, far away from the large bonfire in the middle. Tables were spread across the edges too with food and drinks, as well as papers that people could write on and burn in the Holika Dahan bonfire.

She took a moment to admire their handiwork before acknowledging Nishant.

"Hey," he said.

"Hey."

He motioned at the microphone nearby. "You should welcome everyone to our event, Maya."

Maya started. "What? No, you do it. You're the DJ."

"It's your event," he said, nudging her. "I helped, but you were the first to have the vision of reviving Holi, of bringing back the event that so many people loved."

He said it with such sincerity, that she couldn't help but look at him. His gaze was direct, unvarnished. Maya realized she had been waiting to hear those words for a while, and he was the one to say them. Here, now.

Was he acknowledging that this had been her vision? Was this an apology?

Well, it wasn't the one she wanted.

She stared at him stubbornly. "It's our event. You made this happen as much as I did." She didn't mean for it to come out as angrily as it did.

"But you were the first one to believe. And the Holika Dahan is special to you."

He had remembered? Maya's chest constricted at that realization, softness flooding her heart. She was still angry, annoyed, but that coil of emotions loosened as she remembered her grandmother.

Maya nodded at Nishant and stepped toward the microphone. She started to welcome everyone in, her voice initially shaky and growing in confidence.

"We're so happy to welcome you all to the new Holi Mela. We're kicking things off with the Holika Dahan, the traditional bonfire to celebrate the defeat of evil and the triumph of good. We hope that tonight you can let go of the things that may have been weighing you down over this past year and let them burn away in the bonfire."

Maya looked over to Nishant, who gave her a warm smile. She took a giant breath. "When we first started planning Holi, all I could think about were the different pieces of the event that we needed to plan. Booking the venue or getting vendors. Finding performers, selling tickets. But standing here now, I see that today is so much more. Today is a moment for you to forget the darkness of the past year and to step into the abundance of tomorrow. The potential." Maya threw her hands up and a cheer followed, cheering her on. "Tomorrow we start brand-spanking-new in the afternoon. We'll kick off the festival with food and local artisans and on Saturday, we'll play Holi on the lacrosse field and end it all with a music festival that will go late into the night, all to celebrate a new spring. A rebirth, if you will."

She had meant every word she had spoken. This Holi Mela was so much bigger than just an event for her. Its first steps had been her first steps as Maya 2.0, as the girl—the woman—she she was today.

"Let's kick it off," Nishant said, appearing next to her as another cheer went through the crowd. Their gazes locked and Maya could feel herself smiling back. They were a good team together, which was why it made the rest so hard.

The volunteer committee sprang into action as they kicked off the bonfire, and again, Maya was thankful that they'd had the presence of mind to recruit people to help out in the community.

After the bonfire had been lit and everything was set, Maya finally felt herself relax. They still had time, but this event, this particular one, meant so much to her. Her grandmother would have been proud of this, and Maya was, too.

Maya scribbled something down quickly on the piece of paper she had tucked away before tossing it into the bonfire.

"What did you write?" Nishant said, coming up behind her. The flames of the bonfire cast a bright glow across half of his face, the other shrouded in the dark.

"Can't tell you," she said. "It's like a wish."

"Oh, really?"

"Everyone knows that."

He stepped closer to her, and Maya had to remind herself not to step back, especially as his familiar smell washed over her, the warmth from his presence.

"I'm sorry," he said.

Maya cocked her head at him to go on. She was going to need more than that. Maybe the Maya of old would have taken that *sorry* and run with it, because she had never gotten one. But Nishant had been the one to show her that she could and did deserve so much more.

He ran a hand through his hair. "I think I just freaked out last night, and you took the brunt of it. I talked to my parents, and they really liked you, and I didn't know how to handle it."

"You were an ass to me because your parents liked me?"

"Yes?" he said. "I told you that my one relationship failed, right? And you asked me if I was scared? Well, maybe I am."

She wanted to ask why, when it hit her. His parents had thought she was his girlfriend, and they had liked her—just like his ex and the relationship that had made him swear off them in general. Not a great feeling, she guessed.

"I think I just had a flashback to the breakup and everything that followed," he said, "the way everyone took her side."

"We're not even together, Nishant."

"I know" was all he said. But there was something else in the way he said it, a hint of an unknown, a question. "But my dad thought we were."

Maya didn't mention that she'd had a flashback, too, one that was just as negative, one that convinced her that whatever feelings she might have had for Nishant needed to be put away. She had been right when she had first met him—he was dangerous to her.

Her heart wanted Nishant, and her heart had always led her astray.

But he was still her friend, and something melted in her at the uncertain look on his face.

"Nishant," she said. "You wanted to show your parents, especially your dad, that he was wrong, and this bonfire, this whole weekend is proof. They saw what we've built—what you've built. Your vision is coming to life, and I will tell anyone who asks that it was your vision as much as mine. So if anyone tries to take that away from you, I won't let it happen. I'll fight them if I have to, and I'll have it be known that I can be scary—"

It was like a heavy blanket fell off Nishant's back. He looked at her, his gaze so intense that it nearly took her breath away.

His lips were on hers, soft and firm. Maya was shocked at first, but then she kissed him back, letting go of the storm that had been building up inside her. His kiss turned deeper, closer. Minutes, hours, days passed.

His hands grazed her jaw, her throat, coming to rest on the back of her neck. He rested his forehead on hers as they took a breath.

"Maya—" he started. His eyes swept open, the warmth in them fading away. His voice startled her back into reality, as did the buzzing in her pocket.

Shit. Dev had said he was going to stop by the bonfire. Her heart thudded in her chest.

What was she doing, kissing Nishant?

"This— We can't— This is a mistake," she whispered. Maya could feel Nishant's flinch as she pulled away. Her gaze darted around and when she didn't see Dev anywhere, her heartbeat started to steady again.

"And why is that?"

"We're friends," Maya said, trying desperately to hold on to the thread of what she had realized the night of the HSA formal. That was all they could be.

"Because of Dev?" he said, looking annoyed.

"You're the one who set me up with Dev!"

Nishant bit his lip and looked away. "I know," he said. "And I've regretted it since then."

Maya stepped back. What? Part of her couldn't believe that he meant it.

"Sure. It's not like you've stopped dating," she said.

"Actually," he said, staring at her. "I have. I haven't seen anyone since you came to the open mic." His voice was soft, a little too insistent. "You're the only one who's seen that side of me and not shied away. Who has encouraged me. Did you know after that I submitted my songs to a few competitions? I even got a bite."

"That's amazing," she said softly.

"Maya, if it wasn't for you, none of that would've happened. You gave me a chance, you are— You're special."

Maya tried not to let the words lodge in her heart. She knew what would happen if she sank into that, believed those words. This wasn't the first time she had found herself here, listening to a boy who would never be interested in committing to her.

"You told me yesterday that I wasn't your girlfriend, that you didn't want me to be," Maya said, before she could help herself. "It doesn't seem like you think I'm that different. Or that you're ready."

The words snapped reality back into place, for the both of them.

Nishant looked torn, his jaw tensing and then relaxing. It looked as if he wanted to say it, wanted to admit it, but something was holding him back.

"I didn't say I didn't want you to be," he said finally. "It's just my parents— Look, I know I messed up."

"Then would you want a relationship? You freaked out when I mentioned it." Nishant's silence lasted a beat too long.

Maya shook her head and stepped back. She wrapped her arms around herself, like it might help against the sudden chill she felt.

"Okay," Maya said.

She had made this mistake before. With Ari and then, in another way, with Thomas.

She had picked the wrong guy both times, one who wasn't right for a relationship, one who didn't value her, and look what had happened.

Nishant might like her now, but what would happen when he changed his mind later? Maya clearly wasn't good at making these decisions. It was the reason why she had started using Meet'em in the first place, and then being matchmade. Her heart couldn't be trusted.

Nishant turned back to her, his eyes a little wild, a little confused, a little heartbreaking.

"Maya—I'm sorry, I didn't— I don't—"

"It's good," she said quickly, trying to ignore the way her heart was splitting inside.

She knew this from the beginning. Nishant didn't want a relationship, and after what he had gone through, she understood. Maya couldn't fix him, couldn't change him. It was like Thomas had said.

He had to take that step himself, and he wasn't interested.

Nishant might one day want a relationship, but not with her. Even if he felt the same spark as she did. And now he would say something to hammer that nail in even more, and Maya didn't think her heart could take it. Not now.

"We're friends," she continued, barging ahead. "Clearly, friends who had some sexual tension, but it's a normal thing."

"It is?"

She nodded her head emphatically. "Totally. We're in college. Time of trying things and all of that."

Nishant didn't look convinced, but he stepped away, an inscrutable look on his face. Probably one of relief. "Okay."

She was doing this for both of them. For their partnership. The Holi Mela still had to go off without a hitch, and she didn't want to be the heartsick girl dragging them down, and she would burn up in mortified flames if he thought of her that way, so this was easier. Safer.

Better for her.

Maya turned on a wide smile, hoping it hid the sadness that was clawing up her throat. "Friends."

Nishant cleared his throat and looked away. When he looked back, his normal expression had returned. "Can we be friends that kiss like that again?" He raised an eyebrow at her.

"Probably not," she said. "I do have another date with Dev . . . and I think it's getting serious."

She didn't anticipate the way his entire body seemed to freeze up and shut down at the same time.

"Right," he said. "Of course. He would be an idiot not to lock you down."

Maya glanced up at Nishant's words. The resigned tone of them. His gaze met hers as if he was trying to tell her something, show her something, through it.

But then he looked away.

"I'll see you tomorrow, then?" she said.

"Tomorrow," Nishant said, nodding. He gave her that brilliant smile of hers. "I'll even bring the coffee. Though I might try to sneak in some extra sugar. We're going to need it tomorrow. It's a packed schedule."

And just like that, Nishant was back to normal. Maya forced herself to get back there as well. Thinking about tomorrow did the trick. Nishant was right, it would be a long day and she couldn't afford to let this drag her down.

"I'll see you then?" Maya said. Nishant nodded, and she made an excuse about needing to leave early.

She dashed away from the bonfire and the laughing voices all around her, trying to ignore the sinking feeling in her stomach.

That had gone pretty well, hadn't it? She had saved their friendship and focused on their partnership first, all while letting Nishant off the hook.

It was a success.

And if Maya could ignore the way her heart felt like it was shattering, she might actually believe it.

CHAPTER 23

Nishant Rai: Lewiston Daily wants to interview you.
Maya Sastry: OK. When are you free?
Nishant Rai: Not us. You. I set it up for tomorrow, if that works for you?
Nishant Rai: You deserve this, Maya.

Maya was trying her best not to be a wet blanket, but it was rather hard when she was, in fact, cold and wet. Of course, the morning of the Holi Mela the heavens had decided to open up and pour water down. They were prepared, because Maya had put together multiple contingency plans, but it didn't mean she had to be happy about it—it wasn't even April-showers time yet! Any other day and Maya wouldn't have hated it, would've maybe felt it was fitting, given the horrible mood she was in. Given the storm of thoughts and emotions in her brain after that moment with Nishant the night before.

She had made the right decision. She had, hadn't she?

The rain pelted the window. Maya jumped up.

"Are you okay?" Dev asked, leaning across the table. They were getting an early lunch at the local taqueria, which had her favorite salsa molcajete she had tasted in three states. Even that couldn't cheer her up.

Maybe being an adult and making grown-up decisions was supposed to feel like this. Like soggy, sad, unhappy bread that you forgot you dunked into your soup.

"Still a little wet," she admitted. Her jacket was drying off on the seat next to her, but her jeans were mildly soaked, too. It wasn't like she could take those off to dry.

"Can I do anything?" Dev asked in that sweet way of his. Maya was still getting to know him, but she knew that Dev was definitely a fixer. He was like her in that way.

"No, no," she said. "I'll dry off."

He glanced at her but then nodded. "Okay."

Dev also wasn't a pusher. He was a straight shooter, which she did appreciate, but it also meant that he missed some context sometimes.

"I have a surprise for you," Dev said, leaning forward.

"Oh," Maya said, trying to muster excitement. "I love surprises."

That was true, she really did. And Dev was thoughtful, and he was more like her than anyone she had ever met, so it would be good.

"You said you didn't have concrete plans for spring break. What if you came to India with me?"

What? Maya thought she had misheard at first. "Huh?"

"Um, India? I'm going, and I'd love to have you come," Dev said.

She had not misheard, unfortunately, and her first reaction was utter panic. Looking-for-an-exit panic.

"You could meet my family," he said, his eyes bright, his smile wide. He was so excited that Maya couldn't help but feel some of it rubbing off on her. Only the expectant look on his face made her stay in her seat and not run away, because this? This was a lot. She was not ready for this.

"That's so cool," Maya said, trying to calm herself down. "That you're going to India. Are you sure you want me to come?"

"Yes," he said. "I wouldn't offer if I didn't mean it. I'd love for you to meet them since, you know, I think things are going well?"

He said it as a question, looking at her. Maya grabbed her water and took a huge gulp, giving him a vague nod. Dev seemed to interpret it as a good sign, because he kept going.

"I've already bought the tickets, and I have a complete itinerary and family tree ready for you," he said excitedly.

"Wow, you've thought of everything," she said.

And he had—exactly the way she might have handled it as well. They were two peas in a pod. Cut from the same cloth. She looked at the itinerary he had pushed over to her and saw that there were even breaks for taking photos. And a dedicated time for snacks.

She had wanted a boy who would commit, and this was commitment.

It was everything Maya had wanted, and yet this time, it left her feeling kind of cold. She could picture their entire life together, and while that had sounded like a good thing before, it felt claustrophobic now.

What about color? What about taking a detour or a longer path? Discovery would probably be added to the itinerary.

Maya didn't foresee any risk, any uncertainty, in their life plans together. And while there was nothing wrong with that, she wasn't sure she wanted that anymore.

She wasn't sure what she did want, though. Or more precisely, if she could trust what she wanted.

"Well, not everything," Dev said. "I still have a few time blocks to fill up, and I need to confirm some of my second cousins' spouses names, but it's a start."

Maya looked at Dev, really looked at him. He was smiling at her, oblivious to her thoughts. How could she tell him that his itinerary, which normally would've made her glow with pride, was giving her squeezing heart palpitations?

Dev tilted his head at her expectantly. "So, what do you think?"

When the moment came, Maya found herself unable to speak. It was like the words didn't want to leave her mouth, let alone her soul. A tight grip squeezed her heart, and no matter how she tried to speak, nothing came out.

It wasn't just the itinerary. Or the booked tickets without asking her. It was all of it together. All the detours and missed paths that they'd never take.

She could see their life together flashing before her eyes, and she didn't want it. She had started to love the uncertainty, the challenge life as Maya 2.0 had introduced. There would never be a version of Maya that didn't love cozy, but maybe there was a version of her that wanted multiple things. A chance to explore, to innovate on the life she already loved.

And it felt wrong to lie to him. She knew she had to tell him no.

"Let me think about it" was what Maya ended up saying.

Even in this, she had somehow disappointed herself. Her body deflated like a balloon leaking air. But while something stopped her from saying yes, there was also something lodged in her vocal box preventing her from saying no.

So here she was, stuck in the middle. Utter limbo.

Dev frowned but hid it quickly. "Sure," he said. "I know it's a lot all at once."

"This is great," Maya said, reaching out to him. He wasn't trying to be controlling like Thomas—her gut was telling her that—but it was a lot all the same. "I just need a little bit of time."

A few months ago she would've jumped for joy.

But a few months ago, she never left her apartment.

"Okay, sure." He swiped on his phone quickly, looking something up. "I've got miles, so I can always change the flights or bump it a few days."

Maya gave him a short nod. It wasn't about a few days, but she couldn't explain it to him right now, not when she couldn't even explain that feeling in her chest to herself. So she just kept on nodding.

"Text me, then? I mean, I know you have Holi and everything, so you won't be able to—"

She couldn't do this to him. She couldn't lead him on, even if her head was telling her to wait, to consider it.

Maybe her head wasn't always the right one. Maybe, just maybe, her heart held the truth, even when it was inconvenient.

"I can't," Maya said. "Or I shouldn't."

Dev winced. "It's too soon, isn't it?"

"A little," Maya said. "But also . . ."

"We aren't there yet?"

"Yes."

Maya realized then that Dev was who she had been in the past, someone so desperate to get to the happy ending that they tried to skip through the rest. Sometimes romance shouldn't take the standard path. She didn't need to follow what the movies said love should be.

And even if there had been no Nishant, this would've probably been too soon, too fast. But if there hadn't been a Nishant, Maya probably would've said yes.

What did that say about her?

"But you are right about Holi," she said. "I'm going to be super busy for the rest of the weekend. Let's reconnect after that? Maybe a coffee?"

Dev's face dropped, but he kept the smile on. "Sure," he said, though it was clear to both of them that maybe their relationship wasn't going to last Holi. That maybe they'd only be friends on the flipside.

But how did you end a relationship that had barely started?

When she left the restaurant, she kept the smile on her face until she said goodbye to Dev. And then she let it drop, fully and totally.

Mask gone, feelings fully in her throat. She glanced down at her phone, noting the absence of long, emoji-filled texts. It had only been twelve hours and still, she missed them.

Missed him. Hoped that last night hadn't ruined everything, even though it looked like she had already done that herself.

And then—she got one. A text from Nish about one of the vendors making a last-minute change plus a meme that Maya had never seen before, but it made her laugh. Something lifted in Maya's chest upon seeing his text, knowing that they were still cool. That they were still friends even after that kiss.

Maya looked back down at her screen and then bit her lip.

But what if that wasn't what she wanted anymore? What if she didn't want to pretend their kiss was nothing?

What if she had made a huge mistake?

"Okay, I love you, but you have got to stop baking," Jana said from her seat on the kitchen barstool. "I've eaten so many cookies since last night that I might actually start not liking cookies anymore, and that sounds like a travesty of epic proportions. Plus, I need to fit into my outfit for Holi tonight."

"But it's the only way I can deal with my stress," Maya said, rushing around the kitchen. "I have to handle the interview this afternoon by myself, which means I have to be charming on my own. On my own! And also Macroecon results are online in an hour. What if I've trashed my entire academic record to plan an event that no one will attend?"

"Girl, you have got to chill out," Jana said. "We both know this baking spree has nothing to do with your Macroeconomics exam results." Jana grabbed her arm and tugged her away from the mixing bowl. "We know that this is about your boy issues."

"I don't have boy issues anymore," Maya said. "Because I have no boys anymore! I said no to Dev, remember?"

"Yes, love," Jana said. "I do. And I told you it was the right decision. An hour ago. Then thirty minutes later. And now."

Maya slumped onto a barstool. "I know. I'm sorry. It's just—"

"That you're rethinking and regretting every decision you've made? And taking it out on our poor kitchen?" Jana said. "I've noticed."

"I mean I think I made the right decision. I listened to my heart, but heart is always wrong. My heart also led me to stick around for Thomas," Maya said. "So maybe—"

Jana threw her hands up. "You've got to trust yourself, Maya! And your head cannot fix a heart problem."

"What?" Maya paused mid-stir, and a gloop of batter fell off her spoon. "Yes it can. It can stop me from making another horrible decision."

"Maya, your head isn't always going to be right."

"But New Maya—"

Jana let out a frustrated sigh. "New Maya is awesome! But guess what? I fell in love with Old Maya, and while she maybe needed to explore more and challenge herself and *believe* in herself, she didn't need to be gut renovated."

Her words hit Maya in the soft part of her that had been holding so tightly onto New Maya.

"There's nothing wrong with your heart," Jana said. "It's the best part of you. You can't keep looking for reasons that everyone is going to be like Thomas. Or Ari. Or anyone else who hurt you. It's just not fair. To yourself or to Nishant."

Maya let out a giant sob and attacked Jana with a hug, her spoon forgotten. "You're the best, Jana. But—" She stepped back, realizing what else Jana had said. "To myself or Nishant?"

"Ugh, are you really going to make me say it?" Jana said. "Can't you just admit it and put me out of my misery?" She leaned forward, her chin in the palm of her hand.

Maya stepped back. "How did you know?"

"I'm your best friend. You think I haven't been paying attention to your life? Especially the things you're not ready to say? You came back from every meeting with him just a little more buoyant. A little feistier. And after your first semester, I was so happy to see it." Jana shook her head so hard her earrings swung on their own. "You met his parents, remember that? That's a big deal. Boys don't go around introducing everyone to their parents, especially not a boy like Nishant."

Maya flushed, thinking back to their kiss. Nish's hands in her hair, pulling her closer to him. But just because he liked kissing her didn't mean he liked her. All of her.

Jana raised an eyebrow at her, like she knew exactly what Maya was thinking. Which was impossible. Right? Though leave it to Jana to somehow have developed best-friend psychic powers. Maya wasn't sure she could put it fully past her.

"We kissed," she whispered.

"What?"

"We. Kissed." Maya raised her voice a little.

The reaction was mild at first. Jana's eyes widened, and then she let out a scream. "I knew it! I knew it!" She glared at her. "When?"

"At the bonfire," Maya said, covering her face.

Jana pounded her fists against the kitchen counter. "Oh. My. God. And you didn't mention it? You are sneaky."

"Not on purpose," Maya muttered.

"So he likes you, too," Jana said with a sigh. "But he's clearly also an idiot, because he set you up with so many boys. You both are a pair, that's for sure."

"He's not interested in me like that," Maya said, a little more defensively than she had intended. Hadn't the V-Formal proved that? And what about the way he had acted after the dinner with his parents? After their kiss?

He had apologized, but Maya wasn't sure her heart could handle it.

"He doesn't want a relationship," Maya finished.

Some of the wind went out of Jana's sails. "Maya, why are you more focused on the relationship than the person?"

"I'm not," Maya said. "I just want someone who *wants* a relationship."

"Do you really, though?" Jana said. "Or do you want love? Actual love? Love that could turn into something real? That's what was missing with the others. Not a relationship."

Wow, she had never thought about it like that.

Maya had always been so focused on the outcome that she didn't realize that what she really wanted was . . . love. The rest could come later. She wanted a chance at something real.

That was it, wasn't it? Maya finally saw how she had always put her goal above what her heart was actually telling her.

"I already told him we were good as friends," Maya said. "He kissed me and then pushed me away, and then when he apologized, I got scared."

Jana came over and put a warm hand on her arm. "That's very human. And it's okay. The question is, what do you want to happen next? What do you want?"

The answer was blazingly clear now. Jana seemed to see it on her face.

"Then go and tell him you changed your mind," Jana said. "It's as simple as that."

Maya worried the outer corner of her lip, one simple question rattling around in her mind. It wasn't as simple as that.

"How can I trust myself? After all the mistakes I made in high school and first semester?" Maya said quietly.

Warm hands enveloped her own, and Maya looked up. Jana gave her a wry smile. "Why can't you see the Maya I see? That Nishant seems to see? The one that picked herself up after a tough first semester and is now running the biggest HSA event? Who put herself out there? Who was willing to change her mind and listen to a DJ with some potentially bad ideas?" She patted Maya's hands. "That Maya is fierce. And a fighter. Now go fight some more. Take your future into your own hands. Take the first step."

Maya ducked her head, overcome with emotion. Jana saw her like that? If she was being honest, Nishant saw her like that as well. He had basically told her that. Her body flooded with warmth, certainty. Jana wasn't wrong. Maya had done all those things. She hadn't stayed down after Thomas kicked her off the Meet'em app, either.

She had trusted herself enough then. Why was she doubting herself now? Maya was a fighter. Always had been, even if she hadn't always realized, and that didn't come from some list or from listening to her head over everything.

It came from Maya and from her heart.

And if she were a fighter, what would she do? A tiny voice whispered in her head.

Go and find Nishant. Kiss him again until you both see stars.

"I'm not sure he'll be interested anymore. . . ." Maya trailed off, rubbing her forehead.

"Never say never," Jana said. She tapped Maya on the side of her head. "Fight."

But how? She would have to figure it out, after she nailed this interview. Step one to taking control of her own future.

To truly becoming Maya 2.0.

CHAPTER 24

DRAFT INBOX
Maya Sastry: Nish, can we talk—
Maya Sastry: Nishant, we should—
Maya Sastry: I made a mistake.

Maya walked into her interview, or, well, casual coffee chat, with the *Lewiston Daily* prepared and ready. Any other day and she would've felt like she was on top of the world, even though she was a basket of nerves.

But today, the nerves were dulled, probably because all of her felt dulled. She still hadn't figured out how to fight for Nishant, hadn't thought of any clear way to show him what she really wanted.

The journalist from the *Lewiston Daily* was in the corner, wearing the coral linen blazer she had mentioned in her email.

Maya went over to her. "Isabelle?"

"Maya?" The woman reached her hand out and Maya gave it a firm shake. "It's so nice to meet you."

"Likewise."

They walked over to the counter, discussing the recent spate of bad weather in the area and how trippy daylight savings could be. It instantly put Maya at ease.

They got their coffees—black for Maya, a matcha latte for Isabelle—and found a seat in the back corner of the café. It wasn't long after they settled in that Isabelle leaned forward, asking for all the details on Holi. Maya gave their practiced boilerplate pitch, throwing in a few colorful details here and there.

"Wow, you've done so much already for an event that was once slated to be canceled. How does that feel? To pull something like this off? Pretty good, I bet." Isabelle winked at her.

"Yes," Maya said, laughing. "I know I'm supposed to say I did it all myself, but it's not the truth. My partner, Nishant, brought an exciting musical perspective to the whole event, and I brought a more traditional events perspective. It was a great combination. I actually think teamwork is how to elevate events. To listen to multiple ideas."

"Really? Has that always been the case?"

Maya gave her a half smile. "I have to admit, I wasn't always like that. But through planning this event, I learned a lot. And my partner, he believed when I didn't. And vice versa."

Isabelle smiled warmly at her. "That's so true. Sometimes we all need someone to help us believe."

The truth of those words reverberated in Maya. Nishant had

believed from the start, in the vision for Holi, in them as a partnership, in her.

She had been the one to resist. She had been the one to doubt.

The interview wrapped up shortly after, with a firm handshake and a warm goodbye from Isabelle, who promised to attend the Holi events the next day. It was perfect timing, as it allowed Maya a few minutes to just sit.

Maya took another sip of her coffee and closed her eyes, allowing herself a moment of peace before the storm started.

Well, it had already started, if the number of pings she was getting was any indication. She glanced down to see that most of them were from Zane, probably with ten thousand questions about the mela setup that afternoon.

Maya let out a deep breath and brought herself to her feet, savoring the last sip of her coffee. She was a few steps away from the trash can when she saw a head of curls that were way too familiar.

Thomas was standing a few feet away, coffee cup in hand as he looked directly at her.

Her heart sank.

No, not this. Not now.

Maya tried to dodge away but found no exit in sight. She turned around slowly and started to back up, just as Thomas started to walk toward her.

"Hey, Maya."

"Um, hey," Maya said, trying to duck to the side. Unfortunately, there was a triad of art students discussing the importance of impressionism in the advent of modern art.

"Can we talk?" he said, stopping in front of her with an expression on his face she couldn't quite decipher.

"I think the time for that is gone," she said, shaking her head.

"I know," he said. "I just have one thing I want to say to you." He inhaled sharply. "I'm sorry."

Wait, what? Maya turned to face him.

"Come again?"

Thomas sighed, shifting his feet. "You really going to make me say it again? Okay, fine. I'm sorry, Maya. I was kind of a . . . complete ass to you. And I'm sorry for getting you kicked off Meet'em, too. It was a moment of weakness and I regret it. A couple of the guys from the *Fortnite* club have stopped talking to me over the whole incident, too, once they found out."

"Found out?"

"Yeah, well, they happened to be in the same class as Jana and apparently heard that it was the inspiration for her documentary." Thomas's voice had a note of accusation, but then it dropped. "Then I ran into her, a few days ago, and she reamed me out in the Engineering School. In front of everyone."

If he was looking for sympathy, Maya wasn't going to give it. She blinked at him.

"Yeah, okay," he said. "It sucked, and I was going to call you and I just chickened out, but I saw you today and, well, yeah."

Not the most eloquent of speeches, but Maya could see that it was still an effort from Thomas.

"Why now?" she said. "It's been months."

"I broke up with Suki, and after that, I've been thinking a lot. Like I said, I've been meaning to talk to you, but I didn't know how to," he said. Thomas glanced down at his shoes and then up at her, looking particularly miserable. Old Maya wanted to put him out of his misery, but New Maya wasn't willing to give in.

She met him in the middle. "I appreciate that. And I appreciate your apology."

He gave her a tentative smile, and Maya found that she meant her words. She did forgive him. She wouldn't forget, but she didn't hold on to it in her heart anymore.

"Maya," he said. "I took you for granted. You were kind and you were always there, and I think I just kinda got used to that kindness. And I was there, I don't know if you remember, but it was just a day or two after we had broken up, and I saw you and Nishant at the coffee shop. It was clear he was into you."

"No, he wasn't," she said automatically. "That was the first time we had ever met, and we didn't start working together until a few days later, and by the way, I didn't even want to work with him. I blame Zane."

But she didn't anymore, did she? Zane had brought Nishant into her life like a whirlwind, and it had changed everything for her.

"When I saw you with him at the party, I kind of lost it," he said, sounding a little contrite. He shook his head. "I know it doesn't forgive my behavior, but I wanted to let you know why. And that I wish things had turned out differently."

Maya nodded. "Me too."

Thomas's mouth quirked to the side. "By the way, Holi looks like it's going to be amazing from what I've seen," he said. "You should be really proud. And I know it doesn't seem like it, but I've always believed in you."

His words hit her in an unexpected part of her heart, the part of her that had needed to hear that two, three months ago.

"Thanks," she said, really meaning it. "I hope you stop by."

Thomas smiled, the first real one in their conversation. "Already bought a ticket."

One of his gaming friends came into view, waving at him from across the coffee shop. They said their goodbyes, and Maya took a moment to steady herself.

That had been a lot different than she had been expecting. An apology, for one. Contrition, for another.

But through it all, she kept thinking of one thing.

Sometimes we all need someone to help us believe.

I've always believed in you.

It hit her then, like a lightning bolt.

She knew how she would fight for Nishant.

CHAPTER 25

Maya Sastry: Zane, I have a favor to ask.
Zane Patel: Oh, no. I did not have enough coffee
for this.

In a stroke of luck, the clouds cleared for the second day of Holi, the buttery midday light highlighting the green and blue of the mountains in the distance. A hazy rainbow peeked out from behind the sun as it shone. The crowd, all decked out in head-to-toe white, had started lining up early to play Holi, and the field was filled with long lines of vendors who were still packed despite opening the day before, from local clubs like the knitting club to regional artisans like Sheela Mistry, who made handmade silver jewelry.

They had carved out a space for playing Holi, which was bordered by a line of long tables, all decorated with brightly colored cloths and lined with overflowing plates of food from restaurants all around Lewiston.

Holi had started off well, even though the morning was still wet from the day before. The vendors had opened to a rainy beginning, but it hadn't stopped the flow of people, who had returned in full force. Maya had dressed in her best and whitest of clothes, which was Holi tradition. Every speck of color and dye she got over the course of today would tell a story, one that she knew she would treasure for a long time.

They only had a minor snafu with Paneer Pete's (her forever nemesis now) forgetting to bring the right number of plates. But otherwise, the field wasn't too muddy for playing Holi, and the new colored powder they had gotten shipped from Edison, New Jersey, was leaving just the right amount of dye on everyone.

There was still a lot to get ready for the music festival. She had barely seen Nishant because of it—getting the university sound system ready for a night full of performances was no joke.

So when she saw him standing on the side of the field, talking to one of the artisans, she knew this might be her only chance to see him before he went on for his set later that evening.

Maya nudged one of the volunteers and winked, pointing at one of the steel bowls of gulal on the table nearby and then Nishant. The volunteer's eyes widened and then they grinned, quickly handing the bowl of gulal to her. Maya took a fistful of the colored powder and walked toward Nishant. She kept her hand out of sight and sneaked closer when she noticed that the vendor had stepped away.

Nishant glanced up as he saw her approach, his expression turning sharp. They had mainly been talking over text the last day or so, and this was the first time she had seen him up close since their kiss—and the aftermath.

Her chest constricted at the sight of him in all white, the way his hair was a little less slicked back, and she had a strong desire to mess it all up. But she couldn't kiss him here, and it wouldn't be enough, would it?

"Hey," he said. "What's up? I'm just about to leave—"

She swung around and swiped the gulal across his cheek, fully enjoying the way his eyes lit up in surprise. The pink powder left a streak against his cheek, beads of it falling onto the collar of his pristine white shirt.

"Oh, you are going to get it," he said, after a beat, giving her a slow, devious smirk.

"You'll have to catch me first," she said.

Nishant stepped out and caught her by the wrist, tugging her closer. Maya looked up at him, watching the way his eyes roved over her face.

"Nishant!" someone yelled. The moment broke, and all that was left between them was unspoken words.

He looked like he wanted to say something, but then he let go. Instead, he stole some of the pink gulal from her palm and spread it across her nose. "Now I got you, too," he whispered.

That had happened a while ago, Maya realized.

And tonight she was going to try to keep him.

The rest of playing Holi went off well, except for one hiccup when a few students dumped the wrong gulal and accidentally stained a part of the field, but that was just a part of Holi. Maya hadn't been to a single one that hadn't left some sort of remnant behind, whether physical or in everyone's hearts. If social media was any indication, they had done both this time. Their handle was blowing up with mentions and tags from attendees gushing about their event, and to Maya's embarrassment, her speech at the Holika Dahan had gotten over ten thousand views already.

Sheila Mistry's silver jewelry tent had sold out, Maya had to get out the backup gulal (not from Edison), and Paneer Pete's hadn't stopped having a line since the doors had opened.

Maya checked in with the volunteers and noted that more than five hundred people had shown up since the shops opened the day before. She walked along the edges, taking it all in. The shouts of joy and laughter as friends attacked one another with exploding water balloons and reams of gulal, the messy group photos that followed. Even a few love stories in the making, like the couple in the corner who kept chasing each other around with a small bowl of bright blue gulal.

This is why she had worked so hard, wasn't it? To bring a little bit of home to Neadham. And if the conversations she had overheard were anything to go by, people were buzzing for the night's musical festival, too.

Maya found she couldn't wait, either. After seeing the mela come to life, she found herself excited for the music festival, eager to continue the celebration.

She didn't think she would have said that a few months ago.

But that's the whole point of a rebirth, of Holi, wasn't it? A celebration of the beautiful, colorful mess that was life.

And she had a plan.

Maya bustled over to the stage in preparation for the music fest.

Thankfully, the stage held up (one of Maya's worries), the weather had cleared, and even though most of the performers were on IST (Indian Standard Time), she had planned for that and built an extra thirty minutes into the schedule. Once she had checked everyone in and they were halfway through the performances, Maya finally let out a huge sigh.

Which meant it was time to find Zane.

It had taken a fair bit of planning to get Zane on board with her new plan, but she knew she had him when he dropped his head into his hands and groaned.

"I can't believe I'm helping you do this," he said as she walked up to him.

"Please," Maya said. "We're just adding in someone, it's not even a lineup change. Shouldn't affect the schedule at all. Not a huge change if you really think about it."

Zane huffed, but finally nodded. "Fine. But you owe me one."

"Tons," Maya agreed.

"Can you even sing?"

Maya grinned. "Not even a little bit."

A heavy sigh streamed out of Zane. "And he doesn't know you're going to join him onstage?" She shook her head. "I know you had a fight with Nishant," Zane said. "But I didn't expect that you were going to do something about it in such a public way. You've got cojones, Maya."

Coming from Zane, that was a huge compliment.

"Wait," Maya said, his words sinking in. "How did you know about our fight?"

Zane blushed a light pink and mumbled, "Jana might have mentioned it."

"Are you friends with my best friend and never told me?" Maya said, a little put out.

"She's annoying, but she's a great study partner for Comp Sci," Zane said, in a bit too casual of a way.

"Uh-huh," she said, narrowing her eyes at him.

"You're in luck that I'm a huge romantic." Zane raised an eyebrow.

She mouthed *Thank you* to Zane.

"By the way," he said, "great job, Maya. I know it wasn't always easy, but you both managed to pull this off. You brought the Holi Mela back to life."

Maya flushed. They had, hadn't they?

The flood lights turned on and the audience started to cheer. Zane handed her the microphone. "Break a leg."

Maya took the microphone and a deep, calming breath. She had never been very good at being in the spotlight, but this was her one shot to make things right. So here she was. She took a few small steps so that she was on the stage but still in the back. A few audience members turned and pointed at her.

She leaned into the microphone—just as someone else started to speak.

"Uh, hello? Can you hear me?"

There was a beat of silence and then a chorus of yeses. Nishant stepped out from his spot behind the DJ table, waving at the crowd.

What was he doing? He looked as if he had something to say.

Nishant stepped forward, looking a little unsure at first. He straightened his shoulders and took a step.

"I wanted to dedicate this song to someone. I've been letting the past hold me back from a future I wanted—that I still want. I'm hoping that she will give me another chance."

And then Nishant began to sing. A few seconds later, after a stunned audience took in that DJ Nish was singing a cappella and was really, really good.

Even Maya stood there stunned for a moment.

Nishant was out there, on the stage, singing the song he had written, the one that had been sampled on the song he had played for her in the library. The crowd listened intently, and she could see a few people leaning forward, enraptured.

And he had said—she could barely believe what he had said. Her heart threatened to burst with all that she hoped.

That he had been talking about her. That he had been talking about them.

Maya stepped out and held the microphone to her lips. She cleared her throat and then she sang a few shaky bars along with Nishant.

He immediately stopped and looked at her, his eyes going wide, confusion written all over his face. She motioned at the microphone, and he kept singing, finishing out the song to thunderous applause.

Maya spoke before he could.

"I wanted to say something before the next set," she said. "DJ Nish is kind of a local celebrity, for his beats and for never failing to get us all up and dancing at HSA parties."

Cheers and whoops filled the air at the mention of DJ Nish. Maya felt herself warming up a little, though she was still sweating a bucket. "But what many of you don't know is that DJ Nish is just one facade of Nishant Rai, my co-planner and the ideator behind this concert we're putting on for you today. He's worked tirelessly to get this to happen—"

A voice yelled in the crowd, "So have you!" It sounded suspiciously like Jana.

"And as you've all found out now, he's also an amazingly talented singer. I want to say something to Nishant," she said. "Thank you for coming on this ride with me. For being my partner." She took a deep breath.

The crowd cheered, someone yelling "Go to her!" from the back.

Smart crowd. They had figured out what she was doing, even if Nishant hadn't yet.

"The song's about a love gone wrong, one that could've been changed if certain things had happened differently," Maya said. "I'm hoping you were talking about me before."

Nish was frozen in his spot, staring at her. Speechless, for the second time. The crowd cheered around them, but her vision focused on him and him alone, the stage around them disappearing.

"Nishant, will you—"

He went over to her in a flash, pulling the microphone away from her and holding it down. The song continued in the background, but she could barely hear it with Nishant standing in front of her.

"You want—" he said, his voice lowering. The crowd was only a few paces away, watching everything, but Maya found she didn't care.

"Yes." She didn't even hesitate. "You. Even if I don't know for sure if you want me—"

"Was that you trying to tell me you want me?" Nishant asked.

Maya hung her head. Nishant placed a cool finger under her chin and tilted her face up. "Tell me."

"Yes," she said, the word coming out breathy. Hopeful.

He kept looking at her with those warm brown eyes, and Maya felt all her words spill out of her heart.

"I do, I want you, even if it's scary and uncertain," Maya said. "Do you want to try? This dating thing? But with each other this time?"

Nishant gave her an inscrutable look. And then he shook his head.

"No," he said.

If the floor had dropped right then, Maya wouldn't have been surprised.

"What?"

"No," he repeated. "I don't want to *try* to date you." Nishant stepped closer to her, cupping her cheek. "I want to date you. Not just two dates, but five. Ten. One hundred, if we can make it to that number."

Now it was her turn to look at him incredulously.

"I was wrong before. Actually, I was scared before," he said. "But the idea of losing you was scarier. It's as simple as that. You're the only person I feel like myself with, Maya. You brought me back to myself, to who I want to be."

And that was all that mattered, wasn't it? Not Holi, not New Maya, not event chair.

But this.

This was the new beginning that Holi was bringing them both, one full of love and hope.

Nishant tugged her closer, his fingers tilting her chin up. "Ask me again. Properly this time."

Maya looked into his warm, brown eyes as she asked, "Nishant, will you date me?"

He swept her up in his arms and dipped her low, nearly knocking the microphone stand over on the stage. The crowd went absolutely wild, but Maya wasn't paying attention to them. They were merely background noise in the story that was happening right in front of her. Her heart flew into her throat, catching, hopeful.

"Yes," he said.

Nishant pressed his lips to hers, and it was like the stars in the sky above had burst. This was better than she had remembered the first time. It felt right. The kiss deepened and he tugged her tighter into him, the two of them losing themselves in the moment.

A wolf whistle pierced the air. The outer world rushed in enough for the both of them to realize they were still standing on a stage in front of hundreds of people. Maya flushed, and there was even a faint pink tinge to Nishant's face.

Nishant pulled them both upright but didn't let go of her. His fingers entwined with her own, like they were always supposed to fit that way.

They didn't even notice when the first water balloon hit them. Or the colored powder. In seconds, the entire crowd was cheering, and when Maya and Nishant looked down to the front row, their friends were there, colored water balloons in hand.

"Finally!" Jana yelled, lobbing another one at them. Nishant covered her, letting it hit his back. Pink color bloomed across his white shirt like the petals of a rose.

"So chivalrous," Maya said, smiling up at him.

"Least I could do," he said. "Since you serenaded me earlier."

Maya laughed, the sound climbing up the air around them. They both smiled, wrapped up in each other.

She was wrong. This was the best Holi ever.

EPILOGUE
TWO WEEKS LATER

here was never such a thing as too much butter, at least in Maya's book. But the croissants at this HSA meeting were, daresay, too buttery.

"These are perfect," Nishant said, stuffing one into his mouth.

Maya bit back a sigh, making a note mentally to teach Nishant about the finer points of pastry. Then Nishant paused, making an uncertain expression as he continued to chew.

"But maybe a little too much butter? It seems like the ratio might be off. They were talking about ratios on *Bake Off*, weren't they?" he said.

Maya beamed so hard she nearly fell off her chair. "Yes, exactly. Like the production class you took me to—there's a right mix of beats and bass and melody."

Nishant made an *mmmm* sound in understanding.

Zane walked out at that moment and Maya jumped on him. "Did you get these from the new pastry shop on Cherry Pine Road downtown?" she said.

He blinked at her. "Yes; how did you know?"

"Don't ask," Nishant said. "It's her superpower. Now, can you finally tell us why you brought us both down here and then refused to let us into the meeting?"

Zane cleared his throat and shifted his weight. "Yes, well. We had some things we needed to discuss. Emergency session, if you will, as we figure out leadership for next year."

Maya's entire body tensed, and she wondered if she should just ask. Or would that look too desperate? But she and Nishant had really killed it with Holi, and she deserved to at least know what they were thinking.

Zane quickly put her out of her misery.

"You're not the event chair," Zane said. Maya's throat caught, and she quickly swallowed away any emotion. This was okay. She would be okay. "Because we've decided to get rid of the position."

Maya started to unfreeze and stared at Zane.

"Wait, what?"

Zane grinned at her. "The HSA leadership team unanimously decided that we want to hire a part-time event planner given how big our events have gotten . . . and due to the university grant we received. You both got over a thousand ticket sales." Nishant let out a whoop. "Holi was so successful that we were given a discretionary event grant from the college to keep putting on events that could be 'cultural touchstones,' which means we could even partner with other clubs in the future. It helped that Neadham was quite happy about the sizable donation we sent to the Cultural Center due to the event you two planned. I would ask both of you to take it on, but since DJ Nish seems to be starting a singing career and it's taking off, Maya, would you—"

"Yes," Maya said.

"I haven't even gotten to the best—"

"Yes."

"But, Maya, I had a whole speech written down about how you're the perfect fit for this new, unique part-time event-planner position and why you should consider it."

"The woman said yes," Nishant said, a laugh playing across his lips.

Zane sighed, running a hand through her hair. "Fine. The position is paid, too. Yay." He threw his hands up, and some confetti flew out from them as he frowned at Maya.

"What?" Maya nearly screamed.

"I told you to wait for it," Zane said grumpily.

He couldn't say much more as Maya threw herself at him. Zane nearly toppled over from the surprise hug.

"We get to keep working together, Zane!" Maya said into the wool of his spring sweater.

"I'm so excited," Zane said, sounding as excited as Zane could.

Maya let Zane go and cleared her throat, holding her hand out to him. He shook it, shaking his head as well. "Thank you," she said. "I won't let you down. HSA's events are going to be the best every semester, I'll make sure of it."

"Plus," Nishant said, "DJ Nish is obviously going to perform free for any event his girlfriend plans."

"Does this mean we can all stop pretending like we didn't see you make out in front of the whole school?" Zane said.

"Yup," Nishant said, tugging Maya close to him. "Though you'll have to deal with more PDA going forward, sorry." Maya looked up at Nishant, and he tilted his head down, kissing her lightly on the corner of her mouth.

"Ugh, ew, you two," Zane said, making a noise in the back of his throat. "It'll be fun to have you on board, though, Maya. Welcome to the team."

Maya smiled at him and then at her now-boyfriend. A lot could change in one semester, if this one was any evidence.

And she couldn't wait for many more.

THE END

ACKNOWLEDGMENTS

Thank you to Augusta Harris for believing in this idea and me the whole time. You've been the best cheerleader and guide along this process, from the earliest stages of Maya and Nishant's journey. It's been so much fun working with you and I'd be lucky to do it again.

Thank you to Kristin Nelson, my fearless literary agent who has been by my side for seven years now. Can't believe how the time has flown, but wouldn't want anyone else as my partner.

Thank you to the entire Disney team, including Elanna Heda, Rebecca Kuss, and Candice Snow, for helping shape this story and believing in me. Thank you to Zareen Johnson for this amazing, vibrant cover. Thank you to the tireless marketing, sales, and PR warriors behind the scenes: Matt Schweitzer, Holly Nagel, Danielle DiMartino, Ann Day, Crystal McCoy, Vicki Korlishin, and Marina Shults. Thank you to Guy Cunningham for dealing with all my commas!

Thank you to my husband, my parents, and my sisters, who never fail to lift me up and believe in me, rather like Jana does Maya. And to my word warriors and my NYC writer friends, who always see a path forward.

Finally, as always, thanks to my readers who have followed me faithfully from book to book. I hope you enjoy Maya and Nishant's story as much as I enjoyed writing it.